Two W in June

A novel by
Martin McSweeney

Cover photo: JFK's Motorcade on Patrick Street, Cork City, on 28th June 1963.

Photo taken by Robert Knudsen, White House Photographer

First published by Dog Ear Publishing
4010 W. 86th Street, Ste H
Indianapolis, IN 46268
www.dogearpublishing.net

ISBN: 1-59858-057-4
Library of Congress Control Number: 2005933500

This book is printed on acid-free paper.
This book is a work of Fiction.

Printed in Ireland by ColourBooks Ltd.

Dedication

For Suzanne, Ellen, Aoife and little Isabelle.

Author's Note

Although this novel is a work of fiction, the excerpts taken from The Evening Echo newspapers of the time are completely factual.

Cork City, Ireland

Friday 14th June 1963

Excerpt from the Evening Echo:

PRESIDENT KENNEDY HIMSELF INSISTED ON INCLUDING CORK

Mr. Kennedy had himself asked specifically that Cork be included as part of his Irish itinerary, it was revealed today by Mr. Pierre Salinger, the U.S. President's press secretary. The press secretary told an 'Echo' reporter at the City Hall that he thought President Kennedy's desire to visit Cork was due to the fact that his forbears, the Fitzgeralds, came from Co. Cork.

Mary went to the window and stood next to her mother. "What the hell has he got with him?" her mother asked.

Jack Horgan, her father, was coming down the path, carrying a large cardboard box. The two women watched him negotiate the six steps that fed down to the front door, not once considering that they should go out and help him.

"It's never a bloody pig?" Mrs. Horgan gasped. "Well, if it is he'll be takin' it back up those steps again, I'll tell ya."

Jack entered with the large cardboard box and, from that moment forward, the ambience of the Horgan household was changed forever. It wasn't a live pig he had brought home.

Jack set the box down on the dinner table, which was the centrepiece of the room. There were two rooms downstairs; the living room and a small pantry. The living room was big, but it served many purposes. The dinner table took up a large chunk of space, with the fire taking most of what was left. A small door led under the stairs; the coal for the fire was stored there.

"Jesus Christ," he exhaled. "I just carried that shaggin' thing all the way from Patrick Street."

They lived on Cathedral road, on the north side of Cork, in the parish of Gurranabraher. The parish stretched from Cathedral Road up to Baker's Road and across to the Parochial Hall. From Patrick Street, it was an uphill climb of about two miles to number 13 Cathedral Road. It had often been noted that some people had suffered nosebleeds while walking up the steep hills to Gurranabraher. It has also been said that some people had received nosebleeds while walking through the parish, for altogether different reasons.

Jack planted himself in his armchair. He looked shook, but no one came to his aid. Ann Horgan stood by the window staring at her tired husband.

"Well?" she blurted out. "What is it this time? A time machine?"

"I wish it bloody was! Then I could get the hell out of here for a while." He smiled, assuring Ann that he was only joking. The assurance delivered, Jack turned to Mary. "Clear away the top of the chest of drawers in the corner over there, will ya? It should fit there."

Mary walked over to the corner, next to the window that looked out at their small back garden. She moved the pictures and ornaments onto the chair by the window. When she was finished, Jack rose from his armchair again, took a deep breath and lifted the box once more. He placed it on the ground in front of the chest of drawers and opened it.

"Jesus, Jack," Ann shouted. "We can't afford a telly!"

"I didn't buy it, darling. I just rented it. It's 10 and 6 a week. We can give it back whenever we want to." Jack plugged in the television, lifted it onto the chest of drawers and turned the knob. A screen full of snow greeted them.

No one said anything.

They all stared at the haze on the screen for a minute, and probably would have stared happily for the rest of the night, until Jack pulled the rabbit's ears out of the box and hooked them up.

Ann blessed herself and dropped to her knees. She stared at the picture of the Virgin Mary that filled the screen. The television went BONG——BONG——BONG. It was six o' clock and it was also the first time that the Horgan family had seen and heard the Angelus on TV.

Jack dragged his armchair away from the fire and positioned it directly in front of the television. He sat down just as the Angelus finished. The Kit Carson show started and Jack smiled. Ann got up off the floor and Mary, trying to look unimpressed, left the room.

* * * *

Mary was nineteen and although she liked the new television, she hadn't time to watch it tonight. It was Friday night and

she was going dancing at the Palm Court. She had been dancing many times, but tonight was special. She had never been to
the Palm Court, and had never been out dancing with Louise
before tonight. It was one of the most expensive places in town,
costing four shillings for a single. You could get a double for
that in Francis Hall, where they usually went on Friday nights,
but she had asked the girls to avoid Francis Hall for a while,
because of Willy.

She entered the bedroom at the top of the stairs that she
shared with her younger sister, Louise. There were two small
single beds, a dresser and a two-door wardrobe; a wardrobe they
had inherited from their mother's room when she had replaced
it with a new one. There was nothing wrong with it really,
except for a large hole in the back where her older brothers had
hammered through to get at some hidden Christmas goodies a
few years back.

Mary sat on the bed and started to undress. On the floor
in front of her was a large washing basin, about the size of a
baby's bath. It was filled with warm water she had spent the best
part of an hour heating on the stove and carrying up the stairs.
They had no bath. Hell, they had no bathroom! To get to the
toilet they had to go out the back door, through the pantry and
into a small outhouse with an ice cold toilet bowl. That room
was so cold that the water in the bowl would freeze over frequently each winter. The door to the toilet started a foot from
the ceiling and ended a foot short of the floor. It wasn't uncom-
mon to find yourself sitting on the odd cat late at night. It
would be 1973, and a lot of cold arses later before anyone
realised that the door could and should be changed to one that
fitted the frame!

Louise came into the bedroom as Mary was washing herself. Louise was seventeen and was going dancing for the first
time tonight. Jack wouldn't allow it until she turned seventeen,
and that had been last Tuesday.

"Did you see the telly?" she asked.

Mary nodded.

"Dad's complaining already that the shows are useless. He's gone to O'Keeffe's to get the paper. The Echo boy forgot to deliver it again. Brendan is below too. He and Mam are glued to it."

Mary started to dry herself. Louise opened the wardrobe and took out a pink dress. "Are you sure it's alright?" she asked, holding it against her chest.

"It's lovely. You'll turn some heads tonight."

＊＊＊＊

The two girls arrived downstairs a few minutes after half seven. The rest of the family were in the living room watching the TV. All, that is, except Jack. He was sitting on the chair by the front window, reading the Echo.

"Aren't you watching it, Dad?" Louise asked from the door.

He answered without looking up. "Bloody useless it is. A load of snobs talking shite." He rustled the paper to make his point.

"Watch your language, Jack Horgan!" Ann shouted across the room. She always used a person's full name when correcting them.

Don't you jump in those puddles, Mary Horgan. If I see you with those boys again it will be the end of you, Brendan Horgan, you hear me?

Always the full name, as if the message was clearer somehow.

"Ah, Louise, you look divine sweetheart," Ann said, rising from her chair in front of the TV.

Jack was cute enough to take up her lead. "Let me have a look at my youngest daughter, all grown up." He dropped the Echo and took a long hard look at Louise. "You can't go," he said finally.

Panic filled Louise's face. Her eyes started to fill up.

Jack walked up to her and kissed her forehead. "You'll have to stay here…or you'll break every heart in Cork tonight." His joke delivered and duty done, Jack returned to his paper.

The smile returned to Louise's face. Mary nudged her. "He nearly had you there, ya eejit."

"Turn around and let me look at you properly now," Ann said.

Louise obliged and when she completed her turn, her mother had tears flowing down her cheeks. She threw her arms around Louise. "You're all grown up, my baby." She released her grip and placed both hands on Louise's shoulders. "Have a great time tonight, darling."

"Not too good a time now," Jack added, without looking away from his paper. The two boys, Michael and Brendan, hadn't taken their eyes off the television.

****

The sun was still shining outside, and with the dinners served to each husband, the women of Cathedral Road had come out to pursue their pastime of leaning on their garden gates to gossip. Jack had often commented on this sacred ritual. "If I told Mrs. Murphy at the bottom of the hill that I had killed a man in town, there would be a Garda waiting for me when I reached my front door. The shawl express," he would call it.

The girls climbed the steps and walked the path to the gate. They could almost feel the breeze caused by the turning of heads. Mary let out a sly laugh. "It's going to be a busy walk down to Shandon Street, Lou."

"Let them say and think what they want. I couldn't give two shits."

The women at their gates were not old. In fact, most were young enough to be heading to the Palm Court, but most of these women looked old, old before their time. Some wore heavy black shawls around their shoulders, although it was the middle of June. Others wore aprons constantly, from morning until bedtime. The highlight of these women's lives was gossip. Living their lives vicariously through others gave them something to keep them going. Louise knew that some women would comment on her dress, her makeup, anything they could think of slandering. Some would be harsh, jealous of her. Others would be kind and happy for her, but all would have something to say.

"We could get the bus?" Mary suggested.

Louise shook her head. "I wouldn't give them the soot of it. I didn't get dolled up tonight to get on the bloody number one bus, did I?" She shut the gate behind them and started walking down the footpath, wiggling her behind that little bit more than usual.

Mary looked ahead and could see Angela Browne coming out of her house. Angela was Mary's best friend and she was going with them tonight. As Angela came closer, she started screaming. "Would ya take a look at Louise Horgan? I never thought you had tits before tonight girl."

Louise blushed.

"Just make sure you come back home tonight with them," Angela teased. "Don't let some nobber rub them off ya." She laughed aloud.

The three of them walked down the road giggling and pushing each other, like they were five years old going to buy sweets with their pocket money. The women, standing by their gates, looked on and raised their eyes to heaven in disgust, although most of them would have traded places in a heartbeat.

They turned right at the end of Cathedral road, where the actual Cathedral that gave the road its name towered above them, and walked down Shandon Street. Mary wanted to get some cigarettes for the night ahead. The three of them went into a shop and bought a pack of ten No.6 between them. They would end up smoking at least ten each, but they only bought ten between them to get them started. The lads that danced them and tried to shift them would gladly supply the rest. But they would need some at the beginning, mainly because the lads took so long to even approach them. The dance started at half eight and no man would dream of approaching a girl and asking for a dance for at least an hour.

"Do we have to go all the way over to the Palm Court?" Angela asked as they continued down Shandon Street. Louise looked at Mary and shrugged. Mary definitely didn't want to go to Francis Hall. It was closer, just across the Northgate Bridge, but she knew that if she went there she would almost certainly have a run in with Willy.

Willy was Mary's ex boyfriend, although Mary would argue the fact that they had ever been a couple at all. Willy had pursued Mary, following her everywhere, until she conceded and agreed to go to the pictures with him. She had enjoyed the film and Willy had barely spoken to her at all during the show. It was later that she developed a severe dislike for him.

He lived outside the city, close to the village of Blarney. He drove his mother's car that night and when they pulled up outside Mary's house, he had leaned over and started to kiss her. She left him have that. After all, he had paid for the pictures and the sweets, and a kiss wasn't going to kill her.

It was when Willy latched onto her breast, like it was a doorknob to a room he just had to get into, that Mary pushed him away. It wasn't the romantic moment she had imagined would take place between her and the man she would first sleep with.

"What's your problem?" Willy had shouted, turning angry.

Mary hadn't bothered to answer. She jumped out of the car and ran to the front door. She didn't cry or anything so foolish.

He wasn't worth it and she was stronger than that anyway. She had told Angela about the encounter the next day and Angela had suggested that she would cut his balls off the next time they met him.

Mary stared at Angela now. "It's not that far," she pleaded. "Come on. It will be great."

The penny dropped and Angela sided with Mary. "The Palm Court it is then," Angela announced, linking both sisters. "But I had better meet the man of my dreams tonight, Mary. Okay?"

"Okay," Mary answered, relieved.

* * * *

The band playing at the Palm Court was called The Modernaires. It cost four shillings each to get in and Angela started to protest, but Mary's piercing stare halted her objections once more.

Louise overflowed with excitement as they walked into the main dance hall. Mary looked at her and remembered the first time she had gone dancing, two years earlier with Angela. That night, Mary had thought she would bust with anticipation.

Mary and Angela headed for the women's side of the room. Dance halls all over the world were the same. The men occupied one wall of the room, while the women sat across the empty floor, against the other. Two groups of adversaries, the battleground dividing them.

The two girls sat down and looked back to see Louise still standing by the door gazing around aimlessly. Mary waved to her, snapping her from her trance and she hurried over to join them.

No one was dancing. It was too early. The hall was filling slowly, but no one would venture onto the floor for another half-hour at least. Angela had already started laying out her stall.

Mary watched as she scanned the line of eligible men across the room. To Mary, it looked like Angela was a farmer at an auction, examining the livestock on sale before the bidding started. Angela's eyes moved up and down the line, making eye contact with as many men as possible. Mary knew that Angela wasn't a girl to sit around and hope that fate took a hand. If she hadn't danced by ten, she would cross that floor and do the asking herself.

"See any you could get some milk out of?" Mary asked her.

"Sorry?" Angela replied.

Mary leaned closer. "Do you see anyone you fancy?"

Louise sat listening to the exchange, trying to learn the ropes.

"I can see one or two already, but if this thing doesn't get going soon I'll dance with the fella taking the money at the door, if I have to."

Mary and Angela laughed, followed closely by Louise.

* * * *

As things turned out Angela didn't have to dance with the doorman after all, but she wasn't the first of the three of them to dance. At quarter to ten, a rather small, shy looking lad, who couldn't have been more than seventeen, walked toward them. Angela sat up, pushed her chest out and smiled.

"Would you like to dance?" he asked, a slight quiver in his voice. Mary smiled up at him and drove her elbow into Louise's side. Louise, who hadn't been paying attention, looked up at the young man and realised that he was asking her to dance.

There weren't many couples dancing when Louise took to the dance floor for the first time in her life. She could dance; her mother and Mary had taken care of that, but dancing with your mother or your sister in the front room of your house was like playing with dolls before someone handed you a real baby.

Mary sat for a while and watched her baby sister grow up right in front of her eyes. Louise looked extremely nervous at first and kept her chin buried in her chest, afraid to make eye contact with the equally nervous young man. Then he leaned in and whispered something in her ear. Louise laughed a little, raised her head slightly and smiled. He returned the smile and they spent the rest of the night together, dancing and chatting.

Mary was next to dance. A boy she knew came in, and when he saw her he ignored all others and asked her to dance. She knew that Trevor really fancied her and she thought he was nice too, but he wasn't boyfriend material. They danced for two songs before she excused herself and went to the ladies room. On her return, she was asked to dance again before she had reached her chair.

Angela danced next, but she wasn't asked. After seeing Louise upstage her and Mary get asked to dance a second time, Angela became desperate. She was a pretty girl, but not in the league of the Horgan sisters. She scanned the wall of men standing and sitting on the opposite side of the dance floor.

Desperate times called for desperate measures.

Angela got up and walked across the battleground. She didn't do it timidly. She wasn't by anyone's imagination a shy girl. Strutting across the room, she continued to scan her prey. It took her four seconds to make the walk; not a lot of time to spot a looker and make her choice, especially with the dim lighting. She knew she had to have her mind made up when she arrived in front of them, or else it could turn into a complete disaster. If she picked a smart arse, he would embarrass her for fun and she would be forced to take steps; steps back to her seat.

She arrived at the far wall and with a second to spare, she spotted him. A young man of about twenty, sitting on a stool, made eye contact with her and, as she looked back at him, he gave her the one-two-one look. Once at her chest, then her legs and up to her eyes. Non interested parties would make eye contact, probably by mistake, and look away immediately. He did-n't, so Angela went to work.

"Do you like what you see?" she asked, as seductively as she could. He was shy, she realised. He didn't answer, just nod-ded and giggled. That was all Angela needed. She dragged him onto the dance floor and pulled him close to her, his head dis-appearing into her bosom.

He was a small man.

* * * *

At around eleven the three girls met in the toilet. The dance would be over in thirty minutes and there were decisions to be made. As the three of them admired themselves in the mirror, Angela started.

"What do you think of my fella?" she asked.

"He's lovely," Louise replied.

"Yeah. If you're a fucking midget, he is." Angela added.

The three of them laughed; Angela harder than anyone. She always laughed more at her own jokes.

"I don't care either way, really. I'm still going to the pic-tures with him tomorrow night. We'll be the same size lying down anyway." She paused, "And maybe he is big in other ways, you know?" She nudged Louise, whose face reddened.

"Shut up with your foul mouth, Angela Browne!" Mary said, taking a leaf from her mother's book.

They worked on their makeup for a few seconds without speaking. Then Louise broke the silence. "Justin wants to walk me home."

Mary shot Angela a look that said, *Don't you dare slag his name off. Don't you dare spoil my baby sister's first romance.*

Angela got the message and stayed quiet.

Mary turned to Louise and smiled. "That's great, but remember you must be home by twelve, and don't let him walk you to the gate. We'll walk behind you all the way. Wait for me by Mrs. Sweeney's gate, okay?"

"Okay," Louise answered and left.

Then Angela started, her voice elevated to a south side tone. "I bet you Justin is not from the north side. I'll bet Justin is from Ballyphehane, or maybe Douglas. He'll shit his pants when Louise turns to go over the Northgate Bridge."

Mary didn't answer. She continued putting on her lipstick, trying hard not to laugh. "Come on," she said eventually, "let's squeeze in another dance before the end."

"I intend to squeeze more than another dance tonight," Angela added, giggling.

Mary wasn't impressed. She knew Angela was still a virgin, just like her, and her vulgar tongue would always come out, even if everything else was kept hidden away.

* * * *

The dance hall was next to the General Post Office, a tall limestone building that looked out of place on Oliver Plunkett Street. Mary, Louise and Justin leaned against the wall of the G.P.O. and watched, as Angela kissed the midget goodnight across the street. Angela was almost crouching down to get into a good position and Mary thought that any second Angela would give in and pick the boy up. She didn't pick him up, but she did slap him hard on the cheek.

"Ya dirty little bastard!" she shouted at him.

He laughed and walked away.

Angela crossed the street. "Ya fuckin' midget," she shouted after him. He waved back at her as he went, a large grin exploding across his face.

She joined the others by the GPO. Mary looked at her and shook her head.

"What?" Angela said. "He grabbed me tit," she explained.

Justin laughed and Mary thought Angela would start into him then, but she didn't and Louise looked thankful for that.

"Go on you two," Mary said to Louise. "We'll follow behind you."

Mary turned to head home and came face to face with Willy O'Reilly. He wasn't a midget. Willy was twenty-four, stood six feet tall and looked nearly as wide. Louise and Justin, who had already crossed the street, turned to look back.

"I saw you in there," Willy started, pointing towards the Palm Court. "I saw you fucking dancing with all those men."

For the first time, Mary was afraid of Willy. She hadn't been before, even the time he had felt her up. Now she could see anger in his eyes. She could smell the stink of whiskey from his breath. He wasn't fall-down drunk, but he was on the road to it.

"Go home, Willy." She tried to sound strong, stronger than she felt. She turned to Angela and motioned to her to move. Willy put his hand against the G.P.O. wall, blocking Mary's path. Mary stared into his eyes. She decided not to say anything. She would walk around him and get home as fast as she could.

"Get out of her way, ya fuckin' drunk!" Angela spat at him, obviously with another plan in mind.

Willy dismissed her comment, not even turning to look at her. "Fuck off, slut," he said.

Mary moved to walk around him.

"Where do you think you're going?" He moved to stop her, grabbing her arm and swinging her back towards the wall, too hard.

Mary crashed against the limestone wall and felt a jolt of pain run up her arm. She knew she would be badly bruised tomorrow, if she got to see tomorrow. Louise and Justin had come back, but they stood watching, unsure of what to do. Justin looked like he was about to make a move toward the much taller Willy, when a man taller than both of them brushed past him.

Willy saw him coming and turned in his direction. "What's your fuckin' prob...," were Willy's last words that night.

The man didn't speak. He didn't ask what was going on. He didn't try to defuse the situation. In one swift motion, he drove his open hand into Willy's chin, sending him back against the wall. Willy's head made a sound like an apple bursting against the limestone wall and that was the end of it. He slid down the wall into a crumpled heap on the ground. Nobody knew how to react. The stranger turned to Mary and took hold of her hands.

"Are you alright, Miss?" he asked softly.

Mary felt like she was in a dream. This didn't happen in real life. You only saw this kind of thing at the Palace Cinema. Only Richard Burton or Marlon Brando could do the things that had just happened.

"Are you alright?" he asked again, jolting Mary from her trance.

"You're American," she blurted out, cringing at the sound of her own voice.

"Last time I checked anyway," the stranger replied, smiling.

Mary felt her left arm and winced slightly. The stranger examined it, stretching it out and back again.

"Squeeze my hand," he said to her.

She did. It hurt, but she could do it.

"I don't think it's broken, but you will be sore for a few days." He smiled and all the pain in Mary's arm subsided instantly.

She smiled back at him, oblivious to the others who had gathered around them. People were still coming out of the dance hall and the crowd was growing.

"I think we had better get moving before the cops come," the stranger suggested. Mary nodded and let him lead her away gently. He was so very gentle, she thought.

Louise, Justin and Angela trailed behind them as they walked from the G.P.O. up Winthrop Street and onto the main thoroughfare of the city, Patrick Street. The street was alive with the sound of chatting people, and they soon melted into the crowd.

"My name is Dean Reynolds, by the way," the American said, as they started the long haul up Cathedral Road.

"I'm Mary. Mary Horgan."

"Nice to meet you, Mary. Although I wish it were under better circumstances."

Mary looked up at Dean, who was at least four inches over six feet, and wondered how old he was. He had a tight haircut and was wearing an expensive two piece suit, his broad shoulders carrying the jacket well. She guessed he was about thirty.

"Are you on holidays here with your wife?" she fished.

Dean laughed. The other three, now in front of them, looked back and Louise giggled a little before looking away.

"No on both counts I'm afraid. No wife, and I'm not on holidays either."

Mary didn't know what to say next. A silence descended on them and they walked on slowly for a few minutes.

"I'm here on a little business," Dean said, jumping into the silence. "I'm originally from Washington, the capital that is, Washington D.C.. Are you originally from Cork?"

"Yes," Mary answered. "I'm only nineteen so I've lived here all my life so far, although I'd love to go to America some day."

Dean looked at Mary and she thought she would drown in his eyes, his big blue eyes.

"America would love you, Mary Horgan. You were made for it."

"What do you mean?"

Dean kicked a stone and Mary wondered if he was shy after all.

"Well," he said. "A beautiful woman is always welcome where I come from. We just don't have enough to go around." They both laughed and felt the eyes from the leading group again.

The Horgan house is on the only level stretch of Cathedral Road, and they reached this plateau at five past twelve. The conversation had been friendly, but difficult to maintain. Mary had spent a few minutes explaining where she worked and how she hated it. Angela had already departed, with a wave back to Mary, and now Louise stood by Mrs. Sweeney's front gate, kissing Justin. Mary stopped two gates short of them.

"I think we should stop here and let them have a few minutes," she said.

"Where do you live?" Dean asked.

Mary pointed past Louise and Justin. "See the blue house past Justin's head."

"Yes."

"There you are! Chez Horgan."

Dean smiled and the silence descended again, like an unwanted rain shower. They stood looking at Louise and Justin locked in a passionate embrace.

"I hope you don't mind me asking, but who the hell was the psycho?"

Mary blushed, admiring her shoes.

"I'm sorry," Dean said. "I didn't mean to pry."

"No, it's okay." She cleared her throat. "I went out with him once and he won't leave me alone. I avoided him up to now, but that's the first time I ever saw him like that."

"I hope I haven't made things worse for you now. Does he live around here?"

"No. He lives on a farm on Faggot Hill, out by Blarney," Mary answered. "I think things would have been a lot worse tonight, if you hadn't come along. I never thanked you either in the heat of the moment," Their eyes met. "Thank you," she almost whispered.

"It was my pleasure, Mary," He leaned over and kissed her cheek.

Mary didn't draw back or blush. She wanted him to kiss her, and not on the cheek.

"I think your sister is ready to go."

Mary looked up the road. Justin was on his way toward them and Louise was waving frantically at Mary. Mary didn't want to move yet, but she spotted the hall light in their house was on. Her father was up and he was coming out to check if they were outside, snogging.

"I've gotta go," she said. "My Dad is up." Mary ran to the front gate and joined Louise as Jack Horgan opened the door.

"The princesses decide to come home," Jack said glancing at his watch. "And where are the pumpkins?"

The girls darted past him and bolted up the stairs. Jack stepped out the door and stumbled lazily up the steps. He thought he saw someone at the crest of the hill, but when he rubbed some of the sleep from his eyes he could see no one.

"Bloody prince charming my arse." He laughed as he trundled back down the steps.

Saturday 15th June 1963

Excerpt from the Evening Echo:

The Conclave: Romans Survey the "Papabili"

As Vatican officials today made final preparations for next week's Conclave to elect a new Pope, Rome was discussing the leading "Papabili", Cardinals who are thought to be possible successors to Pope John.

Leading Cardinal, according to Rome opinion today, is 65-year-old Cardinal Montini, Archbishop of Milan.

The princes of the church who represent 31 nations will be locked into the Vatican on Wednesday evening. They begin their secret voting in the Sistine Chapel on Thursday morning, filling in their ballot cards in disguised writing and ritually placing them in a golden chalice.

Jack Horgan stood by his front gate. It was half past nine and the sun was already high in the clear blue sky. He thought about the television. At ten shillings and six pence a week, it was an unnecessary indulgence on his part. He earned eight pounds a week, and with all the children working, except Louise, they were better off than most of their neighbours. So, why not indulge himself?

Of course, Ann complained but she also sat for the night watching the so called 'stupid thing'; finally moving her arse from the chair when a priest on the television said a goodnight prayer and Radio Telefis Eireann shut down for the night. Ann headed to bed; the dishes from dinner still languishing on the draining board, washed but not dried. Jack could not recall a time in all their years together when that had happened.

He had watched the other men head off to work at about half past eight, and in a weird way, he had envied them. It amazed him really. Every Saturday morning he would bitch and moan as he dragged himself out of bed to walk the few miles down to Blackpool. Here he was, with a day off in front of him, and all he could do was stand and watch other people go to work. He hadn't even slept in, but he would tomorrow, after a feed of pints tonight.

The Cellar was a meat-processing factory close to Murphy's Brewery. It was officially called Denny's Meat Cellar, but was more commonly known as The Cellar. Jack spent some of his days shoving sausages and rashers into packaging. Eight sausages and five rashers to a pack, but it wasn't all hum drum stuff. Sometimes they would do full pound packs of sausages and that would mean sixteen to a pack. The fun never ended on those days. Other times, he would be assigned to help with the unloading of the truckloads of pigs or sheep as they arrived. It was better to deal with the unloading of the living than the packing of the dead.

Jack stared at his watch; twenty-five to ten. Tonight, they would go to the Templeacre Tavern, around the corner. He would wish the day away waiting for it. They went there every Saturday.

He looked up to see the bread van turning the corner. He greeted the breadman as if he were a king, bought two bread sculls and licked his lips as he made his way down the steps and into the house. He could taste the butter melting on the freshly cut bread already, could feel the hot tea washing the cheddar cheese and hot bread down his throat. For the moment, Jack Horgan was happy to be off work on this Saturday, and the feeling would last at least until the last slice of fresh bread was gone.

* * * *

Mary was awakened by the sound of her father coming in the front door, singing a tune. She rolled over and was met by the smiling face of Louise. They hadn't spoken much the night before; afraid that their father would have had a fit if they had kept him awake any later.

"Dad's not working today?" Louise asked.

"He mustn't be," Mary paused. "I hope things aren't turning bad at The Cellar."

Louise jumped out of bed. "He deserves a day off though. He's getting on a bit now."

Mary laughed. "He's only forty-five, for Christ's sake."

"Yeah. That's old to me."

"Angela thinks Dad is still a looker."

"Well," replied Louise. "I suppose he's better than midget man from last night." They both exploded with laughter.

Mary lay in bed as Louise got dressed.

"I need your help, sis," Louise said quietly.

Mary tilted her head, unsure of what was coming next. "For what?"

"I want to meet Justin tomorrow night."

"Dad won't let you."

"He won't know," Louise spoke quickly. "We're babysitting for the Fitzgeralds tomorrow night, right? So I will go across to their house with you and when they go out I'll sneak out and meet Justin for an hour or so." Louise made a face like a sad puppy.

"You know what will happen if Mam or Dad finds out."

Louise smiled, knowing that Mary had already agreed. "They won't," Louise said hugging Mary.

Mary let out a scream. "Jesus," she said, holding her arm.

Louise lifted Mary's sleeve and gasped when she saw the huge bruise that covered most of her arm. "That must be sore."

"Do ya think so?" Mary teased, examining Willy's work. She reached out and grabbed Louise's hand. "Not a word to anyone below, or forget about lover boy tomorrow night. Right?"

Louise hesitated, clearly concerned for her sister. "Okay," she finally conceded.

* * * *

In the room next door, Brendan opened his eyes and took in a deep breath. He coughed hard, and almost threw up as the smell of stale farts filled his lungs. "I know you're awake, Michael, ya rotten bastard," he said toward the lump of bedclothes in the bed opposite his own. "No one could drop one like that in their sleep."

Michael giggled under the covers and Brendan joined in, flapping his hand in front of his face. Brendan's bed was against the window so he reached back and flipped it open leaving a warm breeze in to clear the air. Michael, who was twenty three, and Brendan, two years younger, shared a room so small that if you tripped and fell coming in the door you would fall straight out the window.

Finally, Michael surfaced and eyed his brother. "Have you made up your mind yet? Are you going to go with me or what?"

Brendan was starting to get dressed. He didn't answer at first. He still wasn't sure if he wanted to go.

"Look," said Michael. "Come along. And if you don't fancy it you can forget about it. But don't make up your mind without first going at least once, like."

Brendan sighed and nodded.

"Great. We'll head after breakfast. Longy will take us in his car." Michael jumped out of bed and started to dress quickly. Brendan was ready to go downstairs, but waited for his brother.

"I smell fresh bread. Dad must be off today and he's after getting some fresh sculls I'll bet," Michael said, smiling. "Let's go down and bug the shit out of him. I could eat a horse."

* * * *

Jack heard the footsteps of the boys coming down the stairs and he panicked. The girls were already down, but he could cope with them. The girls might have one slice of bread each, if even that much. But the boys would eat his hand off if he left it too close to the bread. Jack cut three more slices and headed for the kitchen.

The girls had taken a slice each and were toasting them in the pantry. Jack buttered his share in the pantry and guarded them like recovered treasure. Michael and Brendan sat at the table and divvied up the remaining chunks of bread, Brendan making excellent work of cutting perfectly even slices. Jack returned to the front room and took a seat at the table. He brought the butter with him and Michael started buttering.

"Any sausages on, Dad?" Michael asked.

"You mean the sausages that you and him ate last night, those sausages? Ohh, they'll be ready any minute now. I threw on a few eggs for you as well and a plate of beans each to get you going. I gave the chef the day off today, but the butler will be in later to answer the front door for ye." Jack bit into his cheese sandwich.

The boys glanced at each other and smirked.

Jack shouted toward the pantry. "Mary, is that kettle boiled yet? Drop me out a cup of tea, will ya?"

"Two minutes," came the reply from the pantry.

"Make a pot altogether," added Michael. He waited to be told where to go.

"Okay."

The three men looked at each other, amazed, and took huge chunks out of their slices of bread. Neither of them spoke again until Mary and Louise came in with the pot of tea and the cups. Brendan threw his arm around Louise.

"Well, little sis, how did it go last night? Are ya getting' married?"

Louise pulled away from him. "Go way, ya fool. I'm hardly getting married."

"Seriously though," added Michael. "Did you have a good time?"

Louise smiled at Michael. "It was great. I even got to dance."

Michael turned to Mary, who was pouring tea. "How did you get on, sis?"

Mary didn't look up. "Grand," she offered.

"And what about that Angela? What poor boy did she corner last night?" Brendan asked.

"She kissed a midget," Louise blurted out.

Even Jack broke into laughter after that comment. The five of them sat together around the table eating until all the food was gone. As they finished their tea Brendan broke the silence.

"Was there anything good on after we left last night?" he asked Jack.

"Not much really. A show called Dragnet came on at quarter to eleven. That wasn't bad. I hope the shows get a bit better or that useless thing will be going back to Patrick Street on Monday."

"Is there anything on it now?" asked Louise.

"Nah," Jack answered, "The bloody thing doesn't start until five and then it's over before twelve." He paused for a few seconds, thinking. "Still, your mother loves it, so that's that."

"So ye won't be going to the Templeacre tonight then?" Michael teased.

Jack didn't answer. He didn't need to. He just laughed a little and threw a glance in Michael's direction.

Michael slurped the last of his tea and got up. "Well, I'm having a quick wash and me and Brendan will be out of your way for the day."

"Me and your mother are going to town. I can't wait," Jack said, throwing his eyes to heaven.

★ ★ ★ ★

The O'Reilly farm was a fifty-acre section of land at the top of Faggot hill, overlooking Blarney village. Willy O'Reilly ran the farm these days. His father had died seven years earlier, leaving Willy and his mother alone. The farm wasn't very profitable when his father was alive, and now that he was gone, it had deteriorated even further over the years. Willy's mother had taken to her bed after her husband was taken away, and she had stayed there since. This left Willy, at seventeen when his father had died, to look after the farm alone.

Willy would have stayed in bed this morning, if his mother hadn't shouted at him until he had to get up. His head felt like a party was still going on inside. He felt the back of his skull and grimaced as his hand landed on a lump. He had woken up, on the ground against the G.P.O. wall, just after midnight. A crowd of people had gathered around him, but no one had made a move to help him. Willy had picked himself up and walked away as calmly as he could. He was still drunk, so he had staggered slightly as he went.

He stood now by the pigsty trying to recall the events that had ended with him in a crumpled heap on the ground. He held the pen gate open trying to get the pigs to gather inside so he could feed them. Although the man had come at him quickly the night before, Willy had seen his face. It was the last thing he had seen. He didn't remember feeling any pain and wondered for a while if he hadn't simply collapsed. It was possible. He had downed a fair amount of whiskey in the pub next door to the Palm Court, before going in and seeing Mary dancing with a few men.

The bastard must have hit me, he thought. If he had, he had moved at amazing speed. Willy hadn't seen the punch coming. He had been in numerous fights during his short life and had never seen someone move that fast. Deciding that the man must have hit him, Willy felt a mixture of shame and anger. He must have looked like a complete eejit, lying in a heap on the ground; the hero probably walking Mary home, probably getting a kiss for his troubles, maybe even more.

One of the younger pigs hesitated at the gate and Willy gave him a kick. Not a hard kick, but one that would get him moving in the right direction again. The pig panicked and slammed into reverse. Willy caught the young pig in the midsection as he backed up, sending the animal into flight across the farmyard. The pig landed awkwardly on its back and proceeded to roll over a few times. It came to rest and lay still for a moment, trying to catch its breath. Willy was on it like a flash, stamping down on the animal's back with his oversized boots, his eyes inflamed with rage. The pig let out a harrowing squeal as its spine cracked under the barrage of kicks from Willy.

Less than a minute later, the pig lay dead on the ground. The rest of the pigs, seeming not to care, continued eating. Willy stood admiring his work, and decided that he would do his best to see the man who had humiliated him the night before in that very same position, soon.

"What's going on out there, Willy?" A voice rose from one of the farmhouse windows. It was Willy's mother.

Quietly, Willy closed the gate, slung the dead pig over his shoulder and headed for the barn. He would have to bleed the pig before it was too late.

He didn't answer his mother.

* * * *

"Mornin', boys," Longy said, as the Horgan brothers turned the corner. Longy, or Kevin Long, lived on Templeacre Avenue, a street running adjacent to Cathedral Road. The houses on Cathedral Road had been built in 1934, but the house that Kevin Long lived in had been built much later. By the time the council got around to building these houses, it was decided that toilets and baths would be included in the construction, or more importantly, that they would be inside the house. This fact didn't do much for Longy's appearance. He rarely washed himself, and everyone would comment that there was always a strong odour of onions whenever he was around.

The car was the only reason that Michael bothered with Longy at all. They had attended school together at the Cathedral Boys' Primary School. They hadn't sat together. Michael was sure he would never have lasted seven years of primary school sitting next to Longy. They were not great friends back then and they sure weren't great friends now. Longy had a Ford Prefect, and that was the only reason that Michael put up with the shitty attitude, and the smell of onions. The car, an old heap, had been part of an inheritance that Longy had received the summer before from a dead grandfather.

The three of them got into the small car and Brendan opened his window. It was June and the sun was shining, but if it had been February and freezing the window would still have been opened. Death by cold weather was a dream compared to

death from Longy's odour. Michael climbed into the front passenger seat and rolled down his window. Longy, oblivious to the
real reason, and wanting to be like Michael, also rolled down his
window.

They drove through Blackpool, headed out towards Tivoli
and on towards East Cork. The car wasn't very fast, but Longy
drove it to the limit. The top speed of a Ford Prefect was around
seventy miles per hour, but Longy would be lucky to get this car
over sixty.

Michael sat with his hand resting on the door, listening to
the music from the radio that Longy had strapped to the dash-
board. A Buddy Holly song crackled through the car and they
all let the moment wash over them.

* * * *

Longy pulled the car off the road a couple of miles beyond
Midleton. He drove through an open gate, where an older man
stood waving him on. The field climbed for a hundred yards or
so and then dipped down out of view of the road. When they
reached the highest point of the field, Brendan let out a long
gasp. There were at least thirty cars parked in a row outside a
large red barn. All the cars were empty and a few men stood
near the entrance to the barn. One of them pointed to the end
of the row and Longy followed the instruction, parking along-
side an older Ford.

Inside the barn was darker and it took their eyes a minute
or two to adjust. Brendan looked around at the gathering. All
men. Not one woman. At least fifty men stood or sat on bales
of hay. The three boys walked to a corner and stood quietly.
Everyone around them seemed to be talking. The men ranged
in age from seventeen to seventy. Michael had been to two previous meetings, but he still felt the presence of these men, the
power and passion that had gathered in that barn.

A tall thin man that Michael and Longy had seen before, but Brendan had not, entered the room and walked the length of the barn. As he passed, the noise level dropped, as faces turned to see him coming. Silence travelled like a wave behind this man's back and by the time he reached the large stack of bales, which had been set up specifically for him, the room was completely still. The birds singing outside in the field could be heard clearly.

The man jumped onto the stack of bales and turned to address his audience. He didn't speak at first. He scanned the crowd, making eye contact with as many people as he could. After a minute, he finally spoke. "Why have you come here today?" he began, his thick northern accent filling the room.

No one offered an answer.

"You have come here today because you care about your country, because you are tired of sitting back and watching what is happening to this country of ours. In fact, I don't know why I even call it a country when it's really only half a bloody country anyway!"

The man spoke and everyone listened. Michael glanced over at Brendan. Brendan was staring at the speaker, his mouth wide open, and Michael knew he was hooked.

"The time is coming, my friends. The time for escalation is upon us. The time for talking is well behind us now. Our words have fallen on deaf English ears for too many years. Maybe the sound of our guns and bombs, they will hear much clearer."

The room erupted, every man shouting at the top of his voice. Michael looked at Brendan again who was screaming and punching the air with his fist.

The man from Northern Ireland finished his speech a few minutes later and stepped off the stage. He shook hands as he went, receiving numerous pats on the back as well. He stopped in front of Brendan and extended his hand. "I'm Andrew Kelly," he said.

Brendan shook his hand, smiling all the time. "I'm Brendan Horgan," he replied.

"I know. Your brother told me about you last week." Kelly shook Michael's hand as well, but kept his eyes on Brendan, like he was trying to cast a spell on him. "Come on, let's go outside and talk."

They exited the barn and walked away from the cars, down the hill. Longy, who had been ignored by Kelly, wasn't asked to join them, so he stayed in the barn, joining one of the many groups of men huddled inside, discussing times past and times to come.

Kelly walked slowly, the two Horgan brothers strolling next to him. "You remind me of a young freedom fighter who also grew up in County Cork." Kelly stopped and put his hand on Brendan's shoulder. "Do you know who I am talking about, Brendan?"

Brendan shrugged.

"Did you ever hear of Michael Collins?" Kelly asked.

"Of course," Brendan said. "Who hasn't? We learned about him in school."

"And do you think he was a good man?"

"I think he was a great man."

Kelly smiled. "Aye, he was a great man. He did things in his short life that we can only dream about doing. But we must do what we can in the time we are in now, and different times call for different tactics."

The two boys nodded their agreement.

Kelly continued walking down the hill. He removed an envelope from his pocket as he walked. "I want you two to do me a favour." Kelly waved the letter in the air.

The boys nodded, not sure what was coming. Kelly laughed. "Don't worry. I'm not going to ask you to kill anyone...yet." And he laughed again. "I want you to deliver this letter to the Evening Echo offices in Cork some time next week.

It's a message for JFK, a little welcome for him. All the instructions are inside, so you don't have to say anything to the reporter. Ask for John Corrigan and give him the letter personally. Okay?"

"No problem," Michael replied.

"Okay?" Kelly asked, looking directly at Brendan again.

"Okay," he replied.

Kelly handed the letter to Brendan. "Make sure you deliver it. It's a welcome, but it's also a warning. A warning to keep his nose out of our business with the English. Deliver it and watch for the paper on Tuesday 25th. An identical letter will be delivered to the American Ambassador on the same day."

Brendan was about to ask Kelly why he didn't post the letter, but before he could Kelly leaned closer and whispered something into his ear. Then Brendan understood the reason.

Michael was close, but not close enough to understand what was said.

A shout came from the barn behind them. A large, well-built man waved to Kelly and he waved back. "I've got to go now, boys. I'll see you back here next week." Kelly removed a small card from his pocket and again handed it to Brendan. "If you need anything call this number, anytime. You won't get me directly, but you'll get someone who can contact me." He shook hands with them again and jogged back up the hill.

By the time Michael and Brendan got back to the barn, Kelly was gone, the barn was almost empty and most of the cars were also gone. Longy stood by the barn door. He didn't look happy.

"What did he want?" he asked.

"Not much," Michael offered.

Longy didn't believe him. "He must have wanted something?"

"He thought I looked like Michael Collins." Brendan smiled.

"Yeah. But he thought you looked like Breda Collins, from Spriggs Road," Michael said to Longy.

Longy laughed, not aware he was the butt of the joke.

* * * *

The journey home was uneventful, until a Garda flagged them down on the outskirts of the city.

"Trying to break the sound barrier, boys, are ye?" the Garda started.

Longy didn't reply. Michael could see that he was trying to assess the Garda, trying to work out which category he fell into; friendly law enforcer or complete bastard.

"You were going pretty fast there, boy. Do you drive like this all the time?"

Longy shook his head.

The Garda leaned his elbows on the car door and stared at Longy. "I hope you don't drive like this at night, lad. What if you met with mist or fog?"

Michael saw the smile appear on Longy's face. Why was he smiling? This Garda obviously fell into the bastard category. He was just building up a head of steam first.

"Well," Longy said, speaking for the first time. "If I did I would take my foot off Mr. Accelerator and press down on Mr. Brake."

The Garda didn't smile. Lifting his elbows off the door, he leaned further into the car and was almost nose to nose with Longy when he spoke. "I said MIST or FOG, ya little smart ass!"

Longy's face drained of all colour. He had heard the Garda completely wrong, and worse than that, he thought he had heard something funny, and friendly. Brendan stifled a laugh and Michael bit his lower lip as the Garda removed his ticket book and started to write furiously.

Monday 17th June 1963

Excerpt from the Evening Echo:

Same Problems Faced Irish

"The Negro problems now in the United States are just the very same as those which faced the Irish in America two generations ago."

This was stated by Mr. John C. Houlihan, Republican Mayor of the city of Oakland, California, when he arrived at Shannon Airport this morning by Pan-American jet, accompanied by his wife, Emily, for a four day visit.

Mr. Houlihan said that the rising demands of the minority races, especially of the negro people, was the greatest problem facing the United States today.

Mary woke at seven to the sound of her two brothers making their way down the stairs for breakfast. Michael worked in the Harbour Commissioners, by the docks. He spent his days unloading and loading crates of drink from one truck to another. The work was hard but he enjoyed it, especially if someone dropped a crate and broke some bottles. Everyone would scamper to the dropped crate with pots, kettles, anything that could hold liquid. They would salvage what they could, and at five o'clock the men would sit around and drink their salvage. Whiskey, brandy or sherry, it didn't matter. They would drink what was given, and pull the bits of sawdust that had gathered with the spilt alcohol from their teeth as they drank.

Brendan worked at the turf stores on Baker's Road. While Michael loaded and unloaded drink all day, his younger brother handled turf for a living. If someone dropped some turf during the day, they bloody well picked it up and carried on. There were no perks on this job like the ones Michael enjoyed.

Mary looked over at Louise in the other bed. She was still asleep and wouldn't get up until eight at the earliest. Louise wasn't working and spent her days helping her mother. Louise had finished school the summer before and hadn't bothered to look for a job yet. Mary thought of Louise as the kind of girl who marries young and never works outside her own home in her lifetime.

She looked at her sister and felt sorry for her. Justin, the little bastard, had given Louise a fifty the night before. She had returned to the Fitzgerald's house, devastated by his no show. Mary had tried to console her, but Louise cried for almost an hour. It was her first bad experience with men, and it probably wouldn't be her last. She had calmed down just before the Fitzgeralds came home. Mary brought her across the street and stayed up talking with her for another hour. In the end they had decided that men were shit and they would never get married. Louise suggested they should buy their own house and live together happily, without men. Mary laughed and agreed, but as she lay down she thought of Dean Reynolds, the American, and hoped she would never share that house with Louise.

* * * *

Downstairs was bedlam. Mary stood at the door and watched as her two brothers and her father spilled milk, knocked over the sugar bowl and duelled with butter knives. Jack looked pretty hung over. He rarely drank on Sundays, but the Eucharistic Procession had been on yesterday and that had meant a trip to the pub afterwards.

Michael and Brendan were no doubt hung over as well, but they had youth on their side. 'For every year after you reach thirty add another hour on to your recovery time from excessive drinking', her father had told them. From the look on Jack's face, Mary thought he would still be suffering tonight when he arrived back home. Her brothers looked shook, but they would be fine after a brisk walk to work.

Michael gulped the last of his tea and shoved a half-eaten piece of toast into his mouth. He grabbed his lunch and headed for the door. "I'll be late," he said through the toast. "It's John's turn to drop a case today." And he was gone.

He had the longest distance to walk and always left first, followed by Mary, then Jack, and finally Brendan.

Mary worked in Cudmore's shop on Patrick Street and had told some white lies to land the position. Cudmore's was a sweet shop and sat on the corner of Patrick Street and Winthrop Street. The front of the shop faced the entrance to Cash's department store, the place where Mary dreamed of working. Unfortunately, only south side girls from good families were awarded jobs in Cash's. It was hard to get any job in the city when they heard you were from the north side, so Mary had used her granny's address in Sunday's Well on her application.

Sunday's Well was a respectable part of the north side, even though the hills and houses of Gurranabraher looked down on the area.

Mr. Thompson, her boss, was not a nice man, and she suspected that he often wondered about where she lived. He would throw questions at her from out of the blue, at least twice a week and she often had to check behind her as she walked home; afraid he would follow her someday and catch her out in her lies.

She liked the job, but hated Mr. Thompson. He was older, at least fifty, and was always leering at her, asking her to go up the ladder to get the apple drops from the top shelf, or bend over and pick up the bon bon jar. His dress code for work was simple. Mary, and Beth who worked with her, had to wear skirts below the knee. This not only made them look presentable, but also worked quite well for Mr. Thompson, when he needed a jar of apple drops from the top shelf.

* * * *

The morning was cool, but the sun was already drying the dew that had settled on the grass overnight. Mary stood at the gate to Angela Browne's house and waited for her friend to make an appearance. Angela worked in the city as well, and they would walk to and from work together everyday. Her job was not as inviting as Mary's. Angela worked in a tailor's shop, sewing hems and letting out dresses for women who had put on a few pounds. She only ever saw the faces of the three other women who worked with her. Mary's job had its problems, but at least she had the variety of dealing with customers all day.

The front door opened and Angela plodded out. Mary knew immediately that something was wrong. Angela's face was always an open book to Mary, and looking up the path at Angela now, Mary thought of Angela's father.

"Is everything alright?" Mary asked, knowing it wasn't.

Angela had tears in her eyes. She glanced back at the house and walked past Mary, obviously wanting to be away from it. "He never came home yesterday after the procession," she started.

Mary nodded and listened. She never knew what to say when this happened.

"He went for his few pints after mass and never came home for dinner. Johnny saw him marching in the procession, but he didn't come home after. He came in last night, just after eleven."

Angela and Mary walked toward the city, neither of them talking for a while. Angela seemed to be searching for the words to describe what had happened. A single tear ran down her face and Mary offered her a tissue.

"It will be better from now on," Angela began again. "It will be better now."

Mary felt like she had to say something, so she did. "What happened, Angela? Did he hit your Mam?"

Angela's father drank heavily, and often. He was of the breed of men who, after getting blind drunk, liked to hit people. The person who was in his line of fire the most was Mrs. Browne.

Mary was lucky. Her father liked his pint, but had never laid a hand on their mother. He had seen his own father beat his mother regularly, she knew from overhearing conversations between her parents. He had experienced what Angela was enduring first hand.

"He hit her really hard this time," Angela answered. "I came down the stairs and saw her sprawled out on the kitchen floor. Her nose was bleeding, but she still managed to smile at me. 'Go to bed, dear,' she said. I stood in the hallway and stared at my father. He was sitting on a chair half asleep. I was frozen to the spot, unable to do anything, afraid he might have a go at me if I tried to help her."

"You must have been terrified?" Mary offered.

"I was...but Johnny wasn't."

Mary turned and looked at Angela, who looked right back, and nodded.

"Really?"

"Really," Angela confirmed, her voice becoming steadier, controlled.

They had spoken in the past about this day, the day when Johnny would be old enough to stand up to his father. Angela had always reckoned that it wouldn't happen until Johnny was at least twenty, if at all. Johnny adored his father and Angela could never picture the scene where Johnny would turn on him. Mary could see that Angela now had a vivid memory of last night imprinted on her brain for all time.

"Tell me about it, Angela. If you want to, like."

Angela took a deep breath and began. "I stood in the hallway, watching my mother bleed all over the floor. My father sat, contented, on a chair next to her. Then I heard Johnny get out of bed upstairs. He had come upon this scene before and had always stood next to me, afraid, as I was, to do anything. I turned to see him come down the stairs, and the look in his eyes chilled my bones. He didn't look like Johnny at all. He looked possessed. Tears ran down his cheeks and his eyes were like, on fire. He ignored me and headed for the kitchen."

They both stopped walking and Angela continued. "Dad was surprised to see him. He wasn't sure how to react. Johnny stood at the table glaring down at him. 'Pick her up,' the sixteen-year-old Johnny said.

"Dad laughed and motioned for Johnny to go to bed. Johnny stood as still as a pole, just staring down at Dad. I was still in the hall, terrified. Dad got up and came face to face with Johnny. 'Go to bed,' he shouted. His voice almost made me pee, but Johnny didn't look frightened at all. I saw him make a fist with his right hand. He swung hard and the next second Dad went flying back onto his chair. His cheek blew up like a fuckin' balloon."

Mary's mouth dropped open. They were standing by the corner of North Main Street and Castle Street, where they usually parted company. It was almost quarter to nine and Mary was late, but she couldn't move. "What did he do?" she almost shouted.

Angela smiled. "Nothing. He did nothing. Johnny stood over him for ten minutes, waiting for him to get up again. He didn't. I helped Mam up and brought her upstairs to my room. Later, I heard Johnny come up stairs, but by the time I fell asleep, Dad had not tried the stairs at all. I think he slept in the kitchen."

The two girls looked at each other, Angela as amazed as Mary was, now that she had told the story for the first time.

"It will be better from now on," Angela said, and she hugged Mary before running off to work. "I'll see you for lunch."

Angela looked a bit happier, but behind the false smile Mary could see the pain, the pain Angela felt for her younger brother, her brother who would carry the burden of hitting his father with him forever.

* * * *

Mr. Thompson was waiting at the door to the shop, looking intently at his pocket watch. Mary could see, through the large shop window, that Beth was already topping up the shelves. At least she wouldn't have to climb the ladder to get extra supplies of apple drops this morning, she hoped. She looked at Mr. Thompson and knew that missing a peek up her skirt was the real reason he looked put out.

"Nice of you to join us, Mary. Will you be remaining with us for the rest of the day?"

"Yes, sir. Sorry I'm late, Mr. Thompson. It won't happen again." She batted her eyelids at the horny old bugger and he melted slightly.

"Okay. Okay, Mary. Get to work. Poor Beth is exhausted from running up and down that ladder, and she hasn't even got down the apple drops yet." He ushered her in the door.

Mary smirked and watched as Beth climbed the ladder, and watched as Thompson scurried over to hold it for her, just in case she fell, of course.

The morning passed quickly and the sweet shop was surprisingly busy. Mary told Beth about her weekend, especially Friday night. Beth was privy to Mary's secret regarding her address, so she didn't have to change the story that much. She showed Beth the bruise on her arm, which was slightly yellow now and feeling better. She told Beth she didn't know Willy at all, that he must have been a drunk, but she did tell her all about Dean, in excruciating detail.

Mary went about her work with a slight glow about her. Just talking about him gave her goose bumps. She knew she would never see him again, but he was at least thirty; way too old for her. The memory was nice, but that was all she would ever have of him. She thought of Tuesday and dreaded it like the arrival of a nasty flu. Tomorrow, the glow would fade and she would be left with a memory that was already starting to fray at the edges. By then his face would start to fade and become vague. By the end of the week, Mary knew she would be picturing what she thought the American had looked like, not how he actually had looked.

She checked her watch; half past eleven. Her break was at one and the day would be over at six. The shop was empty momentarily and Mr. Thompson ventured out from the storeroom. He scanned the counter, then the shelves, and fixed his eyes on Mary.

"Would you get down some more apple drops, Mary? They seem to have sold well this morning."

Mary walked to the ladder, wondering if Mr. Thompson actually hired people to come in and buy bloody apple drops. Thompson stood next to the ladder trying to mask his excitement. Mary wanted to tell him to get his own fucking apple drops, to tell him he was a dirty old man. But girls from Sundays Well didn't say things like that. Girls from Sunday's Well wouldn't notice that Mr. Thompson wanted a look at their knickers, but girls from Gurranabraher did.

Mary put her foot on the bottom rung of the ladder. She glanced at Mr. Thompson and could swear she saw him licking his lips. Her stomach turned and she wanted to run away, out of the shop and home. He had never tried to do anything to the two of them. He just took his peeks when he could get them. She dared not to think of what he got up to in the storeroom. She started to climb and Thompson slithered in under the ladder, holding both sides firmly. Mary climbed quickly and reached out for the apple drop jar. She pulled it toward her, but it snagged on the shelf and nearly tumbled over the side. Mary's heart leapt in her chest. If she dropped that her wages would be dented severely on Friday. Gathering the jar to her chest, she started back down, looking over her shoulder for her footing.

Mr. Thompson's eyes looked like apple drops. They bulged out of their sockets, and Mary thought they would pop any second and go bouncing down the last few rungs of the ladder. He smiled up at her and she felt like vomiting on top of him. She looked at Beth, who stared up at her, a look of empathy on her face. She too had been there, numerous times.

Slowly, Mary turned back, and without hesitation, she let go of the apple drops jar.

It seemed to take forever for the jar to fall. Mary could see the look of pure ecstasy on Thompson's face wash away, to be replaced with a wince in anticipation of the oncoming pain.

The jar hit the sixth rung from the bottom and flipped over, the cap of the jar catching the dirty old man on the bridge of his nose. A dull popping sound could be heard clearly in the empty shop. Blood flowed down his nostrils and splattered onto the floor.

The jar hit the floor next, but didn't break. Thompson raised his hands to his broken nose and howled in pain. Mary looked at Beth who was visibly smiling. Mary smothered a laugh and started down the ladder.

"Oh dear, Mr. Thompson. I'm so sorry. It just slipped out of my hand. I'm so sorry."

Thompson, in too much pain to answer, continued to howl. Mary grabbed a towel from behind the counter and handed it to him. He placed the towel over his face and headed for the storeroom, his howling slowly fading to a whimper.

He emerged seconds later, his coat thrown over his shoulders. "I'm going to the Mercy," he announced and disappeared through the door.

For a couple of seconds the girls said nothing. Then, at the same time they both fell about the shop laughing.

"I've always wanted to do that," Beth said. "I could never go through with it though. Well done, Mary."

"It worked out nicely really," Mary snorted.

"What do you mean?"

"Well, if the jar broke it would have cost me a pound out of my wages on Friday." The girls erupted once more.

"This seems like a great place to work." The voice came from the other side of the counter. The girls stopped laughing immediately. Mary looked across the counter and Dean Reynolds smiled back at her.

"Hello, Mary."

Mary felt her knees wobble, and thought she was going to keel over. That would really impress him. She stood looking at him smile back at her and realised she hadn't spoken yet.

"Ahh…hello, Dean," she murmured.

Beth moved away to the other end of the shop, behind Dean. She turned and looked directly at Mary, mouthing the words, 'Is that him?'. Mary gave a slight nod and looked back at Dean.

Dean pointed to Mary's arm. "How is it?"

"It's fine. It's slightly sore, but I can bear it," Mary replied, rubbing her arm tenderly. "I can still get the jars from the top shelf."

"Your boss might disagree with you about that," Dean laughed.

Mary blushed. He had seen her drop the jar on Mr. Thompson's head. He must think I'm an animal, she thought.

"He deserved it, the dirty old man; peeking up girls' skirts," she said in her defence.

"I agree," Dean offered and Mary relaxed a little.

Another customer came in and Beth rushed to serve him. Dean pointed at the clove rocks and asked for a bag of them. Mary weighed them out and handed them over. The other customer left.

"I hope I didn't make things worse for you the other night," he said, as he handed over the money.

"No. I haven't seen him since, thank God."

Dean started to speak and hesitated. Mary could see his cheeks redden slightly.

"Would you like to accompany me to the cinema tonight, Mary? I don't know anyone here, except you of course; and it's no fun going on my own."

Mary wanted to jump over the counter and wrap her arms around him, kiss him hard on the lips and tell him she would bear his children.

"Okay, so," she whispered.

* * * *

"Ya lucky bitch," Angela said, much too loud, causing a few heads to turn. They were in Thompson's Café on Patrick Street, having some lunch. They lunched together almost every-day, unless one of them was asked to work through.

"Are you going to sleep with him?" Angela added, much quieter this time.

"Angela, that's disgusting," Mary feigned disgust. "I'm going to stay awake the whole time."

They laughed together; inviting more disapproving looks from the patrons.

"I need you to call in home for me tonight," Mary said, when they had calmed down again.

"Why?"

"He wants to take me to the pictures, and it starts at ten past six. I need you to tell Mam that I am working late at the shop, doing a stock take or something. Okay?"

"Stock take. More like taking off your feckin' stockins, ya dirty bitch."

Mary frowned, trying to remain serious.

"Okay," Angela agreed. "You know I'll do it, for God's sake."

"Now," Mary said. "I have some more news."

Angela leaned in, following Mary's lead.

"I dropped a jar of apple drops on Mr. Thompson's head this morning."

Angela tried to hold it in, but a small, sharp snigger escaped her lips.

"I think I broke his nose," Mary added and Angela had every person in the café staring at her again, but she didn't look like she cared.

* * * *

Across the café, not far from the door, Willy O'Reilly sat watching Mary and Angela laugh hysterically. Everyone in the café had looked in the girls' direction at some point. Mary seemed a little uncomfortable, but Willy could see that Angela wasn't the least bit bothered.

He knew what they were talking about, unlike the rest of the patrons of the café. He had left home early that morning, hoping to spot Mary on her way to work, but he had missed her.

His next stop had been on Patrick Street. He picked the corner between Cash's and Roches Stores as the best vantage point to view Cudmore's shop. The sweet shop was on the next corner and large windows on each side of the door afforded a complete view of the inside. He wouldn't risk going into the shop while the boss was there. He decided to see if the old fart took a break before Mary. And he did, a break to the nose that is.

Willy had watched in amazement as Mary dropped the jar of sweets from the top of the ladder onto the old man's face. Even from where he was, a good fifty feet away, he could see the explosion of blood from the man's nose. Willy didn't laugh at this slightly funny scene. Instead, he discovered new levels of hatred for Mary. As he watched Mary pretend to care for her boss, he touched the lump on his head, digging his fingers into the skin, as if he could push the lump back in again.

His chance came when the injured old man came running out of the shop and headed down Patrick Street towards Daunt Square. Willy supposed he was heading for the Mercy Hospital. His time had arrived.

He could now deal with Mary once and for all. She would tell him about this hero who had bashed his head against the

G.P.O. wall on Friday night. Then he would take care of her and sort out the hero later, when he was ready.

He moved away from the corner and walked towards the shop. There was another girl with Mary, but Willy reckoned he could easily frighten her off. What he had in mind wouldn't take long anyway, so if she decided to run for help he planned to be long gone before she came back. He crossed the short distance between the main door of Cash's and Cudmore's entrance quickly, and was almost to the door when he saw the hero. He had almost walked straight into him. Willy changed direction, cutting behind the man and past the shop entrance. He crossed the road, glancing back to see him enter and start talking to Mary. Taking up his original position by Cash's, he watched as they chatted for a few minutes.

When the hero had eventually walked back onto the street, Willy decided to follow him, just to find out where he could get to him later, then he would double back and deal with Mary. He followed the stranger to the Metropole Hotel on Mac Curtain Street, and when he confirmed that the he was staying there, he arrived back at the shop in time to see Mary heading to lunch.

He sat watching them eat now. He couldn't approach them here, too many people. So he decided to wait until Mary was on her way home later. Willy got up and left the café. He had a few hours to get home and do some work. Then he would get back to the shop by six and deal with Mary.

* * * *

Willy turned up the driveway to the farm thirty minutes later. He looked at the house that his great grandfather had built almost a century ago. The house was perched on the highest point of the farm looking down on the road. It was a powerful building; two storeys that looked like they had dropped from the sky and dug their heels deep into the soft ground, deciding they liked where they had landed. The structure of the house was sound, but after years of neglect she was starting to show signs of weakness. The outer paint work was chipped and cracked. The inside of the house had not been decorated or cleaned to any acceptable level for eight years.

Willy looked at the house as he approached it and thought of his father. Things would be different now, he thought, if his father were still alive. His mother wouldn't be confined to her bed now. The farm and the house would be in a healthier condition than they were. Willy's father had died tending to this farm and Willy had hated the place ever since.

He parked the Morris Minor by the front door of the house and could already hear his mother shouting as he walked into the hall.

"Is that you, Willy?"

"No, it's the grim reaper. Your name came up on our list today."

He always said the worse thing he could think of, and regretted it soon after. He loved his mother, but resented the fact that she had given up after his father had died. Not long after the funeral she had taken to bed one afternoon and had rarely got out of it since.

"What did you say?" she shouted down the stairs.

"Nothing, mother. It's only me."

"Where have you been all morning?"

Willy started for the stairs. "I walked Mary to work and had some lunch with her."

He reached the door to her room. It was slightly ajar. He watched her stare out the window as she shouted questions at him. Nearly everything that came out of her mouth was in the form of a question.

"Are you ever going to bring that girl to see me?"

"Are you ever going to get out of that bed?" Willy countered.

She turned and saw him standing in the doorway. She didn't answer; she never answered that question. Willy waited for the subject change that always followed.

"Have you fed the pigs yet today?"

"I'm about to now," he answered, smiling slightly as his prediction came true. "Do you want anything because I'm going out later."

"Where are you off to?" she asked.

"I'm taking Mary to the pictures tonight."

Ever since that one time he had dated Mary, he had pretended to his mother that they were dating. He couldn't face the ridicule she would serve up to him if he told her the truth.

"Make me some tea and a sandwich before you go. That'll have to do me I suppose."

Willy left the house and headed for the barn. It was quarter past two and he had work to do before returning to Patrick Street.

****

Mr. Thompson returned from the hospital at three o'clock. He confirmed that his nose was broken. The skin around his eyes had begun to turn dark and he had a lot of white bandages stuck to his nose. He looked like a heavyweight fighter after a bad night on the canvas. The girls had tried to quell his bad humour by telling him that it didn't look too bad. He didn't seem to realise that Mary had dropped the jar on purpose, much to her relief.

At six, Beth put on her coat and left. Mary continued cleaning up, moving things into place and generally trying to pass the time. She filled two paper bags with an assortment of sweats and put them in her handbag. She showed Mr. Thomp-

son the money she had taken from her purse to pay for the
sweets before putting it in the cash box. She didn't want to be
sacked for stealing on the day she had almost killed her boss,
and got away with it.

At five past six, Dean Reynolds appeared in the doorway,
his face the picture of happiness. Mary felt her stomach do a
cartwheel and could feel herself blushing. He entered the shop
and Mr. Thompson looked up from his sweeping brush.

"I'm sorry sir, but we're closed."

Dean took a long look at Mr. Thompson's smashed face.
"I'm not here for your sweets, mister. I'm here for this sweetie
right here," he answered, pointing at Mary.

Mary's face almost caught fire. She could feel her cheeks,
neck and shoulders filling up. She thought that she must look
like a beetroot at that moment. Looking at Mr. Thompson, the
expression on his face flooded her with mixed feelings. He
looked shocked and that made her feel good, but she knew the
reason for his amazement was that Dean was looking for her,
Mary Horgan. She felt terrible, but then Dean walked over and
kissed her lightly on the cheek.

"Come on," he whispered. "We'll be late."

He helped her put on her coat and held her hand as they
left the shop.

Mr. Thompson said nothing.

The film was called Military Policemen, starring Bob
Hope and Mickey Rooney. They both found it funny and
laughed constantly. Dean was the complete gentleman. He sat
and watched the film, keeping his hands to himself. He leaned
over a few times and whispered comments to her about the film,
his lips brushing gently against the lobe of her ear. The first few
times Mary sat there listening to him, with tingles running
through her body like volts of electricity. Later, she started to
lean over herself, to do a bit of lobe dancing.

They walked out of the Palace cinema at five past eight. The evening was still bright, but the sun was fighting a losing battle with the surrounding buildings.

"I'm amazed at how late the sun goes down here," Dean said. "I couldn't believe it last night when it got dark just before eleven."

Mary agreed, and they discussed some trivial items for a few minutes. They were awkward minutes, but they were a part of almost every first date.

Finally, Dean made a suggestion. "Would you like to join me for a drink?"

Mary hesitated slightly. It was already past eight and her parents would not believe she was still working this late. She should really be home before eight-thirty. She could still bluff her way out of trouble then.

"Okay. I'd love to," she heard herself saying.

Dean suggested they go to the lounge in the Metropole Hotel. Mary had never been inside the Metropole before and agreed enthusiastically.

* * * *

The hotel was on the same street as the cinema so they were back indoors after less than a minute of walking. Dean removed Mary's coat and led her to a seat in a secluded corner of the hotel lounge. He left her briefly and returned, but without drinks. Mary was puzzled. He had asked her what she had wanted and she had told him, but he had brought no drinks back with him. Maybe the barman told him she looked too young, or something like that. Mary started to feel a bit uneasy at the prospect of being asked to prove her age.

"Are you okay, Mary?" Dean asked, as he sat down.

"I'm….I'm fine," she answered, but she wasn't. She had seen a man come around one of the pillars and he was walking toward them. This was it, she thought, total humiliation. The lounge wasn't full, but there were enough people to point and stare as she was escorted off the premises. Mary was so engrossed with the prospect of being ejected from the hotel that she didn't notice that the waiter was carrying a tray with two drinks on it.

"A glass of Murphy's," the waiter announced, and placed the drink in front of Mary. "And a pint of Murphy's for yourself, sir." The waiter smiled and retreated gracefully.

Dean lifted his pint and held it out to Mary. "To great beginnings."

Mary picked up her glass, relief flooding through her body. They touched glasses and each of them took a sip.

"I'm finding it hard to adjust to the local beverage," Dean said, his face contorting as he swallowed the black liquid.

Mary smiled. "It takes time to get used to it. The real problems start when you do get a taste for it."

They both laughed, and the first and last uncomfortable silence followed the laughter. They both took another sip from their glasses. Mary tried to think of something to say. Then she realised there were many things she didn't know about the man sitting across from her, probably too much. "You told me the last night that you were here on a little business. Do you mind if I ask you what your business is?"

"No, not at all. I'm thinking of setting up here in Cork actually," He removed a business card from his pocket and placed it on the table, facing Mary.

Mary read it slowly. "You're an architect?"

"Yes, indeed I am."

"You design buildings for a living?"

"Yes."

Mary was impressed and she didn't hide it from Dean. "Have you designed many buildings, in America that is?"

"Well, you told me you have never been to America, so you wouldn't know the buildings I have designed. I haven't been lucky enough to land the job for a major landmark yet, but maybe here I will get something better."

"And you're planning to set up a business here in Cork?"

"That's my plan."

"So you're planning to stay in Ireland?"

Dean leaned toward her. "If I can get work, I will stay."

Mary's heart pounded in her chest. He was planning to stay. She took another sip of her Murphy's and tried to calm herself down. No point in throwing herself at his feet, not yet anyway.

"I have one major problem though," Dean continued.

"What's that?"

"I don't know the city that well."

"And?"

"I need someone to guide me around." He looked at Mary pleadingly.

The penny dropped for Mary. "Me. You want me?"

"More than you know." He smiled.

The waiter appeared from behind the pillar and approached them again. "Mr Reynolds?" he asked.

Dean nodded. "Yes."

"There is a long distance call for you at reception, sir."

"Okay. I'll be there in a minute."

The waiter left and Dean looked at Mary.

"I'm sorry, Mary. I have to take this call. It's from the States and it will take awhile."

Mary started to get up. "That's okay. I have to get home anyway."

Dean took some money from his pocket and offered it to her. "The doorman will get you a taxi."

"I'll get a taxi, but I'll pay for it, Dean. You paid for the pictures and drinks already tonight. Fair is fair."

"Okay, I'm not going to argue with a smile like that. I can only lose." He paused and helped her with her coat. "Will you meet me on Wednesday night, Mary?" he whispered into her ear.

Mary turned around and he rested his hands on her hips. She looked up into his eyes. She didn't speak. He knew she would meet him. He drew her closer and kissed her gently on the lips.

"Until Wednesday night," he said. "I'll pick you up after work?"

"Okay," Mary whispered and they walked out of the lounge to the reception area, hand in hand. He kissed her again at the door and headed back to reception to answer his phonecall.

She tied her coat as the doorman asked her if she wanted a taxi. "No. I'm fine," she answered, and after checking if Dean was out of sight, she started the journey home, on foot.

* * * *

While Mary and Dean sat in the cinema watching Mickey Rooney, Willy sat five seats back watching them. He rarely looked at the screen at all, focusing totally on them. A few times, he considered taking out the switchblade he had in his pocket, walking calmly down the aisle, and driving the blade into the stranger's neck. Willy convinced himself that no one would see this act and that he could easily walk, not run, out of the cinema before anyone raised the alarm. He convinced himself he could get away with it, but he remained seated and watched them, deciding that if they kissed he would do it.

Once or twice, the man had leaned in close to Mary and Willy had jumped to his feet, hand on his knife. He didn't kiss her, so Willy stayed behind them and left five minutes before the film ended.

He watched them come out of the cinema, and followed them down the street to the Metropole hotel, keeping a safe distance behind. They entered the hotel and Willy walked past, not daring to look.

She was going to sleep with him!

Willy was sure of it. She hadn't let him have so much as a feel, but this fella from nowhere was going to get everything, and on their first night together! He stood on the street, unable to focus. What should he do now? He couldn't go in and demand the room number. Even if he got it, what would he do then? Go up and kill both of them? No. He would never get away with it.

Feeling helpless and distraught, Willy walked back towards the cinema and entered Dan Lowery's bar. He ordered a Murphy's and disposed of it in three wholesome gulps. He ordered a second and brooded over that one a little longer.

He was on his third pint when he spotted Mary hurrying past the window, on her own. Willy felt relieved that Mary obviously hadn't slept with the stranger. He left his unfinished pint on the bar and burst through the exit doors.

Outside, it was still bright and he could see Mary passing the cinema. She was moving fast. The streets were quiet so he trailed behind her, close enough to see in which direction she was going. At the end of Mac Curtain Street, she paused at the corner. Willy prayed she would cross and take the shortcut towards the North Cathedral. If she turned left, she would be heading for Patrick Street, and more people. The shortcut would be nice and quiet for what he had in mind. He stepped into a doorway in case she looked back over her shoulder. Mary stood looking down towards Patrick Street and Willy felt sure she would go that way. She could get the bus outside Easons and it would take her all the way to her front door.

A large truck rounded the corner in front of Mary and came down Mac Curtain Street. Mary crossed the road and headed down Coburg Street; the shortcut home. Willy darted from the doorway and followed her, smiling like a man who had won a prize bond. His luck was in tonight.

When Mary reached Devonshire Street the gap between them had increased slightly. Willy saw Mary check her watch and up the pace even more. He made the decision to catch up to her before she climbed the steps that would bring her onto Mulgrave Street, and from there onto Cathedral Road. He walked quickly, but feared he had let the distance between them increase too much. If he ran to her now, she would surely hear him coming and start screaming. That would blow the whole thing for him.

Mary reached the first step and started to climb. Willy was still thirty yards away. He decided to grab her before she reached the top step and drag her back down. A dark lane shot off to the left at the end of the steps.

He would take her down there.

Mary had five steps left before she reached the main road and relative safety. Willy started up the steps two at a time. He knew it was risky. If someone turned the corner and started down the steps it could get messy. Although, he thought, I'm just a fella running up the steps in a hurry now. If someone came on the scene while he was dragging Mary back down the steps, that could be a problem.

As Mary reached the second last step Willy was almost on her. He reached out his arm as she reached the top step.

He had her now, he thought.

* * * *

Mary heard the car horn to her left as she climbed the last step. It startled her and she swung around to see who it was. Across the street, a Ford Prefect pulled up to the footpath and Kevin Long waved frantically out through the driver's window.

"D'ya want a lift, Mary?" he shouted.

Mary wouldn't normally take a lift from Longy, and had refused him enough times to give him that impression. But Longy wasn't known for taking hints. Tonight, she was glad he had stopped. She wanted to get home and she didn't fancy the long trek up the north side. She checked the road and ran over to his car. Longy didn't hide his joy. She knew he would ask her out; he always did, and she hadn't been in his car before. She hoped he didn't get the wrong idea.

Mary opened the passenger door and was instantly struck by the reek of onions, much stronger than normal. Her eyes watered and she nearly changed her mind. Then, taking a deep breath of fresh air, she jumped in and, holding that precious breath, she signalled him to drive on.

****

Willy lay flat on the steps, out of view of the car. He had dived for cover when he heard the car horn sound. Who the hell was that, and had they seen him? He had missed Mary by inches, and he was glad he had now. Whoever was in that car, if they hadn't seen him already, would definitely have seen him if he had grabbed her. He heard the car door slam and the engine cough and splutter. Seconds later the car was out of sight.

He lay on the steps, totally annoyed with the way his day had gone. What a total waste of time, he thought.

"Are you alright there, boy?" a voiced rose from below him.

Willy raised his head and spotted the old woman at the foot of the steps. She was wearing a black shawl and looked at him with concern in her eyes.

"Ahh…I'm fine. I just slipped there, like. I'm fine really." Willy sprang to his feet and walked back down the steps towards the woman. As he passed her they exchanged smiles.

He felt like giving her a smack in the mouth, to vent some of his frustration. Instead, he continued back towards MacCurtain Street and his mother's car.

* * * *

"Is there something wrong with me, Mary?"

Mary sat in the passenger seat and wished she had walked after all. Kevin had started the conversation by telling her he was up in court in the morning for speeding, and had jumped from that straight into the 'will-you-go-out-with-me' speech.

"It's not you, Kevin. I'm seeing someone else at the moment. I think you're really nice, but I'm with someone else now." She reached for the handle and rolled down her window. The rush of fresh air pushed the onion smell back towards its source. Mary turned her head to the window and took a sharp, deep breath.

Longy smiled, obviously putting his own twist on what Mary had said. She would be with him only that she was seeing someone else for the moment; for the moment.

"Who's the lucky fella?" he asked.

"You don't know him."

"Oh. A south sider, is it?"

"No."

"Then I might know him. I know everyone from the north side, girl. Try me."

"He's an American," Mary said to shut him up. She regretted it as soon as it came out. She might as well have gone home and told Brendan and Michael as well; Longy would anyway.

They pulled up outside Mary's house. The sun was disappearing behind the houses and darkness loomed. Trying not to breathe through her nose, Mary leaned over to Longy and said. "Kevin, don't tell anyone about my American friend, okay?"

She leaned in as close as she could without fainting. Her breast touched Longy's arm, and by the reaction on his face, she knew she could ask him to cut off his arm and he would do it.

"Okay," he replied, the odour of fresh onions intensifying.

"Especially Brendan and Michael. They would tell Dad, and I would be in trouble then."

"Don't worry about them. I know things about them that would keep them quiet for years." Longy smiled at her.

Mary was interested; anything on her brothers would be handy. Against her stomachs advice, she leaned in closer to him. "What exactly do you know?"

Longy hesitated for all of two seconds and then told Mary all about the trips to East Cork and the meetings. He returned to the speeding story for a while, but she guided him gently back on track. Mary got out of the car when he was finished. He drove off and she stood there considering what he had told her. He was making it up, she decided. He had to be. Her two brothers couldn't be involved in something like that.

It wasn't possible.

Tuesday 18ᵗʰ June 1963

Excerpt from the Evening Echo:

Thirty Motorists Fined at Cork—First Speed Limit Prosecutions

The first prosecutions in Cork under the 1961 Traffic Act for exceeding the speed limit were made before District Justice D.P. O'Donovan, B.L., today in the Cork District Court.

Thirty-two motorists were fined sums ranging from 30/- to 80/- for driving at speeds from 36 to 45 m.p.h. Fines totalled £70. Supt. N. Delany, prosecuting, said that since this was the first prosecution in Cork he proposed to go into detail about proof.

The justice said that if garda gave evidence that a car exceeded the speed limit that would do him. Garda Jim Clifford, in the course of his evidence in the various prosecutions, cleared some points about the operation of the radar speed system. The garda said they were allowed a two-mile margin "each way" but on this occasion at the end of the dual carriageway in Tivoli they stopped no one under 34 m.p.h.

Michael arrived home before six, much earlier than the previous night. His friend in work, John, had dropped a case of brandy during the day and they had managed to salvage most of the spillage. At half past five, Michael had made a trip to the shop on the corner and purchased some red lemonade. The brandy wasn't bad, after they had drained most of the sawdust and dirt out of it. Many of the older men drank the alcohol without any mixer, but John and Michael and some of the younger lads used the lemonade.

Michael had arrived home on Monday night at ten and work on Tuesday had been a battle. He was glad to get home tonight at six and planned an early retirement to his bed. He sat down at the table and watched a show called Mr. Ed.

Ann and Louise were in the kitchen preparing the dinner. Michael could smell the bodice and cabbage, his lips watering as he watched the talking horse.

The door opened and Jack made an entrance. "How's everyone?" he shouted.

No one answered. In the past he would get some recognition of arrival, but now the television demanded full attention. Things had changed forever in the living room so Jack went to the kitchen, kissed Ann on the cheek as she continued working, and returned to the living room to read the paper.

Brendan and Mary came in together. Brendan was covered from head to toe in dust from the turf stores. Mary looked as clean as she had that morning. Mr. Thompson had taken the day off, and she and Beth had enjoyed a relaxing day. They must have climbed the ladder a total of three times each; down a considerable number from when Mr. Thompson was around, and not one customer had been left short of what they wanted.

Ann and Louise emerged from the steaming kitchen, with plates of equally steaming food in tow. They dropped what they had and returned to the kitchen for more. Ann came back with two more plates, while Louise carried a large bowl of boiled potatoes. They all gathered around the table and started in. The television stayed on and they all watched, no one speaking.

After a minute or two, Jack shook his head and got up. He walked to the television and punched in the off button. The screen went blank and everyone roared.

"No. I don't care. From now on the telly goes off during dinner," he announced. "If ye keep going like that none of us will be talking to each other. We'll all just sit here every night and watch that bloody box. What kind of a world would it be then, huh? A bunch of zombies, that's what we'd end up like."

He looked around the table waiting to be overruled by all of them. They could do it too. If they all ganged up on him, with Ann behind them, then that television would be on every night. But they didn't. They glanced at Ann, who nodded. With that nod, she said more than Jack had with his mouth. They all shrugged and accepted the rule, not because Jack had made it, but because Ann had approved it. Congress had proposed a bill and the President had signed it.

* * * *

Mary played with her food and thought about what Longy had told her the night before. She decided to test the water. "Dad, were you ever in the I.R.A.?"

Jack coughed and sprayed chunks of potato across the table. "Jesus, what kind of question is that?" he shouted.

Mary wasn't looking at him. Her eyes moved from Brendan to Michael. Brendan didn't flinch, continuing to eat his dinner. But Michael stopped with a fork halfway to his face.

Mary continued. "No, it's just that Beth in work was saying that her uncle was a member, that's all."

Jack drank some water. "And you think I might have been a member of that bunch of bollixes."

Mary saw it clearly this time. Michael glared at Brendan who shook his head slowly, obviously trying to calm him down. Michael looked ready to pop, his face reddened visibly.

"That's enough talk about that now," Ann said. "Mary, I don't want you talking about things like that in this house." Ann was looking at Jack, and Mary thought she saw something pass between them.

Jack laughed, trying to sound amused. "I hate the English as much as the next man, but the I.R.A. never solved and never will solve anything by killing innocent people."

None of them heard Longy beating on the door, until he shouted for Michael through the letterbox.

"Who's that?" Jack asked the table.

"It's Longy," Michael replied, getting up.

"Tell him to get lost. We're having our dinner."

Michael headed for the door. Brendan followed him. "I'd better go too in case he wants me."

Jack dropped his fork and knife onto his plate. "I should have left on the telly. Then no one would leave the bloody room."

Michael opened the front door as Brendan closed the living room door behind him. They both stood, looking at Longy. They could tell something was up with him. He was wearing his father's suit. Michael wondered who had died, but then he remembered the court case.

Longy had told him on Sunday night that the Garda from Saturday had arrived at his door with a summons to appear in court on Tuesday. Swift justice the Garda had joked, and then went on to explain that these were the first prosecutions of the road traffic act in Cork and the judge wanted to tackle all in one day: Tuesday.

He looked respectable in the suit, but as the smell of onions drifted into the hallway and up their noses, all respect they may have had for Longy and his suit disappeared.

"How did it go?" Michael asked.

"I'm alive anyway," Longy shrugged, half smiling.

"How did what go?" asked Brendan.

"Oh. I forgot to tell you. Longy was in court today for the speeding fine that he got on the road to Cobh Saturday."

"That was fucking quick." Brendan laughed a little.

"It's not fucking funny really, Brend," Longy scowled at him.

"Okay. Relax. It's not the end of the world, boy," Michael said.

Longy put out his hand and the two brothers looked down at it.

"What's that for?" Michael finally asked.

"Fifteen shillings each."

"For what?" Brendan asked.

"What do you fuckin' think? They fined me forty-five shillings. You two are going to split the fine with me. You were in the…."

"Fuck off," Brendan shouted, a bit too loud.

Longy didn't flinch. He held his hand out and said nothing.

"Hang on, Brend. Maybe he's right," He turned and winked at his brother. "I'll go upstairs and get my cheque book," he said, turning back to Longy. "Who will I make the cheque out to, Kevin? You, or your fucking doctor?"

The two brothers laughed.

Longy didn't. He dropped his hand to his side and glared at them. "You're not going to box in with me so?"

Michael calmed himself. "Of course not. We didn't ask you to belt back the road on Saturday. That was you trying to show off. And now you want us to box in with you. It's not going to happen, sunshine."

Longy adjusted his tie, pulling it away from his neck. He looked at Michael and then Brendan. "How does your Dad feel about the meeting on Saturday? Maybe I should give him an update on it. Just in case you left something out, like."

Brendan stepped forward and punched Longy in the face. Longy stumbled backwards and fell onto the steps. Brendan stepped out of the hallway and grabbed Longy's coat by the collar. He yanked him back to his feet. Longy's cheek was already swollen, but the skin hadn't broken.

"Listen to me now, ya little fucker. If you even say hello to my Dad from now on I'll have a little chat with our friend Mr. Kelly about you; and I'm sure he can arrange for some guys to pay you a visit some night, soon." He pushed Longy back onto the steps.

Michael hadn't moved. He was in shock. His brother had never acted like this before.

Brendan stood over Longy and pointed a finger in his face. "You won't have to worry about getting any more speeding fines then, ya slimy little bastard, because you can't drive a fucking car with a bullet hole in your knee." He yanked him up again and pushed him up the steps.

Longy didn't wait around, or make any comments. He stumbled up the path, holding his swollen cheek.

Brendan and Michael stood watching him go. For someone who had just hit a person, Brendan looked quite under control. He stood with his hands on his hips looking up at the gate. Longy passed through it, jumped into his car and drove away.

"I'm glad he didn't ask you to pay the whole fine, brother," Michael said as they watched the car disappear out of sight.

Brendan laughed as he turned to go back into the house. "If he did I would have shot him there and then." He smiled at Michael, but Michael could see in his eyes that Brendan wasn't completely joking.

* * * *

Mary sat by the window watching her brothers eat their dinner. They exchanged a few glances, but neither of them spoke. She watched them until they finished and left the room, together. The others settled down in front of the television after the plates and cups were washed and put away. Mary put on her coat.

"I'm going to call down to Granny's for a bit," she announced.

Ann vaulted from the chair and Mary feared that her mother would join her on the visit. Mary liked to visit her granny, but it had to be alone. If her mother came it would develop into a shouting match between granny and her daughter.

Ann ran into the kitchen, and came out with half an apple tart wrapped in brown paper. "Give that to her, will you?" she asked Mary, pushing the tart into her hands.

Jack's head swung round. "I was planning on eating that!" he shouted.

Ann smiled at him. "Sure you can. Go to granny's and eat it with her, if you like."

"No apple tart is worth that torture," he muttered, turning back to the television.

Granny had lived in the same house, on upper Janemount, all her life. Ann had lived there all her life too, until Jack had convinced her to marry him. The house wasn't very big, but it was in Sunday's Well, which elevated it above any bigger house in most areas of Cork. Mary climbed the steps that led up from Sunday's Well Road to Upper Janemount.

She wanted to talk to someone about Dean. Talking to her mother was out of the question. Angela just wanted to joke about the whole thing and ask if she had done it with him yet. She had decided that granny was a good listener and probably wouldn't remember the conversation the next day anyway; she didn't remember much these days.

Mary lifted the flowerpot on the windowsill, picked up the door key and opened the front door. "It's only me," she shouted immediately, not wanting to startle her eighty-year-old grand-mother.

"I'm in the bedroom," came the reply.

Mary giggled to herself. That reply was always the same, always the same from a bedridden old woman. Granny hadn't left that bedroom in fifteen years, but her answer, when some-one opened the door and announced themselves, was always the same; *I'm in the bedroom.* Mary set the pie down in the kitchen for the home help lady in the morning. She would tell gran it was there so that the woman couldn't keep it for herself; not all of it anyway.

The house was dusty, unkempt. Ann visited every two days and did her best, but she had her own house to clean and the job at Mrs. Duggan's for three days each week. She would tidy up and dust a little, but spent most of her visits talking or arguing with her mother. The home help lady did even less. She was supposed to do a bit of house cleaning, feed and clean Granny and make sure the old woman had everything she needed for the rest of the day and night. Looking around the house as she made her way up the stairs, Mary doubted if the home help lady had ever seen the downstairs' rooms.

"I left some appletart in the kitchen for your lunch tomor-row."

Her granny was sitting up in the bed trying to read the paper. Her glasses rested on the very end of her long nose and Mary often wondered how they stayed on. They always looked like they were about to fall, but they never did. It was like a small groove had formed at the tip of her nose over the years. Granny had caught Mary once, trying to get a closer look at her nose. The nose slightly curved at the end, but she couldn't make out any groove.

"Who made it?" she asked, dropping the paper and staring down the bridge of her nose, through the glasses.

"Mam."

"Ohh," she said, not displaying approval or otherwise. "Come and sit next to me, deary. I haven't seen you in ages." She patted the bed and a plume of dust and snuff bounced into the air.

Granny had always taken snuff and the bed was always covered with it. There was a time, in their youth, when Mary and Louise had tried it and had spent the rest of the day sneezing. Granny had taken the stuff as long as Mary could remember, and when Mary was ten she wasn't bothered by the piles of snuff that lay on the bedclothes. She would come to granny's house, run the stairs and vault into the bed, hugging her furiously. She loved her back then, and she did too now, but the snuff revolted her. Mary felt guilty every time she would visit and granny would extend her cheek for a kiss. She would hesitate slightly, but eventually concede. She hated herself for that.

Hating herself, but still hesitating nonetheless, Mary leaned over the bed and kissed her granny's cheek. The old woman turned as Mary kissed her and planted her own lips on Mary's cheek in return. Mary could feel the soft mush of toothless lips pressing against her skin. She looked at the locker in front of her and spotted the set of dentures, resting in the glass of brownish water.

"I was here last Wednesday, Gran. Remember?"

Gran thought hard and finally nodded.

Mary wasn't sure if she remembered or not. She pulled a chair up close to the bed and sat down. Her granny tossed the paper to one side and rested her hands on her covered legs. She smiled down at her granddaughter.

Mary began. "Louise went dancing with me for the first time last Friday night."

For a moment, it looked like the old woman was trying to remember who Louise was. She nodded again and, to Mary, it looked like her mind had finally shifted into first gear.

"How old is little Louise now, child?"

"Seventeen."

She shrugged. "That's old enough these days I guess. In my day a girl wouldn't be out dancing until after her eighteenth birthday."

"You were married at eighteen, gran, weren't you?"

She stared at Mary for a few seconds. "I was indeed. And I didn't go dancing for the first time until my husband, your grandfather, brought me."

Mary loved to tease the old woman. They were weird times. It was okay for a woman to marry and settle down, but dancing before eighteen was frowned upon.

"I met a man on Friday night, after the dance."

"And?"

"He walked me home." Mary paused, watching her granny's face for signs of disapproval. When she saw none she continued. "He came into Cudmore's yesterday and took me to the pictures last night."

"Is he a north side boy?"

"No. He's….He's American." Mary watched and waited.

Granny looked up at the wall in front of her. On the wall was a picture frame with a picture of Pope John and John F Kennedy. It was a new picture, not six months old. Mary had not seen it before and thought it looked a bit weird. The Pope, a dead Pope at that, and the President of America, still alive, in one picture didn't fit in her head. For a minute, they sat there looking at the picture.

"Are you meeting this yank again, my dear?" granny said.

"Tomorrow night."

"Does your mother know about all this?"

Mary bolted upright. "No, not at all, and don't tell her, please."

Granny put her hand on Mary's and rubbed it gently. "I'm not going to say a word. Don't worry about that. I probably won't remember it in the morning anyway."

Mary looked at the old face and saw the sadness under the surface; the sadness of someone who had enough brains left to realise that the rest had already departed. Granny's eyes filmed over for a moment and Mary thought that she would cry, but she didn't.

They talked for a while longer. Granny asked about the boys and Mary gave a brief update. She didn't ask about Jack; Mary was aware of the rift between her grandmother and her father.

"Dad is fine too," she said timidly.

Granny acted as if she hadn't heard the comment. She arranged the bedclothes around her, and just as Mary was about to speak, she betrayed her silence.

"I know he's your father, but he's a bad bugger."

"No he isn't," Mary responded, a bit upset at the cruel words against her father. "He's a good man, who works hard."

"Maybe he does, but you don't know what went on before. Before you were born." She paused and sighed. "I shouldn't be talking about this, especially to you."

"It's too late now. What went on back then? Tell me."

"It's getting late, lovey. Maybe you should go home. I'm feeling tired." She started to arrange the bed for a night's sleep.

"You have to tell me something, gran. That's not fair."

She stopped arranging the pillows and looked at Mary. "Let's just say he had his dealings with the law back then, and that's all I am going to say. Now give your gran a kiss and lock the front door when you go."

Mary complied, feeling annoyed. She had never heard anyone talk about her father like that. Maybe her gran was losing it totally and didn't even know she was talking about him. She had sounded convincing, not like she was imagining it, or drawing up older memories of someone else in error. As she walked home, Mary decided it was nonsense. Her father was harmless and she had no way of finding out the truth anyway;

unless she asked him or her mother directly, and she wasn't about to do that.

Wednesday 19ᵗʰ June 1963

Excerpt from the Evening Echo:

Eighty Cardinals go into the Conclave to elect a New Pope

Eighty cardinals entered the historic Conclave in the Sistine chapel this evening to elect a successor to Pope John.

Today the Princes of the Church attended Solemn Votive Pontifical Mass of the Holy Spirit in St. Peter's to implore divine aid in their task.

The Mass was celebrated by Cardinal Tisserant, French Dean of the Sacred College at the Alter of the Chair of Peter, the first Pope, in the apse of the Great Basilica. The cardinals entered the church in procession, clad in robes of violet, their colour of mourning for Pope John, who died 16 days ago.

The outcome will be made known by the centuries old method of burning the ballot papers in a stove in the Sistine Chapel.

At four o'clock, Brendan reminded his boss, at the turf stores, that he was leaving for the day, an hour early. His boss, a large burly man who had never lifted any turf, and hadn't seen his feet since his twentieth birthday, huffed and puffed a little before letting Brendan go.

Brendan ran the length of Cathedral Road, almost bursting a lung in the process. He got to his front gate and could see spots floating in front of his eyes. His stomach felt tight and he wondered if his lunch had bought a round trip ticket. He paused by the gate, took a few deep breaths until the spots had subsided, and his stomach was open for business again.

Five minutes later, he vaulted the steps outside the front door and was running down Cathedral Road, his destination Academy Street, in the heart of the city. His dusty work clothes discarded, he looked quite respectable in his Sunday best slacks and shirt. He had to force himself to stop and walk when he turned down Shandon Street. Although he was well built and trim from lifting turf all day, he was no long distance runner. He checked his watch and decided he had enough time.

He reached the Examiner Office at ten past five, in plenty of time. The building was on Academy Street and wasn't much to look at. He opened the door and walked into a small foyer that had a large counter blocking any further progress. An elderly woman stood behind the counter and Brendan was next in line after a young girl who was placing an ad for her lost dog. The old woman took the details from the teenager, barking questions out that made the teenager jump each time. *What's his name? What colour is he?*

Brendan tried on one of his best smiles after the young girl had left quickly, but he dropped it when the woman behind the counter didn't look up at him.

"Yes?" she blurted out, sorting some papers in front of her.

Brendan cleared his throat and said, "I would like to see John Corrigan please, Mam."

Now, she looked up at him. She didn't speak, just eyed him up and down slowly. "What for?" she said finally, louder than before.

Brendan could hear the aggression in her voice. "It's a private matter," he replied, hearing the quiver in his own voice.

"Do you have an appointment?"

"Ahh, no."

She smiled, not a welcoming smile, but one of sly victory. "I'm afraid," she began, her tone changing slightly, "that Mr. Corrigan does not see anyone without an appointment."

He leaned across the counter, getting as close as he could to the woman. Now, she looked startled; someone had invaded her private space.

"I'm with the I.R.A.," Brendan heard himself saying.

The three letters seemed to be spoken by someone else, like he was watching from across the room. He felt a tingle down his spine as he said them. The old lady looked at him blankly, as if she was waiting for him to laugh or something. Then she looked frightened. Without speaking, she got up and disappeared through the door to the left of the counter. Brendan stood, wondering if she had indeed gone to get Corrigan, or if a couple of Gardai would come running in the front door in a few seconds and drag him away. He decided to give her a minute, then he would get out of there.

She didn't return, but a man who introduced himself as John Corrigan did. He looked old to Brendan. His hair was grey and he looked very tired, large bags bulging under his eyes. He moved around to Brendan's side of the counter and, walking past him, he secured the front door with the sliding bolt. Brendan swallowed hard, but tried to mask his fear.

"What can I do for you, young Sir?"

He was much more polite than the woman. The way he addressed Brendan with respect, eased his apprehension.

Brendan dipped into his pocket and took out the letter that Kelly had given him outside the barn on Saturday. He thrust it at Corrigan, his hand shaking uncontrollably. But Corrigan didn't raise his hand to take it; he just stared pleasantly at Brendan.

"I can't take that. How do I know you're with the I.R.A.? We get a chancer a week in here claiming they are with one group or another."

Brendan took a deep breath and delivered the line that Kelly had whispered to him in the field; the whisper only he had been privileged to hear, the whisper that had annoyed Michael all week. Corrigan's face exploded with what Brendan could only describe as sheer delight. He had heard the code before and Brendan felt like he had pulled a gun out of his coat. The power rang through him as he handed over the letter. He wished Corrigan hadn't heard him the first time, just so that he could say the words aloud again.

Corrigan reached out and shook Brendan's hand vigorously. "Keep up the good fight," he said, as he opened the door and let Brendan out into the evening sunshine.

* * * *

Brendan stood on the street, basking in the power he felt rushing through his veins. He loved it. Never in his life had he felt such exhilaration. What he had just done was even better than sex, he decided. Better then the sex he had experienced anyway. He wanted to do something, but he wasn't sure what. He glanced up and down Academy Street and searched in his mind for something to do. He looked at his watch; quarter to six.

The time gave him his plan. He walked left toward Patrick Street, not towards home. Cudmore's was only around the corner and he could walk Mary home. But he couldn't discuss his mission. He laughed at the word mission. But he could talk to her about other things.

He needed to talk to someone.

* * * *

Mary and Beth had fought the good fight all day, but once or twice Mary had leaked a giggle in front of Mr. Thompson. He had returned to work that morning and his face had looked worse. His nose was covered with white bandages that continued across his face and under his eyes. His eyes were white dots in the two black rings that circled them. When he spoke he sounded like Mr. Magoo, and it was this more than his face that set the girls off at numerous points during the day.

One good thing came out of the accident, and that was the lack of trips to the top shelf. Not once had Mr. Thompson asked either girl to get anything from the shelf. They had made three trips each during the day and each time Mr. Thompson had not been in attendance at the foot of the ladder. Mary wondered if he knew that she had dropped the jar on purpose.

Mary's anxiety had been bubbling inside her all day, but at six, it had started to boil over. Her knees buckled at the thought of Dean walking in the door in the next few minutes. It was their second date, but she felt that tonight was going to be special. Angela talking about sex during lunchtime only added to her anxiety. The first date was fine. There was no chance of anything happening and with a second date there should be no chance of them ending up in bed together either. But Dean was different from any man Mary had ever dated. He was miles better than Willy O'Reilly and still towered above all of the other men she had dated during the last few years. He was more mature; he was American, and he was the most beautiful man she had ever met. Could she already be falling in love with him? Mary stood behind the counter and wondered if she had not fallen in love with him the first time she had laid eyes on him.

Then she looked up and he was there. Dean smiled broadly as he entered the shop. Mr. Thompson had left at five, with a throbbing headache. Beth eyed Dean up and down, obviously liking what she saw. Dean nodded at Beth and turned his attention to Mary. "Good evening, Mary," he said.

Mary didn't reply. She stared over Dean's shoulder at the entrance. Dean noticed her gaze and turned to follow it. Coming in the front door was Mary's brother, Brendan. His smile was even wider than Dean's. He waved to Beth and, turning to Mary, he said, "Hi, sis. I was wondering if you wanted your brother to walk you home today?"

Brendan barely acknowledged Dean. Mary contemplated leaving it that way, saying nothing; leaving Brendan think that Dean was a customer. She could hand Dean a packet of sweets and let him leave, if he would. Then she thought better of that plan. It would be an insult to Dean. It might end their budding relationship.

"Sis?" Brendan said.

Mary looked at both men, seconds passing. Finally she spoke. "I'm not going home tonight yet, Brendan. Dean, here, is taking me out." She gestured with her hand to Dean. "Dean, meet my brother, Brendan. Brendan, Dean."

Dean smiled immediately, but Brendan's smile arrived on the next train. It came but it was a few seconds too late. The men shook hands awkwardly and then the awkwardness multiplied. The three of them stood quietly for what felt to Mary like minutes, but only ten seconds had passed.

Beth broke the silence. "Mary, you head off and I'll lock up the shop. Brendan, will you help me close the shutters?"

The spell was broken. Brendan turned to Beth and said, "Yes."

Mary grabbed her coat from the back, said a quick farewell to Beth and Brendan, and grabbing Dean's arm, she literally dragged him out the door.

When they were outside, she stopped and checked her hands. "I forgot my purse. I won't be a second."

Before Dean could react, Mary was back inside the shop. Brendan was lifting some jars back up onto the top shelf. He saw Mary return and quickly came down the ladder. He didn't look happy. Before he could say anything, Mary started. "Don't tell Mam and Dad about Dean, okay?"

Brendan stood at the foot of the ladder and laughed. "You must be joking."

Mary looked for Beth. She saw her in the back, getting her coat. Mary leaned over the counter and locked eyes with Brendan. "If you tell Mam and Dad, then I will have to tell them about your secret Saturday meetings." She paused for effect. "With you know who."

Brendan's face paled; he looked like he was going to throw up. "I wasn't going to say anything. I was only joking with you." He tried to smile, but failed. "They don't need to know nothing, okay?"

Mary headed for the back to get the purse she had left behind on purpose. "Okay," she answered, as she left for the second time.

* * * *

Outside the shop, not fifty yards away, Willy O'Reilly stood watching Dean kiss Mary. Mary rested her hand against his chest and Willy felt his stomach tighten. He wanted to go over and pull her away from him. Then he would beat the living shit out of this fella. Mary would have to be impressed by that. She was his girlfriend after all. He had been with her first. She was just playing hard to get.

He watched as they walked along the street. They stopped at the corner and Dean opened the door of a parked car. Mary jumped in and before Willy could react, they were gone.

Willy's car was parked at the other end of Patrick Street. He had lost them already. He turned to walk back to his own car. He was determined to finish it tonight, but now they were out of his reach.

However, he knew where they would ultimately end up and Willy had a back up plan. With time to kill, he slipped down a lane off Patrick Street and into one of the many pubs.

* * * *

The car was a rental and the interior was cleaner than her mother's oven at home. Mary's knowledge of cars ended with the thought that one car looked nice and another looked okay. She sat in the passenger seat and enjoyed the ride. She laughed as Dean tried his best to stay on the right side of the road; the right side being the left, of course. At T-junctions especially, Dean would make the turn perfectly and as he smiled with triumph, he would subconsciously guide the car back over to the right side of the road.

He wouldn't tell Mary where they were going. It was a surprise, although once they had passed Cork Airport, Mary had a good idea that they were heading for Kinsale.

Mary had rarely been to Kinsale. Her father didn't own a car so Sunday trips with the family, when she was younger, were always to Youghal, a small seaside town east of Cork City, with a nice beach and some amusements for kids. They would all travel down on the first train that morning and return, exhausted, on the last train that evening.

Dean parked the car outside Acton's Hotel, and when he started to walk up the pathway that led to the hotel entrance, Mary hesitated. The feelings of inadequacy she had experienced on their last night together, inside the Metropole Hotel, came flooding back.

Dean stopped and returned to her side. "You look beautiful tonight, Mary," he whispered to her, as he led her up the path. "Now, let's show these people who you really are. Let's show them the confident lady hiding inside."

The words energised Mary, and when Dean kissed her neck as he pushed open the door, Mary felt a rush of confidence through her like never before. She strode into the lobby, a new previously unused bounce to her step. She reached the reception desk and realised that she had not the faintest idea what to say. She stared blankly at the young man behind the desk and smiled. Dean arrived and rescued her, announcing that they had reservations for dinner. Mary continued to smile and stride as the young man led them to the restaurant.

The meal was the best Mary had ever experienced. She followed Dean's lead, ordered as he did, picked up each utensil as he did and drank the wine as he did. By the time the fifth and final course arrived, Mary found that the wine had taken hold of her. The room wasn't spinning, but she was definitely more relaxed than she thought she could ever have been tonight. Dean seemed unaffected by the alcohol and when he suggested another bottle of wine, Mary declined.

"You have to drive back, Dean," she reminded him.

He smiled. "Mary, it's only eight and we won't be going back to Cork for hours yet." He reached over and took her hand. "I took the liberty of booking a room here for us. It's booked for the night, but I know you will want to get home tonight and I understand that. But why don't we go up and order another bottle of wine and we can talk in private?"

Mary squeezed his hand and gazed into his eyes. She didn't want to talk to him; she wanted to maul him. She hadn't felt like this with any other man, ever. She had never drunk so much wine before either. "Let's go," she whispered across the table.

The room was amazing. Dean had rented the wedding suite. Mary looked around the room. A four poster bed was the centrepiece of the room, with lace curtains hung around it. A large bay window looked out onto the harbour. It was still sunny and the large yachts, with their tall masts, cast their unending shadows out to sea.

Not long after they arrived, a waiter knocked on the door and dropped off a bottle of Champagne. He left the bottle unopened, and left after Dean had given him a tip. Mary sat on the edge of the bed while Dean opened the champagne. The cork popped and hit the ceiling. Mary let out a small shriek and then laughed at her naivety. The champagne bottle overflowed and spilled onto the carpet. They both looked at the growing stain and after a second of concern, they giggled foolishly. It was Mary's first taste of Champagne; the bubbles shot up her nose and she coughed loudly after the first sip, spilling more drink onto the carpet.

Dean joined her on the bed, dismissing the freshly spilled champagne. Mary was aware of what was happening and although she had felt fear in her heart every time she had imagined this moment in the past, she harboured none of those fears now. The alcohol had taken complete control of her now. The room spun slowly around her. Dean took her glass and placed it on the bedside locker. He held her hand and looked into her eyes for what, to Mary, seemed like an hour.

Finally, he spoke. "Mary, I have only known you a short while, but you have overwhelmed me, like I never thought possible." He leaned in closer.

"Dean, I'm only nineteen," Mary said before he could speak again.

"I know, but I really—."

Mary put her fingers to his lips. "It's my first time," she whispered.

Dean's eyes widened and he pulled back slightly.

Mary followed him. "It's okay. I want to. I really do. I'm just a bit nervous." Then she sprung forward pushing him back on the bed, pushing her lips against his; the room started to gallop around them, and Mary felt like the world was actually going to move.

* * * *

They had devoured each other like lions consuming their kill. Dean had been gentle, while Mary found that she had been quite the opposite. What little pain she had felt was easily surpassed by the pleasure that had reverberated through her body. They lay on the bed, Mary awake, enjoying the afterglow, Dean dozing quietly next to her.

Her mind raced away from her and she could see herself living in America, waiting on the porch of their huge house, waiting for her husband, the architect, to come home from a hard day's work. The children would be playing in the yard, all five of them, three girls and two boys. Mary wondered if maybe one of those children was now growing inside her. She had taken no precautions, bar buying the new panties, and she knew that Dean hadn't worn anything. She dismissed the thought as silly and slowly got out of the bed. No one got pregnant on their first time, did they?

She needed to pee and she hadn't seen the bathroom yet. Checking Dean's watch as she went, she saw that it was only nine o'clock, still enough time to drive back. She didn't want the night to end and was considering staying. Her parents would come down hard on her, but she was nineteen and it was time for her to start making her own decisions.

Mary stopped when she entered the bathroom and saw something truly amazing. She gazed at it and all the other crazy ideas floating around in her head dissipated. She looked back at the bed outside and saw that Dean was still sleeping.

She knew she was going to do it, she had to. Two firsts in one night.

So, in her nineteenth year, Mary Horgan made love for the first time, and on that very same night she also climbed into a real bathtub for the first time. She turned on both taps and the tub filled quickly, steam enveloping the room. Mary stood looking at herself in the large mirror over the sink. Although she didn't look different, Mary felt somehow older, more mature. An unassailable smile graced her face and she stood there for another minute, enjoying her reflection until the steam had covered the mirror and the smiling girl disappeared.

The bath was hot, but she got down quickly. She had added the complimentary bubble bath and now the bubbles rose high above the water. She lay hidden below them, her head the only visible evidence that she was indeed in the bath. She felt her body temperature rising with the heat of the water. Small droplets of sweat appeared on her forehead. She closed her eyes and let her mind drift. Once again she was on the porch waiting for Dean. The children were playing, the unnamed children of her future. Aoife, Ellen, Luke, she tossed names at them as they played, seeing which ones might stick.

"Is there room in there for one more?"

Mary opened her eyes and saw Dean standing above her, naked. She smiled up at him.

"You look like you are really enjoying it," he said.

For a brief moment, Mary hesitated to tell him it was her first time in a bath, ever. Then she scolded herself. If this was going to work there could be no secrets, no shame from her past hidden away. If he really loved her, he would love her no matter what.

"It's the first time I've ever been in a bath," she said.

Dean laughed, not a mocking laugh but just a laugh. "Well," he said. "Here's another first for you." He stepped into the bath and sat down opposite her, his feet coming to rest around the outside of her body.

The water level rose and some tipped over the side, making a gentle splashing sound on the tiled floor. Dean tilted his head back and closed his eyes. "I'm really beginning to love Ireland," he said gently, and opening his eyes again he said, "Especially the people."

Mary closed her eyes and wished that the night would never end. She heard Dean moving, sending a small wave of water toward her. Then she felt his lips on hers and thought, 'How many people have ever made love in a bath?'.

It was indeed a night of firsts.

* * * *

Jack Horgan turned off the television at nine. Brendan objected, until Jack suggested a game of cards. Jack dealt the cards as Mary got into her first bathtub.

As Mary made love for the second time to Dean, Louise and Ann were knocked out of the game, so only the three men remained. They played until quarter to eleven, when Jack finally won. His prize was thirty pence.

"I think I'll buy that yacht I always wanted now," he said, pocketing his winnings.

All the others went to bed, leaving Jack and Ann alone downstairs.

"Shouldn't Mary be home by now?" he asked Ann

"No. She's gone to the Palace with Angela to see that Mickey Rooney film."

"We should go see that," Jack suggested.

"We should go to bed."

They headed for the stairs.

"No, really. How long has it been since we were at the pictures?" Jack asked.

"Okay," Ann said. "Instead of going to the pub this Saturday night, we'll go to the pictures."

"Ahh Jesus no. It's only a bloody film, after all. Arthur Guinness outranks Mickey Rooney every time."

Ann shook her head and continued up the stairs. By eleven-thirty, they were all asleep.

* * * *

With her skin pruning from the hot water, Mary had to be dragged out of the bath by Dean. The drive back was pleasant, the light of the day hanging on until well after half past ten. By the time they reached the city, darkness had taken hold and Mary knew she was late. She checked the time; twenty to twelve. She was very late. Her only hope was that they were all in bed when she arrived. She had told her mother that she was going to the pictures with Angela. The film started at around nine normally, so after doing the math in her head, she realised that she was still okay. The movie would have finished at some time before eleven. The walk home, with a stop for something to eat, would account for the delay.

She relaxed a little and cuddled into Dean's shoulder.

"Are you late?" he asked.

"No," she replied. "It's okay."

He turned onto Cathedral Road and changed down gears for the long climb up the hill.

"Drop me where you left me the last night, Okay?"

"No problem. I wasn't expecting an invitation for coffee or anything." He smiled across at her.

"Next time, maybe," Mary joked.

Dean stopped the car and turned off the engine. "Are you okay?" he asked her.

"I'm fine. Why?"

"Well, it's been a big night for you, a sort of milestone in your life."

"It certainly has," Mary giggled, leaning over to kiss him.

They kissed for a few minutes, Mary finally breaking the embrace. "I have to go. I don't want to, but I have to," she said, opening the door.

"How about tomorrow night?"

"What about it?" Mary teased.

Dean smiled. "I want to show you my new office. It's right in the middle of the city."

"It's a date," she answered and ran off toward home, a warm glow surrounding her. She couldn't remember ever feeling so happy.

* * * *

The sound of the car door closing woke Willy. He was disoriented for a few seconds, half expecting to see the familiar surroundings of his bedroom. He looked around and saw the hedge, the grass he was lying on, the house to his left, Mary's house. He rolled over and got to his feet, crouching so that he remained below the height of the hedge. He stumbled slightly and had to use the hedge to keep his balance. He remembered the feed of pints he had consumed before driving to Mary's house. His car was parked halfway down the road, out of sight.

Looking out towards the road, Willy saw a car drive past, and a man waved in his direction. It was the asshole who had taken him out by the G.P.O. on Friday night; the man Mary was seeing.

When Mary walked through the open gate and turned to close it, Willy realised that the man was waving at her.

Plan B had worked!

Mary struggled with the old gate. He could see that she was trying to be as quiet as she could. Willy glanced at the house. All the lights were out, everyone asleep.

Perfect.

Mary managed to get the gate almost closed and, seemingly happy with her effort, she turned to walk down the path. Willy saw the fear materialise on her face when she saw him crouching by the hedge. She tried to run, but Willy already had his hand wrapped around her arm. He pulled hard and both of them went tumbling onto the grass. Willy recovered quickly, not showing the effects of the alcohol. He jammed his hand against Mary's mouth, stifling her screams. He rolled her onto her back and pushed his weight down on her body, knocking the wind out of her.

"What the fuck are you still doing with him?" he whispered, drooling spit onto her face. "You know we're meant to be together. Why are you fighting it?"

Mary's fearful eyes glared up at him. She tried to scream again, but his hand covered her mouth easily.

"I think it's time I showed you what you're missing."

Keeping his weight on her, he reached down with his free hand and lifted Mary's skirt. He could feel himself harden against her. Undoing his pants with his free hand, he tugged at it, trying to get it down. Mary kicked at him, but her legs were pinned, his weight too much.

Slowly, Willy ran his hand up her leg until he felt the soft texture of her panties. He pulled at them violently and they ripped away under the strain. Mary grimaced in pain, but Willy didn't care.

His pants down by his knees, he started positioning himself on top of her, when he felt one of her hands break free. She didn't tear at him or try to hit him. Instead, he felt her hand on his bare thigh, rubbing it gently.

She wanted him. He had been right all along.

He eased his weight off her gently, allowing her more room to manoeuvre. Slowly, her fingers trailed along his skin, moving around the curve of his leg and up towards his crotch. He thought he was going to explode.

* * * *

Mary rubbed his thigh and felt the weight of his body shift slightly. He exhaled deeply, his face pressed against hers. She could smell the stale beer on his breath. She had more room to move now.

She guided her hand around his leg, feeling his reactions growing more urgent, his breath coming in great gasps. She raised her hand up his inner leg and when she felt her hand brush against the soft gathered skin between them, she grabbed hard and dug her nails deep into his crotch. Almost immediately, she felt the rush of warm liquid flowing across her fingers.

Willy screamed loudly, rolling off her. He grabbed at his crotch and howled in pain. Mary could see his hands blacken in the darkness, the blood flowing freely over them. She rolled away from him and, slower than she would have liked, got to her feet and headed for the steps, and the front door beyond. Willy rolled around in the grass, making no attempt to pursue her. She thought his repeated screams would surely wake all the neighbours, but amazingly no lights came on in any of the houses.

Mary reached the front door and realised that she no longer had her handbag with her. She had dropped it somewhere in the grass. She would have to go back and get it; her keys were in it! Could she knock on the door and hope that Louise heard the sound first and opened the door? No. With her luck her father would come stomping down the stairs, cursing her.

Turning quickly, she assessed the situation behind her. Willy was still incapacitated; his screams trailing off a little as he came to terms with the pain between his legs. Mary took a deep breath and ran back up the steps and looked for her handbag.

"Ohh, you bitch," Willy whimpered, all the pain in the world evident in his voice.

Mary ignored him and searched the grass with her eyes. She saw her torn panties first and then the bag against the hedge. Darting around the crumpled heap that was Willy, she grabbed the panties and the bag and ran for the door again.

She could have walked. Willy wasn't following her anywhere.

She closed the door as quickly and quietly as she could. Her father's deep snoring floated down the stairs to meet her, and Mary knew the reason why no one in the house had heard Willy's moans. She sat against the door in the hall and listened for ten minutes until she heard some movement outside. She lifted the letterbox flap to have a look and caught a last glimpse of Willy as he staggered out of the gate, holding his crotch.

Thursday 20th June 1963

Excerpt from the Evening Echo:

Full Support for Taoiseach's Motion.

The Taoiseach, Mr. Lemass, in the Dail today moved the motion that President Kennedy, on his visit to this country, be invited to address a joint sitting of both houses of the Oireachtas and received unanimous support.

The Minister for Justice, Mr. Charles Haughey, together with the American Ambassador Mr. Mathew McCloskey and Mr. Daniel Costigan, Commissioner of the Garda Siochana, flew into Shannon Airport today together with representatives of the Department of External Affairs and the American Embassy. They arrived in two helicopters to make a last minute check on security arrangements in connection with the visit of President Kennedy.

Mary knew she was bruised before she even tried to get out of bed. She had hardly slept at all. She had lain awake, listening to Louise breathing gently next to her. Pain wasn't the cause of her insomnia, but fear. Mary lay awake most of the night in fear of Willy regrouping and coming back. He hadn't come back, and she had drifted off to sleep shortly before some slivers of light had cut through the curtains.

Now, lying in bed, Mary felt like she had taken part in a prize fight; the prize being her life. She lay there, her body aching from the slightest movement. She managed to get to a sitting position and sat there for several minutes.

Sitting on the bed, the tears came, flowing down her cheeks. Her imagination kicked in and presented her with an alternate outcome to the events of last night.

What if he had managed to rape her? What if he had put his thing in her?

Up to the point when Mary saw Willy crouching behind the hedge, that night had been the most exhilarating night of her short life. He had erased all those good feelings in seconds. She tried to concentrate on thoughts of Dean. He was a breed apart from Willy O'Reilly. Dean had made love to her twice last night, once in the bed and once in the bath. He had been gentle and thoughtful.

Mary lay down slowly and turned back to face the wall. She decided to stay at home and lie in bed for the day. The aches and pains would hopefully ease with a day of rest and the bruises would fade with time. Time was the great healer, her mother had told her often enough.

Sometime later, Louise woke and, thinking that Mary had slept late, she called her. Mary told her she was sick and to leave her alone. Louise got dressed quietly and left the room, closing the door behind her. Mary lay there, images of the ecstasy and the agony of the night before fighting for attention in her mind's eye.

* * * *

Willy woke in more familiar surroundings this time. He lay on his back and stared at the ceiling of his bedroom as his memory tried to put the night before into some coherent order. He rolled onto his side and the pain came quickly, shooting up through his stomach. He looked down to see that he was covered with a towel. The towel was wrapped between his legs, like a nappy for a baby. The towel was white, but a red stain covered the front of it. Willy reached down and gently touched it. The blood was dry, on the outside.

Slowly and painfully, he moved to the edge of the bed. He swung around and put his feet on the ground. Grabbing the sides of the towel, he tried to pull it away from his crotch. The towel moved freely until he reached the red stain. The blood had dried and bonded the towel to his skin. He tugged gently as one would at an old scab that was ready to come free. He bit down hard when the pain came. The towel was stuck against his torn scrotum.

Feeling faint, Willy lay his head back down on the pillow. Tears flowed freely from his eyes. Slowly, he curled up his legs and assumed the foetal position. He slipped his thumb into his mouth and, after a few minutes, when the pain had eased, Willy drifted back into a dreamless sleep.

* * * *

When Mary woke again, sometime after midday, Louise was sitting on the side of her bed.

"Are you okay, sis?"

"I'm okay," Mary replied, trying to smile but failing miserably.

"What happened?"

Mary was surprised by the question, Louise's voice implying that she knew something was wrong, other than her sister being simply sick.

"What do you mean, what happened?"

Louise pointed at Mary's forearm. Along the front of her arm was the print of four fingers. The marks looked like a tattoo, black against her pale skin.

Mary sighed and looked up at her little sister. "He tried to rape me last night."

"Dean?" Louise shouted.

"No!" Mary said. "Willy! He was waiting for me outside last night when I came home. He dragged me into the grass and ripped off my knickers."

"Jesus Christ! How did you get away? Are you alright? Does Mam know?" Louise blasted her with questions.

"Calm down, Lou. I got away from him." Mary looked at her hands. She could see the faint bloodstains on her palms, the caked blood under her fingernails. One nail was broken off at the top.

She didn't volunteer the details of her escape to Louise. She didn't want to try to put into words what she had done. Looking at her hands, she could feel the sensation of the soft skin that she had plunged her long, sharp fingernails into the night before.

"I think I really hurt him last night, physically like," she said.

Louise took her hand. "Good. Maybe now he will leave you alone."

Mary started to weep again. "I'm more afraid of him now than I ever was."

"You should go to the guards. You have to go. Get him put in prison. That will sort him out." Louise squeezed Mary's hand gently as she spoke.

"I can't. They wouldn't believe me anyway. No one else saw it."

"What did you do to him?"

The question ignited Mary's imagination, and images of the night before came rushing back. She saw herself crouched in the hall, looking out the letterbox at Willy, holding his crotch with both hands. His hands were crimson from the blood. She wondered if the path had bloodstains on it this morning. Then she remembered listening to the rainfall during the night. At least something good had happened last night, she thought. She looked up at Louise again. "I tore the balls off him," she said gently, not doing justice to the action she had taken.

Louise tried to remain serious; it was a serious situation. Her laughter came in splutters.

A hesitant smile grew on Mary's lips. "I suppose it's a bit funny, after all," she admitted.

Louise left her laugh escape and soon they were both hugging each other, and laughing.

After a minute, Louise got up and announced that a cup of tea would solve everything. She left the room and Mary proceeded to get dressed. She lifted the dress she had worn the night before off the floor and saw the mud stains on the back of it. She took a deep breath and decided she could cope. Then the shredded panties fell to the floor and Mary was transported back to the garden again. Ambushed by tears, it took her twenty minutes to dress herself and make the journey downstairs.

* * * *

Willy thought he saw his father standing at the foot of his bed sometime before noon; his dead father. The curtains were drawn and although they were not made of very thick material, the gathered dirt and mildew on them did a reasonable job of blocking out the sun. The curtains had not been changed since his mother had taken to her bed years before.

His father stood by the end of the bed shaking his head slowly. He wasn't covered in mud and filth from the grave he had crawled out of to be there. He looked like he had shortly before he had died. He was wearing the clothes that he had always worn while working on the farm: an old brown pants with a blue shirt.

Willy lay there, as he was when he had fallen asleep hours earlier. His thumb stuck in his mouth, he stared in disbelief at the man he had buried years earlier. Slowly, his father started to walk around the bed. He continued to shake his head, staring as he walked.

When he reached the edge of the bed, he crouched down and when his face was only inches from Willy's he said, "What the fuck are you doing?" Now his face was rotten and decayed, as if he had dragged himself back up out of the earth they had thrown on him so many years ago.

Willy jumped up and out of the bed in one swift movement. Pain exploded from his crotch as the towel slipped free from his waist and a corner of it landed on the floor just before his right leg touched down. Taking a further step away from the bed, and his dead father, Willy stood on the towel and, as he moved, the towel was wrenched away from his body. It fell to the floor and Willy stood motionless for a moment, looking across the bed at his dead father.

But he wasn't there.

Then the pain arrived and Willy was afraid to look down. Instinctively, he put his hands to his crotch. He felt the warm blood straight away, could feel it streaming down his legs. He felt faint and was close to collapsing when a voice from outside the room cleared his head instantly.

"Willy, Willy. What the hell are you up to in there?" his mother shouted. "What do I have to do to get a bit of breakfast?" Her voice reverberated around the room. Willy bent over very slowly and picked up the bloody towel.

"And Willy, don't forget to wash your hands before you handle any food, okay."

His mother used that line frequently, but Willy nearly laughed at the irony, as he admired his blood soaked hands. Only the pain kept the giggles away.

* * * *

Mary sat at the table and drank tea with her sister. Neither of them spoke for a while. Louise, only seventeen, seemed to be struggling with the whole situation and probably wished that their mother would come home any minute and take over. Her mother was at work, as were the rest of the household.

Mary thought about Dean. He was collecting her after work this evening. That left her with no choice but to go into town later to meet him, before he made it to the shop. Then she had an idea. She turned to Louise. "Will you do me a favour?"

"Of course."

"Will you go over to the Fitzgerald's? They have a phone. Call the Metropole and ask for Dean. Tell him to meet me by the Cathedral instead of the shop. Tell him I was out sick today."

"What if he's not there?"

"Leave a message for him, but he should be there."

Louise got up, placed a hand on her sister's shoulder as she edged past and squeezed gently. "Everything is going to be okay, sis."

"I know, Lou. I'm fine now, really."

Louise left and the silence came, a wave of anxiety accompanying it, and Mary could feel her heart racing in her chest. Was it possible that Willy would come back today? No, she thought. He would think she was at work now. This rationalisation didn't help.

When someone banged heavily on the front door, Mary knew it wasn't Louise. She stayed in her chair, unable to move. Her hands started to shake as she tried to decide what to do. The bang came again, heavier this time. It was Willy. She was convinced of it. Who else could it be?

She managed to get up. She had to check if it was him before doing anything. Could he break down the door? She didn't think so. Slowly, Mary opened the living room door. The light from the hall spilled into the room. A man was standing outside the door. Willy had come back to finish the job.

Another bang on the door!

Mary jumped as his fist hit the woodwork. Louise would come back any second. Mary moved toward the door, forcing her feet to take each step. She had to do something. She reached for the lock and started to turn it.

Then the man left the door and jumped over the bars that separated their garden from the neighbour's. The same banging again, but this time on the door of the house next door. Mary heard the door open.

"Pops, eggs or veg.?" the man said.

Mary slumped onto the stairs, dropping her head into her hands. It was the veg man.

"Yes, son. I'll have a bag of spuds and do you have any fresh carrots?" she heard Mrs. Hegarty say.

Mary was startled again when the front door opened. It was Louise. Mary looked at her and then the realisation came. The key was in the door all along! If it had been Willy, he could have opened the door and let himself in. Mary jumped to her feet and grabbed for the key. She pulled it free of the lock, and pulling Louise inside, she slammed the door.

"Are you okay?" Louise asked.

Mary didn't answer. She led her sister by the arm to the living room. She closed that door as well and then she spoke. "Was he there?"

"Yes"

"Did you tell him the message?"

"I did."

"And he'll meet me by the Cathedral later?"

"He's coming."

"Good," Mary said and sat down at the table.

Louise stayed standing. After a few seconds Mary looked up at her sister.

"He's coming here, now," Louise said.

* * * *

Willy sat in the kitchen cleaning the gun. He had managed to put on underpants after delicately bathing his testicles in some lukewarm water. His mother didn't speak when he waddled into the room with some tea and toast for her breakfast, and before she could start, he dropped the cup and plate on the bedside locker and waddled away.

His crotch stung as he washed it, and with each stroke, Mary's handy work became more apparent. He could see four deep cuts where she had dug her fingernails into his scrotum. The bleeding had finally stopped, but the pain continued on relentlessly.

The gun was a double-barrelled shotgun that his father had used infrequently before he had died. Willy had watched his father clean that gun on many occasions; sometimes the gun would not have been fired between cleans. His father seemed to get so much enjoyment from cleaning that gun. He would strip it down to its component parts, clean every piece individually and, after many hours, he would put the whole thing back together again.

Six weeks after Willy's father had died, and around the time Willy's mother had decided that there was nothing more to see or do in this world, Willy took the gun out of the linen cupboard and loaded it. He stood at the end of the stairs that day for a long time, not sure in which direction he wanted to go. His mother was shouting at him from her room, her legs perfectly healthy, but her mind unwilling to move them anymore. He stared up those stairs for the longest time.

Finally, he walked out into the yard and, without hesitation, he shot the first pig that crossed his path, blowing the little animal's head clean off. He sat on the steps watching the other animals cower and huddle in each corner of the yard. That night, as he did now, he stripped down the gun, as his father had many times, and cleaned each piece separately.

****

After clumsily introducing herself to the receptionist, Louise had been put through to Dean's room. He answered politely, but took a moment to recognise Louise. She started out with the plan of just passing on the simple message that Mary had given her. All was going well until she said, "She should be okay by tonight, no thanks to that wanker, Willy."

It didn't take much persuading from Dean for her to spill all the gory details down the phone line.

"I'll be there in ten minutes," Dean announced and hung up the phone before Louise could object.

The news that Dean was coming to her house emptied Mary's head, albeit temporarily, of all the memories of the night before. Dean was coming to her aid. Mary glanced in the mirror over the fireplace. She looked like she had been dragged through a bog facedown during a drought.

"You don't look that bad," offered Louise, reading her sister's mind.

"Yah, if I was going to the hospital. Quick, you iron my blue dress, the one with the long sleeves. I'll try to salvage something from this disaster area called a face."

The girls worked frantically, and by the time Dean pulled up in his car, Mary looked somewhere in the vicinity of what she had looked like the night before; early the night before. She walked up the path and greeted him with a kiss on the lips. She knew she would pay dearly for that kiss. Many of the neighbourhood women were out in the sun, with shawls in tow, waiting by their gates for nothing in particular. This incident, this disgraceful behaviour would be relayed somehow to her parents. Like a convict already strapped into the electric chair, with no hope of a pardon, she planted another kiss on Dean's lips.

"Are you okay? Louise said you were in a bad way."

Mary looked down the path at Louise. Louise gave a hesitant smile.

"My sister tends to exaggerate," Mary said, turning to Dean and opening her arms. "Do I look in a bad way?"

Dean smiled. "I don't think you ever could, Mary." They kissed again and then Mary decided she was really pushing her luck. Her mother would be coming down the hill from work any minute.

"Come on," she said, dragging Dean up the path and waving to Louise. "Let's go before some of the neighbours' eyes pop out."

* * * *

With the shotgun reassembled, Willy got up from the table and went to the kitchen. His mother had been shouting on and off at him for the few hours he had spent cleaning the gun. She was hungry; all he had given her all day was the toast for breakfast. A little after five she had become silent and Willy guessed that she had finally fallen asleep, more from weakness than fatigue. Her voice reverberated in his head for ages though.

Her voice was always in his head.

He checked the kitchen for something he could give her. The pickings were slim. Cutting some stale bread, he buttered it and cut some slices of hard cheese to put on it. He boiled the kettle and made a cup of tea, without milk, because there was none.

His mother slept quietly in her bed. Willy placed the tea and the sandwich on the locker and picked up the plate and cup that were there since morning. He looked down at his mother and he wanted to pull back the bedcovers, drag her from her retreat and make her walk again, but he knew that would never happen.

His mother slept on, and Willy thought about waking her so she could have her tea hot, but he didn't want to hear her speak again tonight. He didn't want to hear her speak ever again, if the truth be told. She would wake later to drink the cold tea and eat the stale sandwich.

Willy came back downstairs and went to the biscuit tin in the kitchen that had never seen a biscuit. He removed six bullets from the tin and put them in his pocket. From the table, he picked up the keys to the car, and the shotgun.

Outside, the pigs looked at him as he got into the car. They hadn't been fed in days and some of them were starting to deteriorate. They looked hungry. Willy thought he could see the hate in their eyes as they gathered around the car. He contemplated getting out and blasting one of them with the shotgun. That would remove that look from the others, he thought, and give them something to eat as well.

He started the car and drove out of the yard, stopping to open the gate that led to the main road. He looked up at the farmhouse, as he tied the twine that held the rusty gate in place, and realised that he really had no fond memories of living there.

At that moment, Willy decided he wasn't going to live in that house anymore. He would deal with his business and then he would pack up and move away, move away from Cork even. Hell, he would sell everything and buy himself a ticket on the next boat to America!

* * * *

"Well, what do you think?"

Mary looked around the room. It was big, bigger than her living room at home. Two large windows spilled light in from Patrick Street. She could hear the bustle of the street below as people made their way home. By the windows stood five old mannequins, partly dressed in old fashioned clothes from years before. The rest of the room was filled with boxes covered in dust.

"It has potential, I think," Mary said.

"It's a mess, is what it is," Dean admitted. "But you're right. It has potential. The landlord is going to clean the place out at the start of July and I intend to open for business in September. Meanwhile, I can still scout around the country for prospective clients."

Mary ran her finger along one of the boxes. "You can, but don't bring them back here, whatever you do."

Dean pushed some of the boxes out of the way and led Mary to one of the windows. Mary looked out and was amazed at the view of the street below.

From the window, Mary looked right and could see all the way up to Cash's department store. Looking left, she could see all the way to Daunt Square, where Patrick Street became the Grand Parade. She turned around and smiled at Dean. "Amazing view. You've got most of the street covered from up here. We should sit up here next week and watch Kennedy drive by, if he comes through this way."

"I can't," Dean said. "I'm going to Dublin on Thursday evening until Friday night. It's a pity really because he is scheduled to drive down this Street."

"Why are you going to Dublin?" Mary inquired.

"Oh, just a bit of business. There's a company in Dublin thinking of building in Cork over the next few years. I'm going to present some of my work to them on Friday morning."

"That's a pity. You'll miss Kennedy."

Dean shrugged. "I've seen him before. I was in Washington for his inauguration in '61."

"Go away, you were there?"

"Yes."

"How close?"

"Pretty close."

"Was it amazing?"

"It was okay," Dean said, with a dismissive shrug. Mary could see him hiding a grin.

"Go away, ya liar," she said, thumping his arm.

Dean grabbed two boxes, dusted them off and gestured for Mary to take a seat. She sat down and Dean sat on the other box opposite her. He put his hands on her knees. "Now, tell me what happened last night."

"It was—," Mary began, but Dean cut her off.

"And don't lie to me, Mary Horgan. I can tell when someone is lying to me." He patted her knees, encouraging her with his eyes to start.

Mary hesitated, trying to decide which way to go. She didn't want to lie to him, but she didn't want him to do anything drastic either.

"Okay," she began." When you dropped me off at home last night, after that wonderful night, the best of my life, if I may say so myself." She blushed and Dean leaned forward, kissing her gently on the cheek.

"Okay. When you dropped me off, I was walking down the path when I saw something move in the garden. It was Willy, Willy O'Reilly."

Mary noticed Dean's face change slightly. The eyes narrowed and the muscles at the sides of his jaw flexed. He looked different to her in that split second, scary somehow, as if there was something inside him that he rarely, if ever, left anyone see. That look was there and then it was gone.

She continued. "He grabbed me and basically, I fought him off. I got in home and he left shortly after that. He was very drunk so he could barely stand."

"And that's it?"

"That's it," Mary said and offered a half smile. She could see that the conversation was far from over though.

"What about that?" Dean said, pointing to her hand. The long sleeve of her dress had moved up her forearm, exposing the bruise.

"That's where he grabbed me."

Dean examined the mark. "It looks pretty bad from here, Mary. Now tell me what really happened. It's not as clear cut as you are making it out to be, is it?"

Mary felt the room begin to close in around her. It was one of those situations when you're caught in the moment and you can't think of anything to say, except the truth. She started to cry, a pitiful whimper escaping her mouth to join the tears as they passed by.

Dean fell to one knee, put his arms around her, pulling her tightly against him and burying his head in her chest. "It's okay. You can tell me everything. You have to tell someone." Then he paused and lifted his head until they were face to face again. "Did he rape you?"

"No," Mary shouted, feeling violated by the very mention of the word.

"I'm sorry," Dean said immediately.

"No, it's okay. It just sounds so dirty, that word. You know what I mean."

"I do."

Mary took a deep breath, held it for a few seconds and then exhaled slowly as she started to speak again. "He didn't rape me, but he did manage to rip off my underwear."

Dean held her in his arms; he didn't speak, just ran his fingers through her long hair.

"He was on top of me and I could feel his bare legs against my stockings. I knew then that he had his pants down." The tears came again. Her voice faltered, but she continued. "I knew I couldn't get him off me by fighting him so I started to play along with him, hoping he would think I was starting to like it, the dirty bastard.

"When I felt him ease his weight off me I grabbed his…" Mary stopped short, embarrassed.

Dean kissed her forehead.

"I grabbed him between the legs and dug my nails in as deep as I could."

She felt Dean shudder slightly and knew he was feeling, in his mind, what Willy had felt last night.

"He fell off me. The blood was running down his legs, and it was all over my hands. I ran for the door, but I had to go back to the garden for my handbag; the key was in it. But Willy was in too much pain to do anything. I got in home and sat in the hall until I knew he was gone."

Dean kissed her on the lips. "You were lucky," he said. "It could have been a lot worse."

"Promise me you won't do anything stupid, Dean. I don't want you getting in trouble over me."

"I won't do anything to him. I'd say you've seen the back of him forever after that encounter. He's probably afraid of you now."

Mary smiled, but inside she knew she didn't believe what Dean had told her.

* * * *

Willy pulled the trigger and the shotgun erupted in his hands. He stood at least ten feet away, to avoid being hit by any spray. The bag exploded and the water spurted free. He had tied five bags along the clothesline he had found in the boot of the car. Each bag was filled with water from the stream that ran through the field he was standing in.

He chose this field because it was outside the city and the land was owned by the State. There were no houses or farms for miles, and the closest town was Mallow, still a good five miles away. He recalled his father bringing him there numerous times before he died. His father would sit empty cans on the rocks and, using the shotgun, he would tell Willy that they were the heads of Englishmen. Then he would proceed to blow their heads off.

Willy blasted each bag and reloaded the shotgun as quickly as he could, not exchanging speed for accuracy at any time. He knew it would be important to reload the gun quickly, but going too quickly and dropping a cartridge could be his downfall.

"Keep an extra cartridge in your left hand as you shoot."

Willy heard the voice to his left. He wasn't startled; he recognised the tone. He turned to see his father leaning against a large rock. Willy kept a straight face, waiting to see if he was going to be cursed at, like before, or if his father had come to help him.

"Hold the next cartridge in your left hand, against the barrel. That way when you open the breech you already have the cartridge in your hand. Then you can slam it home and blast the next bastard away." His father smiled and spat on the ground.

Willy removed the next cartridge from his pocket, loaded the gun, removed another cartridge and held it in his left hand.

He aimed at the next bag and fired. The bag exploded. His father shouted, "Blow their fuckin heads off, son."

Willy snapped open the gun and slammed the next cartridge in. He raised the gun again and fired. The last bag ripped open, spilling water onto the wet ground. The whole operation had taken ten seconds.

"What do you think of that, old man?" Willy asked, spinning around. But he was talking to a large rock. His father was gone; obviously the lesson was over.

Willy left the mess he had made and jumped back into the car. It would take him just over half an hour to get back to the farm, where he planned to spend the rest of the evening cleaning the shotgun. He wanted the gun to be spotless when he used it again.

* * * *

When Mary arrived home just after eight, Louise met her on the steps.

"You can't say you were with Angela. Dad called to Angela's house earlier, looking for you. I think they saw you leave in Dean's car. They've been in the kitchen whispering all evening."

"Where are they now?"

"Dad's sitting in his chair reading the Echo. Mam's still in the kitchen pottering around. Say nothing until they say something. They may be totally in the dark."

The two girls entered the house. Michael and Brendan were watching 'The Gallant Men' on television. Michael turned and looked at her. With that look, she could see that Brendan had told him that she knew about their Saturday outings. He looked worried and angry at the same time.

Jack sat reading the paper, not looking up to register her arrival. Mary walked past his chair and into the small kitchen. Her mother was standing at the sink washing clothes.

"Hello," she said sarcastically. "You're feeling better?"

"Much," Mary replied.

"Are you going to work tomorrow?"

"I think so." Mary opened the cupboard, removed a glass and leaned past her mother to turn on the tap.

"Be careful," Ann said.

Ann always worried over her hot water. She spent an hour heating water on the stove in the summer, when the fire wasn't lighting, and she always overreacted when someone came in for a drink from the tap.

"Okay," Mary said and turned the tap gently, not spilling a drop into the sink. She rested her back against the wall and took a drink from the glass.

"Where were you?" Ann enquired.

"I was in town."

"With who?"

Mary decided that her mother knew, so she stopped playing around. She was nineteen. What could they do to her anyway?

"I was with Dean."

Ann Horgan stopped washing. She froze for a moment, her hands half in, half out of the water. "Dean, hmm," she said raising her eyebrows. She didn't sound upset. "And who's this Dean?"

Mary put the words she wanted to say together in her head and after a brief pause she said, "He's an American. I met him last week at the Palm Court. You'd like him, Mam."

"Would I now," she commented, returning to her washing.

Mary started to leave.

"Hang on a second," Ann said drying her hands on a tea towel. "Tell me more about this Dean fella. How old is he?"

Mary turned back and looked at her mother. Her face wasn't the face of anger that Mary had seen in the past. Her mother looked interested, even concerned. Mary softened slightly and said, "He's thirty and he's an architect."

"Good for him. And what is he doing seeing a nineteen year old girl?"

She didn't sound sarcastic. The question sounded genuine. Mary wasn't sure what to say, but her mother spoke first.

"Listen, love, your Dad and me are just worried about you, that's all. I didn't see you leave in that flash car today, but your Dad was walking up the road, and he saw you. He got a right earful off the bats next door as well, which didn't help at all."

"Mam, he's really nice and he treats me like a real woman."

"That's what your father is afraid of."

"Ahh, Mam. You know what I mean. He makes me feel fantastic."

"Jesus, girl. You only know this man a wet week and you sound like you want to marry him."

Mary's answer to that was 'yes' all the way to the altar, but she didn't share that with her mother. Things were going okay and her mother hadn't said anything to hint that they were going to try to stop her seeing Dean.

"Don't be silly. I just like him and he likes me. He's moving here from America, setting up his own business on Pana. He has an office already. That's where I was this evening, looking at his new office."

Ann put the towel down and moved closer to her daughter. "Look," she said, "All we want is for you not to be hurt or taken advantage of. That's all. As you said yourself, you're nineteen now and you can do what you like. Just remember there are people out in the world who would steal the pennies off a dead man's eyes."

"What do you mean by that?"

"Nothing. Just don't go throwing yourself at this lad."

Too late for that, Mary thought, remembering last night in Kinsale. "I'm not stupid."

"I know that. You're a very smart young lady." Ann picked up a dirty shirt and returned to the sink.

"So you're okay with this, Dad and you?"

"We're fine with it, as long as you know what you're doing." Mary turned to leave again.

"As long as Dean comes to dinner on Saturday evening that is," her mother added.

Mary turned back again. She could see her mother was smiling at the sink, trying to keep her head turned away from her. "What?"

"I want you to invite Dean to dinner on Saturday. Is that okay? He does eat, doesn't he?"

"Of course," Mary spluttered. "I'll ah…I'll ask him. I'll have to ring him tomorrow though because I won't see him until Saturday. It's short notice, but I'll ask him."

"That's fine. And if he can't make it on Saturday, ask him for Sunday. We'll manage."

"Great," Mary replied, leaving the kitchen, not sure if she had just been set up or not.

She walked past her father, who was still reading the paper. He didn't look up. He kept singing to himself; a song she had heard as a child about a woman falling for the wrong man.

Mary wasn't sure if he was getting at her or not, so she kept going, trying not to look annoyed. As she closed the door behind her, she heard what she thought was laughter from the living room.

* * * *

"Do you think she will tell them now? Now that her secret is out, she has nothing to lose." Michael glared at his brother.

Brendan was lying in the bed on his back, smoking a cigarette. "I don't think she will, but if she does, she does. We can't stop her, can we?"

"No, but Dad will beat the living shit out of us if she does."

"No he won't."

"Why won't he?"

Brendan looked at Michael. "Because we're bigger than him," he said and slowly turned away.

Michael lay in bed staring at the ceiling for some time, wondering why he had ever brought his brother to that meeting, and why he had ever gone himself in the first place. The next meeting was on Saturday and Michael racked his brain for a way out; a way of not only getting himself out of going, but also stopping Brendan.

* * * *

In the room next door, Ann climbed into the bed while Jack sat on his side taking off his socks.

"Jes, I dunno about inviting this American lad to the house at all," he said.

"Why?"

"What was it you said he was, an archer, is it?"

Ann chuckled. "An architect, ya eejit!"

Jack climbed in next to her and snuggled his head against her breasts. "Nothing to do with arrows so?"

"No."

"Good. I was afraid he would want to hunt for the dinner. Now I'll just buy a shoulder of bacon on Saturday in Paddy Twomey's."

"That'll do," Ann said, turning away from him. She pulled the covers over her shoulder.

"That's great," Jack shrugged. "A shoulder of bacon on Saturday and a cold shoulder tonight. Lovely, just lovely."

Friday 21st June 1963

Excerpt from the Evening Echo:

Cardinal Montini Elected. — Takes Name of Paul the Sixth.

White smoke from the stove over the Sistine Chapel told the waiting thousands in the square below that a Pope had been elected and a great burst of joyful cheering broke out.

Then came the news that Cardinal Montini, Archbishop of Milan, was the successor to Pope John. He took the name of Paul VI.

Cardinal Montini had been the chief name on the list of Papabili since the death of the late Pope.

"About yesterday, Mr. Thompson," Mary started, but Beth waved her hands vigorously from the top of the ladder, nearly losing her balance with the sudden movement. Mary saw the mental image of Beth crashing down on Mr. Thompson's head, snapping his neck like a twig. She smiled involuntarily. Another glance up at Beth and the message was received.

"What about yesterday, child?" Mr. Thompson urged her to continue.

"A man came in looking for you."

"Really. What was his name?"

"He didn't give a name, did he Beth?"

Beth was wiping dust off one of the jars. Mary could see she was hiding her face from Mr. Thompson. "No, he didn't," she managed to say.

"Did he say what he was looking for?"

"No, he just asked to see you and when I said your weren't here he just smiled and left." Mary removed her coat and went into the back room.

When she returned Beth was alone in the shop, Mary scanned the room for Mr. Thompson.

"He's gone for change next door," Beth explained.

"Thanks, Beth," Mary said.

"No problem. He never showed up yesterday either. Are you alright? Were you sick?"

"Yes," Mary lied. "I was getting sick all day yesterday. I must have eaten something bad."

Mary certainly wasn't going to confide in Beth, when she hadn't told Angela about Willy. She fed Beth some more false details about the previous day and gently changed the subject.

Mr. Thompson returned and emptied the change he had brought with him into the cash till. He called to Beth who was in the back room and addressed both of them. "Next Friday, the President of America is coming to town and Mr. Jacobs next door has just informed me that all shops on Patrick Street will be closing for the hour or so that he is here."

"That's great," Beth said clapping her hands together. "I can't wait to see him."

Mr. Thompson frowned at her. "We," he said, pausing for effect, "are not closing our doors."

"But why?" Beth asked.

"Because, young lady, there will be thousands of people lining that street out there to get a glimpse of the great man. Those same people will want something to chew on while they wait for his arrival. That's where we come in. I think it will be one of our best days ever," he said, rubbing his hands together.

Mary returned to work, not caring enough to complain. Beth pouted as she filled up the ground level jars from the storeroom supply. The morning was uneventful and Mr. Thompson had not asked Mary to climb the ladder at all. He had asked Beth three times and Mary had started to feel a little left out. She didn't know if she felt jealous or afraid that Mr. Thompson suspected she dropped the jar on purpose, but the fact that he didn't want to look at her annoyed her in some way she couldn't explain.

At her lunch break, Mary made a call from one of the telephone boxes on Patrick Street. She called the Metropole and talked with Dean for ten minutes. He reluctantly accepted the invitation to dinner. She didn't like the whole idea of him meeting her family, but she played her part in convincing him to come. She was afraid of her parents' reaction if he didn't. Dean asked her what he should bring with him and she told him to bring the charm he had used on her and he would be fine. He agreed, but added that a cake wouldn't hurt either. Mary kissed him down the phone and raced off to meet with Angela at the Pav, already fifteen minutes late.

* * * *

Angela was sitting alone in the café eating a sandwich with a bag of crisps. Mary ordered a sandwich and sat down. "Sorry I'm late,"

Angela shrugged. "It's okay. I was watching that gorgeous fella there behind you eat his dinner. He's feckin' handsome, he is."

Mary turned slowly, as if she was looking out the door. She turned back quicker. "He's only alright."

"Oh, sure he isn't a touch on the American lover boy," Angela teased. "And speaking of lover boy, did you do it last night?

"Go away out a that, will ya," Mary dismissed her. "I told you everything this morning."

"No you didn't. You avoided all my questions, is what you did."

"No I didn't."

"Okay, did you do it?"

"We had a nice meal."

"You did it!"

"I did not." Mary's smile betrayed her.

"You did, ya dirty bitch. Did you have your clean knickers on?"

"Not for long."

After sharing most of the details, and leaving out the part of the night involving Willy O'Reilly, Mary changed the subject. "Is Johnny still going to join the Brit's army?"

"It's a disaster. Johnny told them the other night. Mam took it very badly. Dad sighed and walked out of the room, leaving Mam to cry on her own. I could see that Dad was delighted. That fucker knows that once Johnny is gone he can start practising his uppercuts on Mam again," Angela looked angry. No tears filled her eyes this time. "Well, I'm not standing by and watching them rip each other apart." She reached across the table and grabbed Mary's hand. "I'm leaving home as well," she announced, a broad smile spreading across her face.

Mary wasn't sure what to say, even though she sensed what was coming. She knew the next sentence before Angela had even opened her mouth, and she knew what her answer was going to be as well. Mary tried desperately to put a refusal together in her head; a refusal that let Angela down softly, and one that didn't involve Dean.

"Will you move into a flat with me, Mary?" Angela said softly.

Mary looked across the table and her heart sank in her chest. She was about to tear a huge hole in the fabric that held their friendship together. She nearly blurted out an affirmative, purely intent on sparing her best friend's feelings. But she held her mouth closed until the strength came to say the words.

"I can't, Angela," she said, squeezing her hand tighter with each word.

Angela's face dropped. She had obviously been expecting a 'yes' and nothing else. They had discussed the prospect of taking this step before and Mary had always been the more eager of the two. But now Mary had Dean, and though she dared not to say it, she harboured the hope that she would be living with him in the near future, possibly even marrying him.

"I can't leave home now," she offered. "Mam and Dad need my wages to keep the house running."

Mary could see immediately that Angela wasn't going to accept her pitiful attempt at an excuse.

"You're joking me, aren't you?" she began, a sharp sting in her voice now. "You were always the one wanting to get out of home and now you're using money as an excuse." Her voice rose with every word and others started to stare.

"Angela, calm down."

"It's him, isn't it?"

"No."

"Of course it is. Jesus, Mary, you only just met him. He'll be gone in a week or two."

Now Mary went on the defensive. "No he won't. He's starting his own business here."

"The only business he'll be doing in Cork is in your knickers," Angela shouted across the table. Some people smothered laughs at nearby tables.

Mary flushed, her face pounding with embarrassment. "We'll talk about this later," she said as she got up, her sandwich untouched on the table.

"Why bother," Angela replied, getting to her feet.

They both barged out of the restaurant and took off in separate directions. Mary felt the tears welling up in her eyes as she walked along Patrick Street. She had thought that all her tears had been spent yesterday, but slowly they arrived and spilled down her face, dragging mascara along with them. By the time she reached Patrick's Bridge, she looked like a sad clown.

* * * *

Willy's father had visited him again during the night, staying much longer this time. They had chatted about things into the early hours of the morning. Willy hadn't loved his father when he was alive, but this man impressed him. He knew what Willy was going through, and most of all he sympathised with him, advised him on what steps he should take to rectify the situation. It was his father who came up with the idea that he shouldn't feed the pigs. "Do you know that pigs can eat a human being in no time at all," he said. "And they don't leave anything after them. They eat it all, flesh and bone."

When Willy had finally drifted off to sleep, the sun was beaming shafts of light into his room, through the filthy curtains.

He awoke to the sound of the pigs grunting and squealing in the yard. He knew they were starving, but he had no intentions of feeding them. He wanted them as hungry as possible. They were crucial to his plan. Checking the clock by the bed, he saw that he had slept through breakfast and lunch. It was four o'clock and he was hungry. He got out of bed, washed his face, checked his groin (it was healing well), and went downstairs. His mother's door was closed and he was surprised that she hadn't screamed him awake earlier. She must be sleeping now, he thought, and decided to leave her be.

The cupboards were bare, almost. A mouse sat in the bread cupboard munching on a week old pan of bread that looked darker in colour than the mouse. Willy swept the vermin out onto the floor with the bread and searched the rest of the pantry.

Nothing.

His stomach reminded him that he hadn't eaten for over a day, echoing a loud rumble around the small room.

He grabbed the keys to the car. He had a pint and some sandwiches in mind at a hotel in Blarney. I deserve a treat, he thought, as he stepped out into the bright sunlight.

The pigs scurried over to him, grunting loudly. Some of them looked pretty bad. He hadn't fed them since last weekend, when he had killed the little bastard who tried to run away from him. He looked around the yard and saw that some of the pigs were lying in the shade around the barn. They looked too weak to get up.

"It won't be long now, my lovelies," Willy said, as he kicked some of them out of his way to get to the car.

* * * *

Kevin Long had paid the fine with his own money and, after walking around sulking for the rest of the week, he decided it was better to have friends who wouldn't split a fine with him, than to have no friends at all. He could see their point as well. He had been the one driving after all. Deep down, he still held a grudge inside, but his chance at revenge would come, someday.

The week had been a drag. He worked as a deliveryman's assistant. They drove all over the north side delivering bread to houses and shops. His boss was getting old and Longy hoped the bastard would drop dead soon so he could take over the job himself. Work had been as boring as usual all week, but after falling out with the Horgan brothers, his nights were as empty as the bread van at three o'clock.

With his mind set on reconciliation, he drove the Prefect up to the turf stores a little before five. The morning fog had lifted by lunchtime and the sky was a canvas of blue with a spectacular sun rolling slowly across it. He arrived as Brendan walked out of the stores. Pulling the car up next to Brendan, he pushed the horn. Brendan bent over and looked in at Longy.

"What do you want, boy?"

"Ahh, come on. Don't be like that. We just had a little misunderstanding, that's all," Longy reached over and opened the passenger door. "Come on, get in Brend. Let's collect Michael and go for a spin out to Blarney or something." Longy looked up at him with sorrowful, lonely eyes.

Brendan sighed deeply, got in and said, "Let's go, my man."

Longy pulled away from the step and drove down Cathedral Road. He didn't notice Brendan casually blocking his nostrils with his hand as he rolled down the window.

They drove past Brendan's house and spotted Louise sitting in the garden. They pulled over and, after Louise told their mother that she was going, she got in the back. The three of them cruised down the road searching the footpaths on either side for Michael.

* * * *

Dean Reynolds stepped out of his room in the Metropole Hotel carrying a large metallic case that was slightly larger than a normal briefcase. He walked down the hallway toward the lift. On his way he met with Andy Dineen, the night porter. Dean had struck up a friendship with the old man during the past week. As the old man shuffled toward him, Dean looked at his wristwatch. "A bit early today?" he said to the porter.

"Hotel is busy. They asked me to come in and help out. Can't complain about being busy, I guess."

"That's true," Dean replied.

"Not dressed in one of your usual suits today, sir?" the porter asked. Dean could not get used to the Irish way of being nosy but nice at the same time.

"I'm going out to take a closer look at your countryside today." Dean lifted his arms. "Are these clothes okay? I feel a bit awkward." He was wearing a pair of slacks with a collared T Shirt and leather jacket.

"Anything looks good on a good looking person, sir," the old man said, as he edged past Reynolds.

"Well, that's good enough for me," Dean said, as he started for the lift again.

His rental car was parked outside the hotel. Dean placed the case in the passenger seat next to him. Before starting the car, he surveyed the street around him and the hotel entrance, for a few minutes. He had to ensure that he wasn't being followed. Happy that nothing was out of the ordinary, he started the car and drove away.

He had studied plenty of maps of Cork and the surrounding county so he managed to negotiate his way onto the Blarney road without many wrong turns.

Three miles later, he arrived in Blarney but didn't stop there. He turned right and drove north towards a place called

Waterloo. Large trees hung over the road from both sides, blocking out the sun completely, and it gave Dean the impression that he was travelling through a tunnel. He emerged a few miles later at a public house called 'The Waterloo Inn'.

He turned right, over Putland's Bridge after the pub and, consulting his map, he confirmed that the next village was over five miles away; a tiny place called Grenagh. After about two miles, Dean pulled the car off the road and parked it as close as he could to the ditch. He didn't want to block traffic and draw attention to the car; but then again, he hadn't seen a car since Blarney.

Carrying the metallic case, Dean opened the gate to the nearest field and started walking. The field was empty of any animals and the grass grew high around him. Climbing over the next gate, which was locked, Dean entered a field of wheat. The crop rose to a level just below his chest and he found it difficult to walk through it. He looked ahead and spotted the start of a wooded area at the end of the field. The trees ran along the side of the field, obscuring anything that lay beyond them. Dean glanced back over his shoulder. The road was out of sight.

Perfect.

He placed the case on the ground in a clearing before the wood. The ground level had dropped slightly as he approached the trees and he couldn't see further than two hundred yards in any direction. He took out his keys, popped the smallest one into the lock, and turned it. Popping both catches at once, the case sprang open to reveal a soft grey sponge insert with grooves and compartments cut into it. Dean admired the disassembled rifle. It was the first time he had seen it. Each component was still wrapped in clear plastic, but he could already tell that the rifle was a work of art.

He had commissioned an expert in firearms, from Boston, to make it. In the course of the last year, he had met with the gunsmith several times to discuss the kind of rifle that he wanted. The end product had cost two thousand dollars, and Dean had paid the complete fee in advance. The gunsmith was surprised by this transaction, telling Dean that no one had ever paid him before the job was done. "What if the rifle has problems?" the man had said to Dean as he took the cash. "Then you will have problems," Dean had replied, smiling.

Removing each section of the rifle, Dean removed the plastic wrapping and set about assembling it. Each part fit perfectly together. The gunsmith had done a near perfect job, and no parts had been damaged during the long journey the gun had taken to Ireland, alone.

With the body of the rifle assembled, two more components remained in the case. Dean removed the silencer first, and positioning it at the end of the barrel, he lined up the threads and the silencer swivelled round the end of the barrel until it was secure. The telescopic sight slipped onto the top of the rifle without much effort. He held the rifle away from his body and gazed at it. In his line of work, he had held many weapons, but nothing impressed him more than the one in his hands now. It was truly a joy to behold. It hadn't fired a single shot yet, but Dean knew it would be destroyed in less than a week, never to be used again. The rifle had taken two months to manufacture, but it would only be used twice.

He put the rifle down next to him and turned back to the case, removing the grey sponge insert that had held the rifle components in place. Under the sponge was another compartment. It contained twenty normal bullets, as requested by Dean, and five mercury tipped bullets, designed to explode on impact. These bullets looked exactly the same as the other twenty. The gunsmith had drilled the tips of these bullets, inserting the droplets of mercury himself and, sealing the holes again with lead, he had filed the tips until they were perfect. Dean could only tell the explosive bullets from the normal ones because of the pre-agreed positioning in the case.

He left the rifle and case and walked along the tree line, counting his paces as he went. After counting two hundred paces he stopped and looked back to where he had left the rifle and case. He picked a tree that was visible from the position of the rifle. He removed a piece of paper from his pocket, unfolded it, and using a penknife from his other pocket, he stuck the paper to the tree. Marked in clear red ink on the paper were three circles, each one smaller than the last. The smallest circle was about three inches in diameter.

He returned to the rifle and picked it up. It felt good in his hands, not as heavy as a normal hunting gun. He dropped to one knee and raised the rifle to his head. It took a few seconds to locate the target, but when he did it looked no further than forty yards away, through the telescopic sight. The crosshairs in the sight looked to be dead centre. Dean was surprised; normally these would need adjusting to line them up properly. He thought of the gunsmith, afraid that something would go wrong with the gun and afraid of Dean coming to visit him. He had obviously checked the sight himself, and lined it up.

He brought the rifle back down to his waist, pulled back the bolt and slipped the first normal cartridge into the breech. He raised the rifle and, looking through the sight, he searched for the target. The red circles appeared and Dean slowed his breathing. He crouched motionless for a few moments, waiting for his heartbeat to slow. He lined up the crosshairs in the centre of the middle circle on the target and, exhaling slowly, he squeezed the trigger.

There was much less recoil from the rifle than he expected and the silencer worked perfectly, the noise escaping the barrel sounded like someone muffling a cough. He left the rifle again and walked to the target. The bullet had hit the tree but had missed the target entirely. It had entered the tree low and to the left. A small entry hole remained, as proof of his shot.

He returned to the rifle and fired three more shots without changing the settings of the sight. The results were all the same: low and left. Happy that the sight was the problem, he adjusted the screws that held the sight in place and fired again. This time, when he checked the target up close, he was still slightly low and left but inside the outer circle on the target. He returned to the gun and turned the screws a quarter revolution.

His next shot struck the target inside the middle circle. Another shot entered the tree inside the circle but slightly to the left of his last shot. The next entered the hole made by the first bullet that was on target. This brought a slight grin to Dean's face.

The gun was perfect.

He walked to the tree, the gun this time under his arm, and replaced the target with a new one. Instead of three red circles, like the last target, this one had a sketched picture of a man's face.

Dean returned to his firing position and shoved another bullet into the breech.

* * * *

Less than three hundred yards away, behind Dean's back, four people lay in the tall wheat looking down the field at him.

"He doesn't look like a fuckin' architect to me."

The others could detect a slight quiver in Longy's voice. He was obviously afraid. Louise lay next to Michael and she was terrified. She had spotted the car as they passed it, and convinced the others that it was Dean's car. Longy drove past the car and pulled in after the next bend, by the gate of the next field.

"How do you know it's his car?" Brendan had asked.

Louise knew it was his. "The number plate is the same, and I remember seeing it yesterday, outside our house."

They had agreed to take a look in the field, in case Dean was out of petrol or something. Michael suggested they go into the field where Longy had parked. "We don't want to walk in on him and Mary if they're messing around."

The four of them climbed the gate and walked through the field. Without their knowledge, they ended up flanking Dean's position on their left. After walking through a few fields, Brendan announced he was turning back. They entered the wheat field and, after a few steps, Michael heard a cough, or what sounded like a cough. He looked left and saw Dean crouched by the trees with a rifle in his hands. He dragged the others to the ground as another muffled report sounded from the rifle. They lay in the grass watching Dean. He fired another shot, got to his feet and started walking in the direction of where he had fired.

They all watched as Dean inspected his aim. Then he took down the target and put up a new one. None of them could make out what was on the target. Dean turned and they all ducked down into the wheat, afraid to look up for a few minutes.

* * * *

Dean returned to the case and pulled back the bolt of the rifle once more. He took aim and fired, hitting the picture of the man's head between the eyes. With his next shot he hit the left eye, followed by the right and a fourth shot into the gaping mouth of the sketch. Happy that the gun was ready, Dean removed a tube of balsa-wood cement and squirted the contents over the grub screws that adjusted the telescopic sight. He lit a cigarette and waited for the cement to harden. After twenty minutes in the evening sun, the cement was hard and Dean loaded the rifle with one of the mercury bullets. He followed his ritual of aiming once again and fired.

The target exploded, sending fragments of paper flying into the air. When Dean retrieved his penknife from the tree, he observed a small crater in the tree where the bullet had entered. The bark of the tree was splintered and nothing of the target remained. He returned to the case, disassembled the rifle and put it back in the case. He put the first target and what remained of the second in with the rifle. He left the field as he had found it, except for the tree with twelve bullets lodged in it for all time.

* * * *

Dean left the field, but the others remained, sprawled out on the crushed wheat, staring up at the evening sun. No one spoke for a few minutes. Louise lay on her back, horrified by what she had seen. She didn't try to contemplate what Dean was doing firing a rifle at targets in a field in the countryside. The thoughts that filled her mind were the thoughts of her sister, Mary. Whatever Dean was up to, Louise knew that it spelled trouble for Mary. After her ordeal with Willy on Wednesday night, Louise knew that Mary would not be able to deal with anything else right now. She decided to speak, to break her own train of thought and the thoughts of the others.

Then Longy said, "What did you say he was, an architect or something?"

"Yes," Louise replied.

"And they draw stuff, buildings and shit like that, isn't it?"

"Yes."

Longy shook his head. "Maybe his hobby is shooting? Maybe he just likes to blow the shit out of stuff?"

Louise looked at Brendan and Michael. Her brothers were staring intently at each other. Michael had a familiar expression on his face. She had seen it before. He always looked like that when something really bad had happened. Brendan looked different to her. His face looked older somehow, more than its twenty-one years. He stared at his brother, unmoving, and Louise could see that Michael knew what his brother was thinking.

"What do you think, boys?" she asked.

Brendan didn't look at her. He continued to look at Michael. Gradually, he started to get up. "We don't think nothing about it, right Michael?"

Michael hesitated, looked at Louise and then back to Brendan. "Right," he said finally.

"I think Longy's right," Brendan continued.

Louise could take a hint, but Longy couldn't. She could see that Brendan wasn't telling them what he really thought. Michael, the older brother, was obviously going along with his younger sibling.

"Or maybe he's some hired killer or something, and the drawing thing is just a cover up." Longy stood and dusted dirt and wheat off his clothes.

"Or maybe the whiff off you is screwing up your head," Brendan shouted.

"What fucking whiff? I don't smell."

"Well, something smelly is following you around, Longy, cause you could knock a fuckin' donkey with that smell."

Louise couldn't help but laugh and Michael was already turned away, his body jerking uncontrollably.

"I don't smell," Longy shouted in his defence.

"Yah, and my shit don't stink."

Longy closed the distance between him and Brendan surprisingly quickly, but Brendan saw him coming.

"Ya fuckin' prick," Longy screamed, as he lunged forward.

Brendan planted his feet and threw his closed fist. Longy changed direction in mid flight and fell to the ground, holding his face in his hands. When he turned over, Louise could see the blood seeping through his fingers. She looked up at Brendan, who looked uncharacteristically calm. Longy screamed in pain on the ground and Michael went to his aid. Louise watched Brendan and knew then that he had deliberately caused the scene before her. All talk about Dean had ceased, and Brendan looked pleased.

"Come on," he said. "Let's go home. It's getting late any-way." He bent over Longy and said, "I'm sorry, buddy. Come on, I'll buy you a pint." Longy shoved him, still holding his nose.

Brendan started to walk away. Louise followed him.

"Come on," Brendan said again. "A pint will fix the pain in your nose, and maybe it will cure the smell from you as well, ya weak bastard."

They left the field and Michael drove Longy's car back into the city. No one mentioned what they had seen. Louise sat in the back with Longy, tending to his bloody nose, while she discreetly covered her own nose to block out the smell of, what had to be, stale onions.

* * * *

Mary arrived home in a daze. She genuinely could not remember walking home from town. Mr. Thompson sent her home with a reminder that it was her turn to work on Saturday. A full day alone with a nobber was not what she needed right now.

She had paused outside Angela's house and her heart sank. What had happened at the café was the icing on the cake. Coupled with her assault on Mr. Thompson, the attack on her by Willy and the fact that she had to work tomorrow, Mary felt like her world was coming to an end.

When she stepped into the hallway at home, she could hear her parents inside messing around. She could hear them arguing about the dinner and Mary was determined to stay out of their game. She opened the door to the living room and popped her head in. "Mam. Mam. I'm not feeling well, so I'm going straight to bed. Okay?"

Ann emerged from the small pantry wiping her hands. "Is everything alright?"

"Fine," Mary lied. "I think I'm just tired is all." Mary started to close out the door.

"Hang on a second, will ya? Come in here and talk to me."

Mary wondered if Louise had spilled the beans. If she had told her Mam about Willy, things could get very uncomfortable for her. For a start, Mary knew that her father wouldn't stand by and let the Gardai deal with Willy O'Reilly. And if he did something to Willy, then he would be in trouble himself.

"Sit down there now," Ann said, pointing to a chair at the table.

Jack got up, as if on queue and headed for the toilet.

"Mam, I'm really tired, like," Mary moaned.

"Ahh, two minutes won't kill ya."

Mary sat down and Ann sat in the chair next to her. She placed her hand on Mary's. "I was talking to Louise this morning," she started.

Mary grimaced, waiting for the explosion of anger for not telling them about Willy, or the sympathy overload from a mother to her daughter.

"I asked her about Dean and she said he was a lovely man."

Mary lifted her head and looked at her mother.

"Now if you like him as much as you say and, well, he likes you back, well, then you might be overcome by your feelings for each other."

Mary tried to interrupt, but Ann raised her hand to stop her speaking.

"Let me finish now. All I'm saying is that he might…. and you might too… you might want to….. well, what I'm trying to say is that he might want to…"

Mary nearly laughed. For a moment she was going to help her mother out, but decided she could do with the entertainment.

"Well, you know what I mean," Ann finished.

"I'm not sure I get what you're saying, Mam."

Ann shifted in her seat. "What I'm trying to say is that he is a man and you are, well, a woman."

"Right."

"And well you know what happens between men and woman."

"They fight."

"No."

"Then what?"

"Well….they….when a man loves a woman…"

"Mam. Are you planning on singing?" Mary smiled at her mother.

"You know what I'm talking about, don't you?"

"Of course I do. And don't worry. I know what I'm doing." She leaned forward, kissed Ann on the forehead and got up. "Now, I'm going to bed because I'm exhausted and I have to work again tomorrow."

"Will I bring up your dinner?"

Mary had reached the door. "No, I had something at work before I left." The truth was that Mary hadn't eaten all day. Her lunch had been left behind after the spat with Angela, and after that her appetite had all but disappeared.

"Good night, Mam."

"Oh, is he coming tomorrow night?"

Mary's heart jumped in her chest. Because of the fight with Angela, the dinner with Dean had slipped her mind.

"Yes. Yes, he is. What are you cooking?"

"I was thinking bacon and cabbage, a traditional Irish meal for a visiting American."

"He'll like that," Mary said, not knowing if he would and not really caring at that moment. "He said he'll be here by seven, okay?"

"Grand. Good night, love."

Mary managed the stairs and undressed quickly. She stood in her underwear and examined her bruises in the mirror. The bruise on her forearm was turning a shade of yellow. The red scrawls on her thighs, where her knickers had been torn against, were already fading. The real scars were not visible in any mirror and were far from healed. Mary thought of all the women who had been attacked by men. She couldn't imagine how the ones, who were not as lucky as her, had coped.

How could they go on?

She pulled on her nightdress and climbed under the covers. It was Friday night and Mary couldn't believe what had happened in the week that had passed. She had met the man of her dreams, had finally given her boss what he deserved, and had almost been raped in her own front garden. Mary knew that all the bad things would fade with time and hopefully Dean would still be there when the fog cleared. She should be floating on air, but Mary felt something hovering over her, like her own personal rain cloud. Surely, nothing else could go wrong? Then she thought about the dinner tomorrow night and a feeling of dread rose inside her. What's the worst thing that could happen? she thought, trying to calm herself. An image of her Dad throwing Dean out of the house flashed by her mind's eye. No way! Her father cared too much about her to do something like that, didn't he?

Exhausted, Mary turned towards the wall and drifted away into mixed dreams of passionate nights in Kinsale and dispassionate nights in her front garden.

* * * *

Michael stopped the car outside 13 Cathedral road and Brendan warned them all to keep the events of the evening between themselves. "I mean it, Louise," he said. "Don't you dare tell Mary about this. This could be nothing, so I don't want her worried or running to Dean to tell him we saw him, okay?"

Louise looked into her brother's eyes and for the first time in her life she was afraid of him. He glared at her and she wondered what he would do if she refused to go along. She didn't want to find out. Timidly, she said, "Okay," and got out of the car as fast as she could.

The three men stayed in the car and, as Louise walked down the path to the house, she could feel Brendan's eyes digging into her back. She reached the door and turned, but they were already gone. She ducked inside and felt relieved to be away from her brother, the one she had always been closest to in the past.

"Where's Mary?" she asked Jack in the living room.

"She's gone to bed. Not feeling well. I think she has work tomorrow too."

Louise worried about her sister, but also felt relieved that she didn't have to sit next to her for the evening, and lie to her.

"Did you hear we have a new Pope?" Ann asked Louise.

"Really," Louise replied, not too interested.

"Well, don't you want to know his name?"

"What is it?"

"Paul the sixth," Ann announced, blessing herself.

"Great," Louise offered.

"Where did you go?" Ann asked, obviously put out by her reaction.

"We went to Blarney, in Kevin Long's car."

"That was nice. That Kevin Long is a nice young man, I think."

"Yah," Jack added. "Except for the bloody smell of onions off the bugger."

"Jack!"

"Am I right, Louise?"

Louise sniggered and nodded. Ann smothered a smile as she headed for the pantry.

"Can I put on the telly?" she asked her father.

"Why not. I think that Dragnet thing is coming on soon."

Louise flicked the switch on the TV and it brightened up the room.

* * * *

Willy O'Reilly had his pint and sandwich in the Blarney Castle Hotel. In fact, he stayed on to have a lot more pints than were in the original plan. He drove up the driveway to the farm, bashing the Morris Minor off the hedging that lined both sides of the drive. The car stopped in the yard and was immediately surrounded by pigs. They always managed to get out of the pen somehow.

It was dark, way past eleven, and Willy couldn't see properly. He stepped on some of the pigs' hoofs, and kicked him out of his way as he went, almost falling over a few times. One of the pigs tried to bite his shoe and Willy swung his leg wildly, catching the pig in the snout with the toe of his boot, sending him squealing off to the barn.

He entered the hallway and listened for a minute.

Nothing.

Mother was asleep, he thought, as he flicked the light switch on in the hall. Everything swirled around in front of him with the addition of light. He realised how drunk he was then. Slowly, he moved toward the living room door and opened it.

When he turned on the light he saw his father, sitting at the dinner table, cleaning the shotgun.

The old man looked up and smiled at his son. "Come on over. I want to talk to you a minute," he said.

Willy swayed a bit as he made his way to the table, but he managed to make it to a chair. "Hi Dad," he said.

His father did not respond and Willy identified the mood of his father immediately. His father was being serious and that meant Willy would have to be serious as well, or else he would get his ass kicked.

His father placed the gun in front of him. "What do you intend to do with this, son?"

Willy thought for a moment, searching his father's eyes for the correct answer. "I'm....ahh....I'm going to kill them."

"Who are them?"

"That Mary and that bastard friend of hers."

His father smiled. "He's no friend of hers, my boy." He leaned in closer to Willy and whispered, "You know he's fucking her, don't you, son?"

Willy picked up the gun and, after two tries, managed to stand up. "I'll go and kill the bastard now," he said and stumbled backwards, falling onto the chair.

His father placed a hand on his. "No, not tonight. It's not time yet."

Willy nodded. He couldn't see straight anyway.

His father continued. "Wait till Sunday night. It's bonfire night. The streets will be busy and you can move about unnoticed."

"Will you come with me, Dad?"

"Of course I will, son. I wouldn't miss you do your first kill, now would I?"

Willy threw his arms around his father and they hugged for a long time. Willy fell asleep not long after his father left him. He slept at the table, unable to make the short journey to his bed.

Upstairs, Willy's mother was silent.

Saturday 22nd June 1963

Excerpt from the Evening Echo:

Kennedy To Have Talks On Our Common Market Position.

PRESIDENT KENNEDY plans important talks with Government officials on his European tour and while in Dublin his conference agenda will include this country's Common Market position, world problems and U.N. issues.

A confident President Kennedy is due to take off from Washington in the early hours of tomorrow morning for Germany to begin a European tour which he hopes will help put new spirit into the Atlantic Alliance.

When Michael opened his eyes, Brendan was already dressed and sitting on the edge of his bed. He was smoking a fag and offered the butt to Michael.

"Will ya fuck off with that. I haven't even woken up properly yet and you're shoving a fag in me face."

Brendan smirked and continued smoking.

"What time is it?" Michael asked.

"Eleven."

"Okay, give me a drag off it." He took the cigarette, put it to his lips and inhaled deeply. Brendan got up. "Keep it, and get dressed. We have to leave in a few minutes."

Michael could feel his heart sinking in his chest. It felt like it was leaning against his rib cage, pushing against the bones, trying to escape. He took another drag. The events of the evening before tumbled back into his head; the trip to Blarney, the rifle, the target practice.

What did it all mean?

"I'm leaving in five minutes, with or without you," Brendan said casually, as he left the room.

"Okay, okay. For fuck sake, let me at least get dressed, ya bollix."

Jack was downstairs. Ann and Louise had already left to visit Granny Ellen in Sunday's Well. Michael walked in as Jack started on Brendan.

"So, where are you off to today?"

"Nowhere special."

"Anywhere unspecial?"

"No"

"I hope you're not up to anything stupid these days, lads," Jack said, as he saw Michael enter.

Michael could see Brendan was about to cross the line. "If you can call cruising for woman stupid, then we're guilty, I guess."

Jack seemed satisfied with Michael's reply. Brendan stayed quiet and Michael nodded towards the door.

"Be home by six thirty latest tonight, okay. Your mother warned me to tell you," Jack added.

"Why?" Brendan asked, knowing the answer.

"You know why. Mary is bringing her new boyfriend for dinner, and your mother wants everyone here."

"Oh, ya. I forgot about that," Brendan lied, heading for the door.

They walked up the hill to Longy's house. The Ford Prefect was parked outside and Brendan suggested that they forget about bringing Longy along. He reckoned he could get the car started without the keys. Michael asked him if he could explain it to the Gardai, if they stopped them again. They went to the front door.

Longy's nose looked much worse than the night before.

"You should really go to the North Infirmary with that," Michael said.

"No way," Longy replied. "If I go down there they'll probably remove my appendix by mistake."

"Or maybe they'll insert a brain in your head," Brendan added.

"You're a real funny man, Brend. You should be on stage."

Brendan turned and walked down the path. "Yah, and you should be in the circus, ya fuckin' freak."

Longy started down the path after Brendan. Michael stepped in front of him.

"Look, we have some serious shit to do today. Never mind him. He's just messin' with ya." Michael patted Longy on the shoulder. "Get your keys and we'll go to this fuckin' meeting."

As they drove into the same field as the week before, Michael felt the adrenaline pumping through his veins. He glanced back at Brendan, pretending he was looking out the back window. Brendan was sitting calmly in the back looking forward. In one week, Brendan had changed personality completely, and Michael wasn't sure if he liked what he saw. He had seen the fear in Louise's eyes the night before, when Brendan had warned her not to tell Mary anything. Longy was too stupid to realise that Brendan had changed. Michael thought that Brendan wouldn't think twice about seriously hurting Longy, if he had to. Would he think twice about hurting someone closer to him? he thought, as the car came to a halt by the barn.

Kelly was already addressing the crowd. They shouted comments and cheered at the end of each sentence. Michael felt the same rush he had felt all the previous times he had been here. Kelly cursed the English and promised that Ireland would soon rise up against their British oppressors and claim back what was rightfully theirs. People will die for this cause, but they will not be forgotten, he told the crowd. The men cheered, unperturbed by his promise of death.

"At the end of this week," Kelly said, "the President of America will be here in our country. We embrace America as our brother, but we must also warn them." He paused, surveying his audience. He spotted the three of them and motioned to Brendan to join him on the makeshift stage. Without hesitation, Brendan waded through the dense crowd and jumped onto the bales of hay. Kelly put his arm around him and pulled him closer.

"We have warned President Kennedy that he must not, under any conditions, acknowledge or condone British occupation of Ireland. This man here has delivered that message for his country and you will all see it soon, displayed for all to read."

A large roar echoed off the metal roof of the barn. Kelly shook Brendan's hand and together they left the stage. As Brendan made his way back to Michael and Longy, he was patted on the back; his hand was pulled in every direction and shaken vigorously. Kelly trailed behind him, guiding him through the crowd.

Kelly motioned to Michael to follow them outside. Longy followed with Michael. They stood outside for a few minutes as the crowd dispersed slowly, each man shaking both Brendan's and Kelly's hands. When everyone was gone, Kelly turned to Brendan. "You did deliver the letter, didn't you?" he said, his northern accent floating across the field.

"Yes, I did."

"Good lad." Kelly frowned slightly as he looked at Brendan. "You have something else on your mind though. I can see it."

"Yes," Brendan almost whispered.

"Well. Spit it out. You have nothing but friends around you here."

Brendan hesitated, as if he was searching for the proper way to start the tale. "Yesterday evening, the three of us and my sister, Louise, went for a drive in Longy's car." Brendan gestured towards Longy, but Kelly didn't acknowledge the inadvertent introduction. "We went out toward Blarney, and beyond."

"Right."

"Well, we spotted the car of an American fella who is jagging my other sister, Mary." Kelly nodded, looking slightly impatient.

"We went into the field to have a look and we saw him shooting at a target with a rifle."

"So?"

Brendan looked puzzled. To Michael he looked like someone who had just realised that he had overreacted to the whole thing.

"It wasn't just a hunting rifle," Michael offered.

Kelly turned to Michael. "What do you mean?"

"Well, it didn't make much noise, but the tree the target was hanging on looked pretty damaged from the bullets."

"A silencer?" Kelly said, looking at the ground now. He remained silent for a moment, but when he spoke there was urgency in his voice. "Did he see you? Did you talk to him?"

"No," Brendan said. "We were lying in the wheat behind him. He didn't know we were watching him."

"And what is he doing here?"

"We don't know. Louise said he's an architect. He only got here last week. He's trying to set up his own business, according to Louise."

"An architect with a sniper rifle?" Kelly rubbed his chin and walked around in a small circle in front of them.

"Does your sister, the one he is seeing, does she know this?"

"No," Brendan answered, an air of confidence back in his voice. "I warned the others not to tell her. If he's up to something then I didn't want her warning him."

"Good lad, Brendan. Okay, maybe it's nothing, maybe it is, but either way we've got to learn more about this fella. What's his name?"

"Dean Reynolds."

One of the men with Kelly took out a small notebook and started writing.

"Describe him."

"Well, he's about six four, with black hair. He's well built. Looks like he could handle himself."

"What part of America is he from?"

"Louise said he's from Washington."

Kelly nodded slowly, taking it all in. The other man was writing it all down. "Do you know where he's staying?"

"Yes, he's in the Metropole Hotel, on Mac Curtain Street."

"Excellent."

"He's coming to dinner at our house tonight," Michael blurted out.

Kelly swung around to face Michael. "He's what?"

Michael swallowed hard. Kelly's stare made his bladder contract. "He's coming to our house tonight."

Kelly looked at one of his companions. The large man with the notebook looked up from the page he was writing on and nodded.

"Okay!" Kelly said quickly. "You go to dinner tonight and act as if everything is normal, okay?"

"Right," the two brothers replied in unison.

Kelly looked to the sky, as if the plan for the evening was engraved on the blue canvas above. "What I want you to do is this. Hit him with questions now and again. Not too many together. Just make it like you're getting to know him. Ask him about being an architect. How long has he been doing it, find out what he did before that."

The brothers listened intently, following Kelly as he paced in front of them.

"At some point you're going to have to ask him about the rifle." Kelly smiled at them. "Relax, I don't mean you ask him right out about it. You'll have to lead up to it. Talk about shooting rabbits or something and then casually ask him if he ever fired a gun. Talk about hunting. They all hunt in America."

"And if he says he never fired a rifle?" Brendan asked.

"Well, then he's lying and we have trouble."

"What trouble?" Longy said, joining the conversation.

Kelly didn't look at Longy. Instead he asked Brendan, "Can he be trusted?"

"He's okay."

"Right," Kelly continued, not answering Longy. "You have my number. I want you to ring me tonight, after dinner. Then we'll decide what to do next."

"Okay."

Kelly shook his head as they all headed for their cars. "I wish you hadn't delivered that letter now, Brendan."

"Why?"

"Because we have more or less, in the eyes of the public anyway, threatened Kennedy with this letter, and if this fucker is for real he could only be here for one thing."

"I could go to the Examiner office and get it back. They won't publish it until Tuesday anyway."

"They wouldn't give it back now, and even if they did, we sent the original copy to the American Ambassador this morning."

The two men with Kelly got into a large car by the barn. Kelly walked the three of them to their car. "Phone me tonight, and remember don't give away that you know. It will be hard, but just get through tonight and I'll take over from there, if I need to."

Kelly's car disappeared over the crest of the hill and the three of them sat in Longy's car for the longest time before starting the journey back. Michael sat in the back on the way home, and as they left the field and turned right for Cork, he swore that he would never come back there again. He didn't share this personal oath with the others.

* * * *

When Mary arrived home at half past six, the house was a hive of activity. She opened the living room door and could feel the heat coming from the pantry. Jack was setting the table and Mary wished she had a camera. The table, which was normally about five feet by four, was now about eight feet by four. The design of the table allowed each end to be extended by another foot and a half. Mary had only ever seen the table that way on Christmas day.

Jack was placing the cutlery on the place mats that reminded Mary of Christmas as well.

"Has Santa arrived yet?" she asked.

Jack grumbled, "If he does he'll have to sit on the armchair over there, because the table is booked out." He put down a fork on the left and a knife on the right, and then after puzzling over it, he switched the order again.

Mary walked over to the table and planted a gentle kiss on his cheek.

"What's that for?"

"For making an effort," she said and kissed him again.

The kitchen was like a sauna. Ann stood by the stove tending to the four pots that bubbled noisily, sending plumes of steam upward to the already moist ceiling. The back door was open but gave little relief to the tiny room. Louise stood by the sink using a towel to wipe the glasses they would use at dinner. The glasses were not a complete set; in fact, only three actually resembled each other, while the other three varied in size and design.

"How are things going, you two?"

Ann turned and smiled at Mary. "We'll get there. The meat is done now and the poppies won't be long after. There's two blocks of ice cream in the fridge and Jack got a lovely apple tart from O'Keeffe's earlier."

Mary leaned forward and kissed her mother. "Thanks, Mam."

Ann's face lit up, as if she had been paid a hundred pounds for her efforts. She reached out and hugged Mary tightly. "Anything for you, dear."

Then she let go and screamed, "JACK, THE MEAT IS DONE! CAN YOU PUT IT OUT TO COOL?"

Jack appeared at the entrance to the pantry, a stupid grin on his face. "Did someone call me?"

While Jack struggled to get the large slab of bacon out of the enormous pot on the stove, Mary turned to Louise. "Where are Brendan and Michael?"

"They're upstairs," Louise answered, barely lifting her head. She continued shining the glasses, looking out the back door. Mary wondered if something was wrong with Louise. Maybe she was feeling a bit left out because all the attention was on Mary and Dean.

"Out of the way," Jack said, holding the plate of bacon, while he manoeuvred past them and out the back door. He placed the cooked meat on the windowsill.

"That should be ready for cutting in about twenty minutes," he announced to his audience, when he turned around. "Now if that's it, I'm going to grab a few minutes to read the paper."

"Not so fast," Ann blocked his path. "There's one more thing."

"Ahh, Jesus, can't a man get a break."

Ann planted a smoochy kiss on his lips. Mary and Louise watched and smiled.

"Thanks for helping."

Jack patted her on the behind as he went. "I'll have to help out more in future," he said, rubbing his hands together as he left the room.

* * * *

Michael's hands were shaking and he felt like he was going to throw up. Brendan, on the other hand, was sitting on his bed casually smoking a butt.

"Jesus Christ, do you feel anything anymore?" Michael spat at him.

"Relax, will ya! All we have to do is ask him some questions. If he answers correctly we can forget about the whole thing. If he lies, Kelly will take over. Either way we're off the hook. You have nothing to worry about."

"Are you mad?" Michael swung his legs off the bed and sat facing Brendan. "If he's a professional killer and we start asking him questions about guns and the like, he's going to cop on and who knows what he might do then. I don't think he's stupid!"

Brendan laughed. "Two episodes of fuckin' Dragnet and you think you're Agent Friday."

"Two fucking meetings and you think you're fuckin' running the IRA," Michael countered.

Brendan laughed again and continued smoking. Michael looked down at his hands and watched them shaking. It felt like he was holding a jackhammer.

Then a scream erupted from downstairs and they both ran for the door.

* * * *

Jack sprang like a cat out the back door, but he was too late. The plate smashed on the concrete, sending broken pieces scattering across the yard.

"Ya little fucker," he shouted, picking up the nearest weapon he could find, which happened to be a coal shovel. He threw it down the yard.

The dog vaulted over the corrugated sheeting that was the boundary fence, bits of the bacon falling from his mouth as he scampered through the line of trees on the other side. Jack picked up a rock and threw it over the fence, missing the mutt, but slamming it into an old glass window that had been discarded at the end of a neighbour's garden. The glass shattered, sparking off a rally of barking from all the other dogs in the adjoining gardens.

The dog disappeared from sight and Jack stood watching the spot where he had made off with their dinner.

"Oh, Jesus," Ann said at the back door. "Oh, Jesus."

Jack turned, and in a few steps was past her and into the house. He didn't speak, but the expression on his face said everything he was thinking. Mary and Louise cleared a path for him through the pantry, tears falling freely from Mary's face. She had been casually looking out the door when the dog had grabbed the bacon from the plate.

Jack reached the hall as Brendan and Michael came running down the stairs.

"What's up, Dad?" they asked.

Jack kept up his pace as he answered them. "Sweeney's dog ran off with the bacon." He opened the front door and vaulted up the steps, turning right at the gate and marching down the street.

Inside the house, Mary was inconsolable.

Ann brought her into the living room and sat her down. "It'll be alright. I'll put on something else in a minute."

"Ahh, Mam, it's nearly seven. He'll be here any minute. It's all ruined," Mary wailed.

Ann and Louise tried to calm her down. Brendan stood at the hall door alternating between watching the front door for Jack, and the living room to see Mary. Michael carried on out to the gate. Both of them smothered slight grins on their faces.

"He's coming!" Michael announced, at the top of his voice.

"Who?" Brendan shouted back.

"Dad."

Michael watched his father coming out of the Sweeney's house, carrying a plate with a large side of bacon perched on it. A large smile exploded on his face when he turned to come back up the road.

"He's bringing home the bacon," Michael relayed to Brendan.

"He's got the bacon," Brendan said to the women in the living room.

Ann looked up. "What do you mean 'He's got it'? It's ruined. We can't eat that now!"

Jack came down the steps followed by Michael. He held the plate at chest height, as if he was about to present the king with his crown. Entering the living room, he walked over to Ann and the girls and placed the plate on the table in front of them.

"One side of bacon for dinner, me lady," he announced.

"We can't eat that after the dog had it, ya fool."

"I know that," Jack answered, "but we can eat this one because it's not the one the dog had."

They all looked at him, puzzled. Then they examined the bacon. It looked in tact, clearly not the same one the dog had dragged across two gardens. Then they all looked at Jack again.

"The Sweeney's were just sitting down to dinner too, and as luck would have it, they were having bacon. I showed them their dog sitting in their back garden eating our bacon and then I told Paddy that I would accept their side of bacon as compensation."

"And he agreed?" Ann asked, still looking confused.

"Let's just say that I convinced him it would be in his best interest to hand it over."

"So what are they going to do now?" Ann asked.

Jack laughed. "From what I saw, I'd say Paddy is going to have the fuckin' dog for dinner."

A gentle knock reverberated through the room from the open front door. They all swung around to see Dean standing in the doorway.

"I'm not too early, am I?" he asked, smiling.

For a moment, everyone stared at him, standing there with a bunch of flowers in one hand and a box of chocolates in the other. He looked like someone who had stepped out of the television and walked into their house.

****

Dean walked forward and presented the flowers. "These are for you, Mrs. Horgan."

Ann took the flowers and a jaw-bursting smile lit up her face. She thanked him giddily.

"And these are for you," Dean added, handing the chocolates to Louise.

Louise took them and nodded her appreciation. Brendan and Michael stood back watching the visitor work the room.

Dean shook hands with Jack. "It's a pleasure to meet you, sir. Mary's told me all about you."

Jack patted Dean's shoulder as they shook hands. "She can't have told you everything, boy, cause she don't know the half of it. Come in. Sit down. Dinner is nearly ready."

With the mention of dinner, the women were jolted back to reality. The three of them bolted for the pantry, Ann stopping to take the plate of bacon with her, Mary stopping to greet Dean. The women disappeared into the pantry and Dean turned to shake hands with Brendan and Michael.

"I know Brendan," Dean said, "but I never met this young man." He extended his hand and Michael took it.

"Michael."

"Nice to meet you, Michael. I'm Dean Reynolds."

I know, Michael thought, I saw you firing a sniper rifle yesterday, ya bastard.

"Nice to meet you," Michael repeated, trying his best to smile.

"Sorry, guys, but I didn't bring anything for you, except a little something for after dinner." Dean patted his breast pocket.

Fear crept up the back of Michael's neck and wrapped its cold claws around his throat. In his head, he could see them finishing dinner and Dean pulling a small, tidy pistol from his breast pocket. They would all be dead in a matter of seconds;

Dean would sit down and drink a cup of tea before leaving, gently closing the door behind him. It would be days before their bodies were found.

Michael glanced at Brendan, but he was smiling at Dean. He looked like he was enjoying the American, savouring every moment. Michael wondered if it would be his brother who would show up after dinner holding a gun.

* * * *

The dinner was served and Dean proclaimed that he had never eaten bacon and cabbage in his life. He then proceeded to eat every morsel put on his plate. The conversation was light and consisted of Jack and Ann asking questions of Dean. Mary, Louise and the three brothers were more spectators than participants. There was an awkward moment when Jack made a passing comment about archery, but it sailed over Dean's head and was quickly passed over by Ann.

Dean asked Jack about life in Ireland when he was a boy.

"Oh, it was tough," Jack started, amidst a few moans and groans.

They had all sat through the story of Jack's youth more than once. Mary explained to Dean about their lack of enthusiasm and he laughed out loud.

Jack, unperturbed, continued his long recollection. "You see, Dean, kids today are spoilt. They have it all. In my day, we weren't taken to Wimpy bars. Christ, I was working at twelve."

"It must have been tough?" Dean said, looking intrigued.

"It was, mind you, and I didn't get to keep money for bloody sweets, I'll tell ya. It was all handed up to me mother."

Jack drove on, recounting his memories of the house he had lived in as a child. Five houses on the block and only one toilet to be shared between them. He told Dean how his mother had tended to ten of them, with a drunk for a husband, beating down on her every night.

Mary, sensing her father was about to get teary eyed, broke in and managed to change the subject. They talked about America for a while and Dean entertained them with stories of his earlier years. Jack looked unimpressed by Dean's sheltered upbringing, but he listened.

Then Brendan opened his mouth for the first time. "They do a lot of hunting in America, don't they, Dean?"

Dean turned to Brendan. "They sure do, Brendan. Some of them will shoot anything that moves, once it's in season of course."

"Do you ever go hunting yourself?"

"I did before, with my father, when I was younger. I love shooting. The feeling of a gun in your hand is second to none. Have you ever tried it yourself?"

Michael exhaled silently, but it was deep and full of relief. What they had seen yesterday was nothing more than Dean pursuing his favourite pastime.

"I haven't," Brendan replied, looking slightly relieved, if not disappointed.

"Of course," Dean added," I haven't held a gun in my hand now for about ten years; since my father passed away."

Mary seemed not to notice, but Louise, Brendan and Michael all looked ill at once. Ann sympathised with Dean on the loss of his father and Mary was too involved with Dean to notice the others' reactions to Dean's lie. Brendan gestured to Louise and Michael to calm down. They couldn't blow it now.

"I used to do some hunting a good few years back," Jack said. "We used to dazzle rabbits at night and then blow their heads off. I could set it up for you some night, Dean, if you're interested, like."

"I'd like that," Dean replied, and Mary looked elated that her father was taking a shine to her man.

"Are you going to see Kennedy on Friday?" Michael blurted out, not sure why he had said it.

Dean shook his head. "No, I can't. I'm in Dublin Friday on business, but I've seen him back home a few times. Make sure you go to see him though. He's a great man, Kennedy."

Yeah, thought Michael, a great man to dazzle and blow his head off, ya bastard.

"I think I will," Michael said.

"Well, lets get this table cleared," Ann announced, getting to her feet. "There's dessert to come yet."

Dean rose with her and started to collect the plates.

"No, Dean, love. Leave it to me and the girls. You continue chatting with the boys."

Mary and Louise helped their mother clear the table. Dean got up and went to the armchair where his jacket was. He reached into the inside pocket. Michael got ready to run. Dean pulled out three large cigars and turned back to the table, displaying all three in one hand. "Do you indulge?"

"Sure, we'll try anything once, boy," Jack almost sang, jumping out of his chair.

Brendan and Michael accepted the cigars, but said they would save them for later. Then they made some excuse about having to meet Longy in ten minutes and almost ran for the door.

Dean thanked them both for their company and bid them goodnight. Then, he and Jack settled into a chair each by the fire. The fire wasn't lighting, but they sat there anyway. They lit the cigars and continued talking.

* * * *

"Well," Jack said, "What are your plans for Ireland?"

"I'm starting my own business. I'm an architect."

"I've heard."

"Yes, I'm trying to rustle up some new clients and make a go of it."

Jack nodded his approval. Both men puffed great wads of smoke toward the dormant fire. Some of the smoke shot up the chimney, but most of it rose gracefully toward the ceiling, slowly filling the room.

"You know if you upset my daughter, I'll kill you, don't ya," Jack said, trying the apple tart.

Dean shrugged and returned the smile. "I would expect nothing less, sir."

Both men laughed and Jack seemed to like the new addition to their inner circle. They exchanged stories of bygone times for thirty minutes, never once running out of topics. Jack delved deep into his past, speaking of the poverty he had dragged himself out of as a boy; how he had seen it all and had never set foot outside of Ireland. Dean, being much younger, had little to offer in terms of competition, but what he did put up Jack listened to intently.

"What are you two up to for the rest of the night?" Jack asked.

"I'm not sure," Dean replied, looking wary of a trap.

"Me and Ann are going to the pub later for a few refreshments. Why don't you and Mary join us for one or two?"

"Sounds good to me."

"Excellent. We'll have a laugh."

Mary came out of the kitchen and sat on the arm of Dean's chair. "I hope he's not boring you. Dad loves his old stories."

"Not at all," said Dean. "Your father's an interesting man."

Jack nodded at Mary, visibly delighted by the remark.

Dean looked up at Mary. "Your Dad invited us to the pub for a drink. Isn't that great?"

Mary looked at her father who was trying to contain his amusement. "Just dandy," she muttered.

* * * *

"Why do we have to tell him?" Michael pleaded with his brother as they walked up the hill to the phone box.

"Don't be stupid, will ya," Brendan said, striding forward. "We have to do something. He's up to no good. Jesus, he lied to our faces."

"I know. I know, but why do we have to get involved?"

Brendan stopped at the phone box. "Look, Michael. I'm just going to ring Kelly and tell him what happened. What he does after that is up to him. We're out of the game, okay?"

"Alright."

"Good."

Brendan opened the door and entered the small yellow telephone box. Michael held the door open so he could hear. Brendan put some money in the slot and dialled the number. Both brothers looked at each other silently for a few seconds. Michael prayed that the phone at the other end wouldn't be picked up. Then Brendan pushed the 'A' button on the body of the black payphone and started speaking. Michael let the door ease shut. He leaned his back against the side of the box and rested his hands on his knees.

This is not the end of it for us, he thought.

He looked through the glass at his brother. Brendan was speaking quickly, recounting the events of the evening down the receiver to Kelly, or whoever had answered. A sly smile appeared on Brendan's face and Michael knew then that this was far from over, and they were far from finished with it.

* * * *

Dean opened the front door of the Templeacre Tavern and coughed loudly as the wall of smoke hit him. "People really like to smoke over here, don't they?" he said, as he struggled to get a clean breath of air into his lungs.

"It's the only enjoyment most of these people have, Dean." Jack clapped him on the back and gently pushed him in the doorway.

The four of them stood for a moment by the door. The scene resembled one of the many westerns Mary had seen at the pictures. The crowd didn't become totally silent, but the noise level did drop quite a bit. Heads turned as if on swivels. Dean, in his impeccable two piece suit, stuck out like a sore thumb. It was obvious that he wasn't a local, and definitely not Irish. Mary ran her hand into his and squeezed it tightly. She looked up at Dean, but he seemed unbelievably calm. He gazed around the room making eye contact with everyone, almost daring them to keep looking at him. Most of them did turn away, but a few lowlifes, not knowing better or caring, continued their vigil.

Jack glided over to a table where Angie Murphy and Joan Fitzgerald were sitting with their husbands. Jack greeted them all, but as they returned the greeting they all stared past him at the American.

Ann nudged Mary and the three of them followed Jack to the table. The others moved around the long seat, sliding their drinks along the table with them. Mary and Ann scooted in next to the other women. Jack introduced Dean to the table in record time, not giving anyone the chance to ask questions. When the handshakes were done, Dean turned to Jack and said, "What's your poison, sir?"

"It's Jack, Dean and my poison is grumpy old women, but I'll have a pint of Beamish with ya."

Dean asked Ann what she would like and headed to the bar. Mary followed him with her eyes and watched closely as he chatted with the people sitting on the long bar stools by the bar. He returned with the drinks and Mary pointed at the Beamish in Dean's hand, knowing he didn't like it. He shrugged, nodded to her father and mouthed the words 'When in Rome'.

It didn't take long for Joan Fitzgerald to stick her oar in between Mary and Ann.

"Who is that handsome young man?"

"He's Mary's new boyfriend. He's American," Ann said with a proud voice.

Joan zeroed in on Mary. "You've done well there, girly. You'll do well to hang onto him."

Mary smiled politely and sipped her drink, trying to search her mind for a plausible excuse to get out of there. She looked up at Dean, standing next to her father, chatting with the other men. He looked like a regular already, laughing and joking with men he had met only a few minutes before. She watched him for ten minutes, while Ann fended off Joan. Her stomach tightened. The words from Joan swam in her head.

'You'll do well to hang onto him.'

In that moment, Mary felt inadequate to the task. She felt the stares again, the speculation that was going on at each table. How could she manage to keep onto a man like Dean? Then she looked up at him and as she did, he turned and looked back. The smile she had drifted to sleep on all week appeared on his face and he winked at her. The fear flowed out of her and she knew he loved her; that what she was feeling was working both ways.

"I suppose you'll be moving to America then?"

Mary turned to see Joan sitting next to her. She looked up to see her mother heading for the toilet. Shit, she thought, here we go. "What makes you think that, Mrs. Fitzgerald?"

"Well, I assume he'll be going home at some point."

"Actually," Mary said, "he's setting up his own business here in Cork." She regretted saying this immediately. All Joan Fitzgerald wanted was information and Mary had fallen into the trap.

"Is he now? And what does he do for a living?"

"He's an archer." Mary hid her smirk with her glass.

Joan gazed across the table at Dean. "Really," she said slowly.

Mary wasn't sure if Joan really knew what an archer was, and she wasn't about to elaborate more. She sat back and finished her drink. She was about to get up and tell her father that they were leaving when another glass of Beamish was thrust into her hand. Mary knew then that it was going to be a long night.

* * * *

The pub closed and the four of them literally fell out the door. Even Ann had kept pace with the drinking spree. Mary, who had only started drinking the year before, had consumed five glasses of Beamish, but the men were having two to every one delivered to the women.

As the barmen called time, Dean and Jack were making a toast with a shot of whiskey each, and another pint of the black stuff was waiting for them on the bar. They downed the whiskey and Mary thought Dean was going to fall over. He steadied himself, holding onto the pint on the bar. The glass seemed to give him the balance he was looking for and he laughed heartily at another bad joke delivered by Jack.

Outside now, the moon lit the way home and the quartet staggered down the hill.

"A great crowd had gathered outside of Kilmainham," Jack started singing as he went. Amazingly, Ann joined in with her husband. Mary had never seen her mother sing. Jack put his arm around his wife and stopped walking. They sang the whole song together, staring into each others' eyes. "For above all the din rose the cry 'No Surrender', 'T'was the voice of James Connolly, the Irish Rebel."

When they had finished, Jack kissed Ann on the forehead. Dean clapped in appreciation of the song. "That's an excellent voice you have their, Jack," Dean said. The 'Sir' had been completely dropped after the third pint.

"That song, boy, is a tribute to a famous IRA man. One of the saddest songs you'll ever hear on these shores."

"They'll write a song about you someday, honey," Ann announced.

Jack kissed her again. "I'm sure they will, love. And it will be one of the saddest songs ever. They'll call it 'The Jumping Jack'."

Jack let go of Ann and danced his way down the street, jumping from foot to foot while making a flapping motion with his arms. The others walked on behind him.

"Your father is amazing."

"I know," Mary answered. "He's the best you could get."

They arrived at the house and Jack pointed to the car. "You can't drive that home, Deano. Leave it there until the morning."

"I think you're right there, boy." Dean raised his voice on 'boy', trying to copy Jack's accent. No one noticed.

Jack and Ann said goodnight and left Mary and Dean alone by the car. Mary waited until her parents were inside before wrapping her arms around Dean's waist and burying her head in his chest. "You must think we're raving alcoholics?"

"No, no, but I think I might be."

Mary snuggled into him, rubbing her hands along his lower back. Dean kissed her head, and as he did, he staggered a bit. Mary helped him regain his balance. "You had better walk back to the hotel alright."

"I think so," Dean agreed. "Just point me in the general direction."

"Will you be alright? I could always ask Dad if you could sleep on the couch."

"No I'm fine. I could do with the walk."

Then he kissed her. His balance held and it was Mary who felt dizzy afterwards. Dean held her by the shoulders and said, "Mary Horgan. I really do love you. I think you're the first woman I have ever loved." He paused then and Mary saw a look of sorrow on his face.

"What's wrong?"

"We need to talk."

"Go on. You can tell me anything."

"No, not here. We'll talk on Monday night, when both our heads are clear. Okay?"

"Okay," Mary said, but she saw something in his eyes that frightened her, something she had not seen before.

"We could talk tomorrow night," she offered. "It's bonfire night. You could come see the fire."

"I can't tomorrow night. I have to make some calls to the U.S. about my old business back there. Tie up loose ends and that." He kissed her again and then broke the embrace. "We'll talk on Monday night. I'll pick you up after work."

"I'll see you then," Mary said, and she watched him stumble away.

What could he need to tell her so badly? Was he going back to America? Her heart leapt in her chest. Maybe he will ask me to go with him? she thought. What if he is going back, but without me?

She scolded herself for thinking that. He just told you he loves you, silly. He's hardly going to dump you straight after saying that.

Again, Mary went to bed with a mixed bag of thoughts swirling around in her head. Louise slept silently across from her and she could hear her brothers snoring in the other room. The house was too small, and as she drifted off to sleep, Mary imagined what her new house in America would be like.

Sunday 23rd June 1963

Bonfire night

Inside the house with the number thirteen on the door, Mary sat watching The Flintstones. It was almost half past seven and she was already bored. Ann had tried to persuade her to join them later, outside at the bonfire, but Mary had refused. She felt too old for that sort of stuff. She had loved bonfire night when she was younger. Back then the women on the road would start collecting pennies from the workmen as they made their way to and from work each day. When bonfire night finally came, all the pennies were exchanged at O'Keeffe's shop for a variety of sweets. Mary remembered that their house, which was directly across from the spot where the bonfire was set up each year, was always used as the distribution point for the sweets. Each child would be brought into the house in turn and given one tour of the table to select four sweets.

That little tradition had faded away as Mary had grown and was now completely discarded. She wondered if they would still be lighting bonfires on this night fifty years from now, and would she be in this country to witness it if they were. The night before, Jack had explained the whole event in detail to Dean. Dean seemed genuinely intrigued and proclaimed that Thanksgiving was the biggest holiday in America, after Christmas of course.

The Flintstones finished and the ads came on. Mary looked towards the pantry, where Louise and Ann were washing the ware. She contemplated getting up, but decided against it. They had enough hands to cope with what little there was to wash. Brendan and Michael had disappeared soon after tea, but

Jack sat by the window half reading the Sunday newspaper, half looking out the window. He kept glancing back and forth, unable to settle on one thing. As she watched him, he checked his watch and, obviously surprised by the time, he dropped the paper and jumped to his feet.

"Well," he announced. "I'm off on my annual tour of the bonfires of Cork." He looked towards the pantry and shouted, "I'll join ye back outside in an hour or so, okay?"

"Right," Ann replied blindly. "Is anyone going with ya?"

"No. I'm on me own again this year."

To Mary, her father looked sad admitting that his children weren't interested in taking a walk with their father anymore. His head drooped and he shook it slightly.

"Aren't you going to come out later, sweetheart?" Jack asked her, raising his head again, looking hopeful.

She couldn't lie to him. She shook her head. "Nah."

"I suppose you're getting a bit old for all that crap, really."

"Yah," Mary replied, nodding now.

Jack rubbed the tiredness from his eyes as he walked out the door.

* * * *

A little over three miles away, four pigs lay dead in the yard of the O'Reilly farm; starved to death. Afraid they would all die, Willy had given them some feed and fresh water on Saturday to keep them going. They literally ate like pigs, diving over each other to get at the trough. The stronger pigs ate well, while the weaker and younger ones licked the base of the trough after the others had finished. The four dead pigs had been the weakest of the bunch, not even strong enough to get to their feet and make an attempt at the trough.

Willy had spent Saturday packing the car with anything in the house that would fit, and was worth selling. After lunch, he left for the pawnshop on Shandon Street and returned a few hours later with a wad of cash stuffed in his pocket. The pawnbroker had looked at him warily when he filled the shop with ornaments, pictures and even some old clothes from his mother's wardrobe. He had entered the room quietly that morning and taken all but one of her dresses. She hadn't moved at all, even when Willy banged his shin on the bed. The rest of Saturday he spent packing his own belongings into a suitcase.

Now, Willy sat at the table cleaning the shotgun. He knew this was the last time he would ever clean it. Tonight he would use the gun on a person for the first time and then he would get rid of it for good. He glanced at the clock on the wall, over the fireplace. Ten minutes to eight. The sun was still high in the sky. He decided he would leave at around ten, as dusk came. Fires would be burning all over the city by then, billowing black smoke up into the night sky.

He wiped the gun affectionately and looked across the table at his father.

"Are you okay, son?"

"I'm fine, Dad."

"It's a fine gun, isn't it?"

"A fine gun," Willy said, running the cloth along the two barrels. He reached the end and continued down the underside of the gun.

"You're not havin' second thoughts, are you?"

Willy shrugged. "No, not at all."

"I can see it in your eyes, ya bastard." His father's voice made him wince. "You know they deserve it. They made a fuckin' fool out of you. And they'll continue to as well, if you don't shut them up once and for all." His father banged the table with his clenched fist.

At that same moment, Willy thought he heard a gentle knocking on the front door, or maybe it was his mother knocking on the ceiling.

Slowly, Willy rested the gun on the table. He looked at his father, who mouthed the words, 'I think it's the door', and pointed.

The knocking came again, slightly louder this time. It was the front door alright, but who could it be? Willy picked up the shotgun and put it back into the cupboard on his way to the door. Before opening it, he motioned to his father to stand out of view. The old man jumped up and retreated into the living room.

Willy turned back and grabbed the handle. He undid the latch and the door flew at him, smashing into his face and sending him reeling across the floor. Blood poured freely from his nose and he knew immediately that it was broken. He looked up at the doorway.

He couldn't identify who was standing there, but he could make out the size and shape of what looked like a man.

"Hello, Willy," the shape said, and in one swift movement the unknown visitor lunged at him, kicking him squarely in the groin.

Willy howled in pain as, for the second time in a week, someone hurt him in the worst place imaginable.

The man bent over Willy and whispered in his ear. "That one is a gift from Mary Horgan. You know Mary, don't you, lover boy?"

Another kick, this time in the lower back, causing Willy to straighten out momentarily before curling up again. His eyes cleared slightly and he searched the room for his father. Surely, his Dad would come to his aid now, of all times. His eyes darted back and forth around the room, but his father was nowhere to be seen. The bastard had run away!

"What are you looking for, lover boy? Something to fight back with? A knife perhaps." The man pointed to the cupboard. "Or maybe something with a little more kick, huh?"

Willy rolled over onto his back and faced his attacker. A black balaclava masked the intruder's face completely, and instead of wondering who was under the mask, Willy was filled with an overwhelming dread. The man didn't look human at all. He looked like the grim reaper, come to drag him, kicking and screaming, to a dark and dreary place, where no one came back from, ever.

"Are you afraid, Willy, are ya?" the mask said, almost laughing the words. "Don't worry, son. It will all be over in a few minutes."

The words chilled Willy's heart and he knew then that he was going to die. He knew he should try something, try to get up and run, or fight this bastard. But he didn't dare move. He lay on the ground, blood flowing down his face.

"Planning on a trip?" The hooded man pointed to the suitcase against the wall.

Willy said nothing. He wasn't sure if the man wanted an answer or not, but it didn't matter anyway; he couldn't speak.

"That's great, Willy. You saved me the bother of doing it for you." The man pulled out a chair from the table and swung it around in front of Willy. "Okay," he began, "I'm going to let you get up now, but if you try to run or anything stupid, I can't be held responsible for my actions. Understand?"

Willy nodded and slowly got to his feet. He had no intention of running. He felt like a bowling ball was resting on his groin as he moved. The pain was rumbling deep inside him, waiting for a sudden movement to set it free again. He felt sure that fresh blood was flowing from the cuts on his groin. He staggered to the chair and fell onto it, almost knocking it over.

"Easy there, big fella. Don't want you hurting yourself now, do we?"

Willy listened to the stranger's voice for the first time. He had heard everything the man had said up to now, but he hadn't listened to the voice. He thought he recognised it, but he couldn't put a face to it.

"Who are you?" he heard himself asking. He could tell the man was smiling under the knitted material.

"Me. Well, let's just say I'm Mary Horgan's watchman. And you've been very disrespectful to my… well, let's say a person who is very dear to me."

Willy sniffled. "Are you going to kill me?"

"Jesus, Willy. That's a very direct question. You like getting to the point, don't you?"

The man circled the chair and Willy could feel him standing behind him. He heard the whoosh of the man's balaclava being removed. The soft empty hat landed in Willy's lap and he instinctively reached for it before it fell to the floor.

"Turn around, Willy."

He didn't.

"Come on. Turn around."

Willy stayed still. He knew if he saw this man's face, what little chance he had of surviving was gone. He stayed facing the window, looking around again for his father.

"Okay, Willy. Have it your way."

The click of the pistol hammer caused Willy's bladder to falter, and his pants changed colour in seconds. He barely noticed that he had wet himself. He watched the window, praying someone would come and stop this madman from killing him.

No one did.

Willy thought he saw his father, out in the fields walking around. A small boy was walking next to him, holding his hand. They were both smiling. It took a few seconds for him to realise who that small boy was, but when he did, it brought a tiny smirk to his face. He watched his father chatting to that little boy, pointing out things as they went. His thoughts turned to his mother, upstairs in that room, all alone. He felt ashamed then, ashamed of what he had become and the life he had led.

He gazed out the window at the father and son walking the fields and he longed to see his father again. He wanted to be with his Dad.

Then the gun went off.

* * * *

The killer stood by the window, looking down the dusty path that led out to the main road. He knew that nobody was going to come running. The nearest house was more than a few fields away, and even if someone heard the gun go off, they would surely mistake it for a car back firing or something. He turned away from the window and surveyed the room.

Willy had been thrown forward, off the chair and onto the ground. He lay face down, a small pool of blood circling his head. The killer moved around the body, trying to find a starting point. He settled at the corpse's feet and started to untie Willy's boots. When he pulled off the first boot, he was greeted by the smell of unwashed socks and seldom washed feet. He removed the second boot and then both socks. Next, he pulled off the pants and underwear. They were wet and stunk of urine. The man continued unabated, removing the dead man's shirt and cutting his vest off with a scissors.

He opened the suitcase, squashed the clothes inside and slammed it closed again. The smell in the room was putrid and he struggled to catch his breath. Leaving the now naked corpse, he started up the stairs. He needed to check that Willy had actually packed all his clothes in the suitcase.

What he found was totally unexpected.

The first room he entered was Willy's room. He stood in the doorway, wondering how a person could live in such filth. Mould encroached on every corner of the room. The ceiling was black, where white paint had once been. The bedclothes were an unnatural colour and a stain that looked like blood, started in the centre of the bed and spread out in a large, almost perfect circle. He moved around the bed toward the wardrobe. It was empty, the door slightly ajar so he didn't have to touch it.

He left Willy's room, but as he made his way to the stairs something caught his eye. Another bedroom door was slightly open, only a crack, but enough to see in at a glance. The stranger thought he saw someone in the room, lying in the bed, but he had taken an extra step towards the stairs and was no longer able to see through the open door. Slowly, he retraced his step back and he saw that there was someone in the room. He moved swiftly to the door and, placing his hand on the handle, he pushed gently.

The woman in the bed wasn't asleep. She stared up at him and he felt rooted to the spot. The odour that invaded his nostrils was like nothing he had ever experienced in his life. The woman stared at him and he was forced to turn away. On the table next to her bed were multiple cups of what he guessed was tea. A half dozen plates with hard, moulding bread were scattered across the table. Flies buzzed around the room, moving from plate to plate. Slowly, the man's eyes returned to the woman lying in the bed. She continued to stare up at him, and if he stood his ground she would have stared at him for all eternity, stared at him with her eyeless sockets; the eyes long gone from the skeleton that rested under the blankets. He was no expert, but he guessed that the old woman must have died at least four years before, if not more.

He came back downstairs. Willy lay as the man had left him, and now he held new levels of contempt in his heart for the naked corpse. He opened the front door. It was still bright and the sunlight surprised him momentarily. Outside in the yard some pigs scuffled around, banging into each other as they went in search of food.

After some effort, he managed to get the body over his shoulder, fireman style, and made his way out of the house. Quickly, the pigs gathered around him, a new lease of life pulsing through them. Blood dripped from Willy's head, landing on the ground as the man carried him across the yard. The pigs followed expectantly. Some stopped to lick the ground where the last droplet of blood had settled, others continued on, hopeful of much larger rewards.

He reached the pen, and without much hesitation, he pitched the body over the low fence. It landed with a dull thud on the dried up mud. The pigs bashed at the fence, unable to control their hunger. Some vaulted at the fence striking the wood half way up and falling back onto the ground. The noise grew as other pigs joined the barrage. He moved quickly to the gate, and after some difficulty, managed to free the clasp; the gate swung open.

The pigs slammed against it, one managing to get in before it swung shut again from the force of the others. The man kicked at the pigs with his leg and when they retreated slightly he opened the gate again, swinging it all the way back this time. He didn't wait to see what happened. He reached the door to the house quickly and didn't pause to look back in the direction he had come.

The smell inside the house had eased somewhat. One pig had not followed him to the pen and was eagerly lapping up the pool of blood in front of the chair. The stranger pushed him away with his foot. The pig eventually gave up and ran out the door, squealing his discontent.

Five minutes later, the man left the house, suitcase in tow, with Willy's overcoat draped over his shoulders. He loaded the suitcase into the Volkswagon Beetle and drove away. Behind him, in the house, he left a smouldering fire in one corner of the room, close to the window and the curtains; one that would not look staged, but would grow over time. He estimated that it wouldn't take the house for another few hours, but it would ultimately engulf the whole building and burn it to the ground.

The man knew that by the time attention was drawn to the house the fire would be out of control, and Willy O'Reilly would be long gone.

* * * *

The flames climbed high into the night sky. It was nine o'clock and a large crowd gathered around the huge bonfire. Ann and Louise sat on milk crates, close enough to feel the heat from the flames, but far enough away to endure them. Young children danced around the perimeter, while older children fed the beast. They tossed old furniture into the middle of the flames; the offering immediately devoured in a splash of sparks and smoke. The fire crackled as the wood split and splintered from the heat. A lad of about sixteen appeared with a large car tyre. He swung it back and forth for a few seconds, the force of his swing depreciating with each try. He let it go and it bounced into the fire, disappearing from sight. Almost immediately black plumes of smoke rose into the night air. The wind rose momentarily and sent the black wall of smoke into the faces of some of the crowd. Some ran, others stayed. The older women simply raised their black shawls over their faces until the wind corrected the trail of smoke.

"Can you see your Dad yet?" Ann asked Louise.

"Oh, ya, I can. He's been over there for a while now, chatting with Mr. Sweeney." She pointed through the fire.

Ann couldn't see at first. Then the flames shifted and she could see Jack standing next to Paddy Sweeney. Both men were laughing and Ann wondered if the topic of conversation was related to bacon and dogs. She raised her hand and waved. Jack spotted her and waved back. She motioned for him to join them.

"A fine fire this year," he said crouching next to Ann.

"Did you see much of the others?" Louise asked.

Jack pointed up St. Enda's Road. "There's a fine fire burning in the field this year. Although, I think ours is about the same size now."

"What were you and Paddy talking about?" Ann asked.

"I asked him how the dog was."

"And?"

"Said he hasn't seen the bastard since last night." Jack laughed and Louise stifled a smile.

"No sign of Mary, nah?"

Ann looked toward the house. "I asked her again before we came out, but she wanted to be on her own."

"No doubt to dream about that boy," Jack said

"He's nice though, isn't he, Jack?"

"He's alright."

Ann thumped him in the arm. "Would ya go away out a that. Weren't you nearly up in his feckin' arms by the end of the night last night."

"I was not."

"Go away," Ann said, dismissing him. "I thought you were going to give him the kiss goodnight instead of Mary."

Jack took the joke. "Well, he is an attractive man."

The three of them laughed, but Ann stopped first, staring across the road at her house. "I'm worried about her though."

"Why? She's having a ball." Jack put his hand on Ann's knee and squeezed it gently.

Louise met her father's eyes, but she didn't speak. Jack winked at her and turned back to Ann.

Ann sighed. "There's just something about her. She seems to be up and down all week. One minute I think she's on top of the world and the next she looks haggard." Ann turned to Louise, who was still eyeing her father. "Has she said anything to you, Lou?"

Louise admired the fire. "No," she replied, as casually as possible. "I haven't spoken to her all that much this week."

Ann leaned forward and took Louise's hand. "You'd tell us, wouldn't you, dear?

"Of course, Mam. But there's nothing wrong with her."

"Right," Jack said. "I'm heading in to watch that telly thing a bit."

Ann and Louise sat by the fire for a while longer. The flames roared at the blackness of the sky.

"Well, summer won't be long going now," Ann said. "It's all downhill after tonight."

Louise nodded slowly.

Monday 24th June 1963

Excerpt from the Evening Echo:

KENNEDY WANTS $21M. FOR PLANE

President Kennedy today asked Congress for the first instalment of about $21 million dollars to help finance an American supersonic airliner, it was announced in Bonn where he was meeting with German leaders on his European tour.

The plane is being developed in a race with the French and British Governments, who are already producing the 1450-miles-per-hour Concorde airliner. The Americans are expected to build a bigger and faster plane.

President Kennedy recently decided that the Government should aid the aircraft industry in developing the airliner.

The Fire Brigade arrived at the O'Reilly farm at half past twelve, two large vehicles full of uniformed men, who had already been to five separate fires earlier in the evening. Bonfire night was always the busiest night of the year for the fire department.

Unable to enter the house, the firemen simply sprayed the walls and roof with water, not making much of a dent in the fire itself. They were unsure whether anyone was inside the house, but it didn't matter by then. The house was fully detached from the rest of the surrounding buildings, so the firemen kept a vigil until the fire had finished its business with the farmhouse, and having nothing else to feed on, it started to die away.

At ten the next morning, Sergeant Higgins arrived at the scene. He had gone to bed early the night before, and had not welcomed the late phone call until he heard the voice on the other end. He had decided there wasn't much he could do until the following day, so he left his squad start their work without him.

The firemen were starting to gut the house. Smoke still rose into the morning sky, as it did all over the city on this day, every year.

Higgins got out of his car and walked around the perimeter of the farm. He was a burly man, well fed and, at fifty, unable to keep his weight under control any longer. When he joined the force some twenty years before, he had been a tidy eleven stone. Now he was pushing a portly seventeen stone, most of it piled on in the last decade.

He circled the house and then the barn, coming to a stop at the pen that held most of the pigs. He had spotted a few dead pigs in the yard when he had arrived. At first, he wondered if the fire had killed them, but on closer inspection they looked thin and starved.

He stood by the pen and watched the remaining pigs. Most of them were asleep. They too looked malnourished, but not as bad as the dead ones. Scanning the pen, he noticed stains on the dry ground. It looked like oil or some sort of dark liquid. He was about to climb the fence for a closer look when one of the firemen called out.

"I've got one," he shouted.

Sergeant Higgins left the pen and returned to the house. The fireman who had called out was inside the hall of the house, bent over next to a section of the fallen ceiling. Higgins looked at one of the firemen standing in the doorway. "Is it safe?"

"Yeah. The ceiling collapsed hours ago. Just don't go too far in. A lot of the roof is still up there."

Higgins stepped into the hallway and looked up. The house was a shell. He was always amazed at what fire could do to a building. The second floor was gone, heaped in piles at his feet. Parts of the roof remained, but enough had fallen to allow the climbing sun to illuminate the house from gable to gable.

In front of Higgins, a fireman carefully moved charred pieces of wood to the side. Higgins looked over the man's shoulder and a human skull gazed up at him. He knew immediately that something was wrong. The skull was burned, black from the heat of the fire, but there was no skin. With all the fires that Higgins had attended down through the years, he never forgot the condition of bodies when they were dragged from the ashes of a fire. The skin burned, but it left marks on the bones and sometimes internal organs were left intact inside the body, cooked but intact. Looking at the skull now, Higgins could see it was hollow and had been for some time before the fire.

"This person didn't die in the fire," the fireman said, voicing Higgins's thoughts.

Higgins left the house and returned to his car to radio for more Gardai. "Call the state pathologist as well," he told the dispatcher.

ingHis backup on the way, Sergeant Higgins left his car again and walked toward the pen. He couldn't piece it all together in his head yet, but he had a good idea what had taken place here.

****

Mr. Thompson's eyes still had a yellowish tinge about them when he walked into the sweet shop at eleven. The bandage was gone and his nose was still badly bruised. He looked like a boxer after walking into a straight right. He went into the back and removed his coat. There were two customers buying sweets, so he stood at the entrance to the storeroom and watched the girls serve them.

Mary glanced up at him and knew immediately that he was not happy. She looked at Beth and darted her eyes back at Mr. Thompson. Beth nodded her agreement.

He wasn't happy.

They served the customers and when they left the shop Mr. Thompson called the girls to attention. "Okay, girls. I've just come from a meeting with the other retailers and it appears that I can't keep the shop open on Friday while Kennedy is passing through." He sighed deeply.

"At least we'll get to see him?" Beth said.

Mr. Thompson eyed Beth up and down, pausing noticeably longer at her legs. She was wearing a skirt, while Mary was again sporting slacks. "I've decided that we will use the time on Friday to do a stock take. It's a great opportunity for us, girls. Get everything right and so on."

Beth shook her head. Mary wasn't surprised.

"Something wrong, Beth?"

"No, sir."

"You, Mary?"

"I'm just fine," Mary heard herself say, with too much severity. She turned away, concealing her face from him. He would flip if he saw her smiling.

When she had herself under control again, she turned back to face him and said, "Your nose looks much better."

"Yeah," Beth added.

"It feels better too." Thompson wiggled it slightly. "Thank you, girls. Now back to work."

He disappeared into the storeroom and closed the door behind him. The girls laughed silently.

"What a dick," Beth snorted.

"Pity it's on his face though," Mary added and they were inconsolable.

"He doesn't like the pants." Beth pointed at Mary's legs.

Mary did a little turn, shaking her ass as she did. "Well, if he has a problem with them, I'll just have to drop another jar of sweets on his nose, but this time I'll make sure the jar is full."

Mary looked at Beth, expecting laughter. Beth looked pale, like she was about to vomit. She wasn't looking at Mary. Her gaze drifted over Mary's shoulder, towards the storeroom door. Mary didn't need to turn around. She knew the door was open and that he was standing there, listening to them.

Beth swallowed hard as Mary turned slowly to face Mr. Thompson. His face was a kaleidoscope of colours; the shades from his injury mixing with the colours produced from the fury that flowed through him now.

"What did you just say, Mary?"

He whispered the words and she could see tears filling his eyes. She didn't think he was going to breakdown and cry. His eyes were welling up with anger.

A young woman entered the shop and started toward the counter. "We're closed," Mr. Thompson barked at her and she fled.

He kept his eyes on Mary.

Beth wasn't sure where to look. She stood, frozen to the spot, looking over Mary's shoulder. Mary wondered if he had heard everything. She looked at him again and his face confirmed it. She searched her mind for a way to spin the whole thing around. If I was wearing a skirt now, she thought, I would lift the bloody thing over my head and give him a prince's view. What could she say? There was no way back from this. Nothing she said now would reverse what he had heard.

"What did you say?" he asked again.

Mary took in a deep breath. "I said, if you look up my skirt again I'll drop another jar of sweets on your nose."

Mr. Thompson gasped. "I never looked up your skirt, Mary. What kind of man do you think I am?"

Mary could feel her head of steam rising now. "Are you joking me? You've seen my ass more times than I have."

"You dropped a jar on me. You broke my nose." He sounded hurt, unable to believe what he was hearing.

Mary stood looking at him. She felt a momentary pang in her heart, a moment of pity for him. Then he spoke again and it disappeared as quickly as it had arrived.

"I want you to get your coat and get out of here now," he said.

"You're firing me?"

"I don't see any other option."

Mary was surprised. She knew it was coming, that he was going to say it, but the words, when said out loud, stunned her.

"That's fine with me. I don't like working for a nobber anyway."

"How dare you!"

Mary brushed past him on her way to the storeroom. She grabbed her coat and returned to the shop. Mr. Thompson was standing next to Beth, whispering to her.

"That's right," she said. "Make sure she doesn't rebel on you. She has a much nicer ass than I do."

"Mary, could you please leave with your foul mouth?"

"That's another thing. You see I have a foul mouth because I'm not from Sunday's Well, as I told you. I'm from Gurran. Born and bred on the north side." She paused to leave the revelation sink in.

Thompson looked genuinely shocked. Mary had thought that he secretly knew, but left it go because he liked her ass. Looking at the expression on his face now confirmed that he was unaware all along.

"That's right. You've been admiring a norry's ass all along, ya dirty old man."

"Just get out, you despicable girl. Get out!" All the fury was gone from him now.

He looked somewhat afraid. Mary moved a step toward him and he cowered behind Beth.

"Don't worry. I'm still a lady, you sorry excuse for a man." Mary walked up to Beth and hugged her tightly. "You're the only thing I'm going to miss about this place, girl."

Beth was crying now. What little humour there was a moment ago had disappeared.

"Take care, Mary."

Mary leaned in closer and whispered in her ear. "Make sure the jar is full when you drop it on him."

Beth both laughed and cried. Mr. Thompson stood back, not once looking away from Mary.

She walked toward the door, but felt she wanted to do something more. She wanted to leave her mark on the place. Unable to think of anything mind blowing, she paused by the last jar of sweets, by the exit. She lifted the lid on a huge glass container of liquorice laces. Reaching deep into the middle, she pulled out a long solitary lace. She looked back at Mr. Thompson.

His mouth dropped open.

Mary tilted her head and put the whole lace into her mouth, leaving only the last centimetre protruding from her lips. Slowly, she grabbed the end of the lace and pulled it back out, saliva dripping off the long red strand. It looked like she was performing a magician's trick. When the lace fell free of her mouth, Mary smiled ruefully at Mr. Thompson and rammed the wet lace back into the full jar. She placed the lid back on and gave them both a petite wave as she sauntered out the door.

* * * *

She was proud of herself for not crying in front of him, but now, as she walked along the front of Cash's department store, she felt the reality of what had happened engulfing her. A wave of dizziness came over her and she felt like she was going to faint.

She paused by the entrance to Cash's and steadied herself against the wall. People walked in and out of the store. Some ignored her or didn't see her, while others stared candidly into her face.

Bile rose in her throat and she felt nauseous. She watched the people go by, each of them blurring into the next. She had to get moving soon or she would throw up on the front door of Cash's.

That would look great.

One of the haughtiest stores in Cork and the norry vomiting all over the door. Cautiously, she started walking toward Patrick's Bridge. She didn't want to go home and face her mother. Of course, she would understand. Hell, she would probably want to go and give Mr. Thompson a thumping! She raised her head as she walked and saw the road ahead leading over the bridge towards MacCurtain Street.

Dean.

The thought lifted her, and her destination was set. She desperately hoped that he would be there. Her pace picked up and the nausea subsided slightly. She trundled over the bridge, and by the time she turned the corner onto MacCurtain Street, she was almost running, tears streaming down her face.

The porter saw her coming and lunged for the door, as if he was afraid she would go straight through it if he hesitated. The receptionist was a woman and Mary silently thanked God.

"Are you alright, dear?"

Mary wiped at her red eyes. "I'm fine. I just had a bad experience in town."

Compassion flooded onto the woman's face. "Were you attacked or something?"

"You could say that."

She lifted the phone. "Will I call the guards?"

"No!" Mary reached out and gently lowered the woman's hand with the phone. "Can you call up to Dean Reynolds's room and see if he's there?"

"Sure, honey. Why don't you take a seat there behind you?" The receptionist pointed to an armchair next to a coffee table. Mary walked over and plonked herself down, feeling the relief ease through her.

She watched the lady behind the desk dial Dean's number. Mary's heart sank when the woman held the phone to her ear and didn't speak.

Then she said, "Hello, Mr. Reynolds. I have a…" She pulled the phone away and looked at Mary.

"Mary Horgan."

"A Mary Horgan to see you, sir." A slight pause. "Very good, sir."

The woman smiled. "He'll be right down, Miss"

"Thank you," Mary said, so happy that a woman had been on duty.

A minute hadn't passed when Dean came out of the lift. He walked casually toward Mary until he saw her face, and covered the last few yards in a heartbeat.

"What's wrong?" he said, falling to his knees in front of her. He wiped a tear from her cheek, but his touch brought more pouring down. Mary hiccupped and took an involuntary intake of air. She couldn't speak.

"Come on," Dean said, pulling her out of the chair. "Come up to the room."

Mary couldn't remember her feet touching the ground on the way to the lift. In the lift she slouched against Dean, her head buried deep in his chest. He didn't speak; didn't try to get her to tell him what had happened. He stroked her hair with one hand, while holding her up with the other.

He spoke to her again when she was lying on his bed, propped up against the pillows. "Now, tell me what happened to you. Are you hurt?"

Mary shook her head and a nervous giggle escaped her mouth. "Now I feel really silly."

"What happened?" Dean asked again.

"I got fired." The words, spoken aloud, brought fresh feelings to the surface and Mary raised her hand to her face.

"Hey, hey, it's okay. Everyone gets fired at some point."

"But I didn't deserve to get fired!"

"Why don't you tell me what happened?"

Mary dropped her hands and gazed into Dean's eyes. She wanted to get lost in those eyes, float into his head and live in there for the rest of her life. "Mr. Thompson fired me because he found out that I dropped the jar on his head on purpose."

"And he fired you because he found out? Who told him?"

Mary hesitated, feeling stupid now. "Ahh, I did actually."

"You told him?" Dean had a puzzled look on his face.

"Not on purpose, stupid. By accident."

"And he fired you there and then?"

"Yes."

"Well, you're better off away from him, the dirty old man. Who knows what may have come next?"

"Him, most likely." She had said it before thinking.

There was a moment's silence before Dean burst into laughter. Mary laughed, relieved that he wasn't disgusted by her sick sense of humour.

He leaned in and kissed her on the forehead. "Look, I have to go out for an hour or so. Will you stay here and wait for me?"

"Okay."

"Have a rest, or take a bath. I know you like baths."

"Especially with you in them."

"Give me an hour and I'll gladly join you, okay?"

"Yeah"

Dean kissed her again, on the lips this time. He removed her shoes and pulled the quilt over her. Mary snuggled down under the cover and sighed. "I could get used to you looking after me."

"You'll have to," Dean replied and got up to leave. "One hour," he said, holding up one finger. "Order some room service in thirty minutes, and it will be here by the time I get back."

"What would you like?" Mary asked, startled by the thought of ordering room service for the first time in her life.

"Surprise me," Dean answered and disappeared out the door.

* * * *

Dean arrived at the entrance to Cudmore's sweet shop and stopped short of entering. He pulled back, away from the door and walked around to one of the large display windows. Inside the shop, Mr. Thompson was under the ladder, both hands holding on tight. The girl had barely moved up far enough for him to take up his position.

She climbed higher and Dean watched from the window. Thompson's head spun around. He looked at the door and spun back again. Dean started to duck, but Thompson had already turned back before he could move. He had checked the door only, to see if any customers had come in. Dean returned to his voyeuristic position and watched the scene play out.

The young lady fumbled with a large jar of apple drops, while Thompson slowly moved his head in towards the rungs of the ladder. As he moved in, he tilted his head back to improve his view. Dean couldn't see Thompson's face, but he knew he was grinning from ear to ear. An image of Mary up that very same ladder, fumbling with the same jar, popped into Dean's head. Unable to stomach what was happening right in front of his eyes, in broad daylight, Dean moved toward the entrance.

* * * *

On instructions from Kelly, Brendan had pretended he was going to work, as normal, that morning, but had doubled back around and walked down Blarney Street. Michael had said he would too, but when Brendan had opened his eyes this morning Michael's bed had been empty.

Brendan knew that Michael wasn't comfortable with what was happening, but he had never felt so complete in all his life. He was finally a part of something real, something that mattered. His head swam as he thought of the implications of what Kelly believed Mary's new boyfriend was planning. He, Brendan Horgan, from the north side of Cork, could end up playing a part in saving the life of the President of the United States of America.

He stood across the street from the Metropole Hotel from half past eight onwards, as he and Michael had the night before, watching the door. These were Kelly's instructions. "Do not enter the hotel," he had told Brendan on the phone on Saturday night. "Just watch from across the street. If he leaves, follow him, but from a distance. The last thing we need is him catching on to us now, before he tries anything."

Now, at a little before noon, he wasn't sure what to do. He had watched his sister enter the hotel lobby. Even from across the street, he could see that she was upset. Maybe she knew, he thought.

When Dean came storming out of the hotel fifteen minutes later, Brendan decided to follow him. Breaking into a sprint, Brendan ran up the street after Dean. He reached the corner and stopped running, taking it slowly while he admired a shop window. When he saw Dean crossing the bridge, he picked up the pace again, being careful to keep a safe distance behind.

* * * *

"What colour are they?" Dean asked from the door.

Thompson sidestepped to his right and turned around, a wide grin on his face. "Can I help you, sir?"

Dean didn't return the smile. Thompson's manoeuvre looked practised, perfected over the years. The young lady turned her head to see who was speaking. He saw the recognition on her face.

"I said, what colour are they?" he repeated, turning his attention back to Thompson.

Thompson wrinkled up his face. "Sorry, sir. I don't know what you're asking me."

Dean walked forward, closing the gap between him and Thompson. " What colour are her panties? You've just had a good look at them, haven't you?"

Thompson looked ill, like a boy caught stealing candy. "How dare you!" he spat out, but there was no venom in his voice. The 'you' came out with a slight quiver and Dean knew he had him.

He kept his eyes on Thompson as he walked around the counter. Thompson didn't move. He seemed hypnotised by the peering eyes of Dean. Beth remained up the ladder, watching the scene play out below her. A smile fought its way onto her face.

Dean towered over Thompson. "Let's have a chat, shall we?" And before Thompson could speak again, Dean grabbed his collar and hauled him into the storeroom, slamming the door shut behind them.

With a final heave, he sent Thompson flying across the small room. Dean stood blocking the only exit. "Do you know who I am?"

Thompson righted himself and looked at Dean. "I've seen you before, last week, collecting Mary."

"Do you know who I am?"

"Ahh, no."

Dean walked forward and Thompson cowered in the corner. "Don't hit me, please."

"I'm not going to hit you, you worthless piece of shit." Dean rested his hand against the wall, trapping Thompson in the corner. "You see, Mary Horgan is a gift from God to me. And that makes you the devil. Do you understand?"

Hesitantly, Thompson nodded.

"Mary is more special than you will ever realise." Dean pointed at the closed door. "That girl out there is special too. Understand?"

Thompson nodded again.

"Okay, good. And when you leer at them, you slowly strip away their dignity."

Thompson spoke. "Mary can come back. I'll give her a raise. It'll never happen again."

"Mary is never coming back here. She deserves so much more than this life, and I'm going to give her that." Dean dropped his hand and grabbed hold of Thompson's crotch.

Thompson would have crumbled to the floor except Dean showed no signs of moving down with him. He remained standing, a low moan escaping his mouth. Dean moved in closer and said, "If I ever catch you again, even looking anywhere below the neckline of any woman, you'll be wearing these around your neck." Dean squeezed for effect and Thompson yelped.

He released his grip and Thompson crumbled to the floor, gasping with relief. When Thompson managed to look up again, he was alone in the storeroom.

* * * *

Brendan had seen the confrontation in the shop; had seen Dean grab the older man by the collar and yank him into the back room. It took him some time to piece it together, but when the pieces fit, he knew his sister was alive and well. He was just defending her honour.

His thoughts now moved to the old man in the storeroom with Dean.

Was he dead?

Dean came out of the shop and Brendan turned away. He was standing at the spot where Dean had watched from earlier. Brendan leaned against the window and examined Winthrop Street. Dean passed him and headed back toward the hotel.

Brendan waited by the shop window, watching Dean walk up the street, but also watching the shop to see if Beth screamed or not when she looked into the back room. As Dean crossed the bridge, the old man came out of the room. He hobbled, more than walked, and he looked shook. Brendan wasn't concerned about him anymore. He turned and took off in pursuit of his quarry.

* * * *

The room service arrived and Mary opened the door. She was still dressed; afraid to chance the bath until the food had arrived. The trolley was full of sandwiches, cut into little triangles, a plate of cakes and a pot of tea with two cups. She realised she was hungry, but decided to wait for Dean.

He arrived moments after the food and paused in the doorway, admiring the trolley. "It looks good, Mary. You did well."

"I sure did," she replied, kissing him.

"No bath running, I see."

"Jes, I couldn't. I had to wait for the food to come. Enough people have seen my knickers already."

Dean laughed. "You're a funny lady, Mary Horgan."

"A hungry lady too," she added.

They sat on the bed and nibbled at the food. A comfortable silence enveloped them while they ate. They looked at each other intermittently and exchanged smiles. When they had their fill, Dean put down his cup and announced, "Well, I definitely need a bath."

"I could do with a soak myself."

Ten minutes later, completely naked, they settled into the hot bath. It was bigger than the one in Kinsale the week before, and Mary was able to lie back on Dean's chest. She pulled the bubbles up over her breasts and leaned her head back.

"Mary."

"Yes."

"There's something I have to talk to you about."

"Go ahead. You can tell me anything."

Silence.

Mary turned her body partially and looked at Dean. "Is everything okay?"

"Yes, but this is not the time or place for it. Will you meet me for dinner tomorrow night? We'll talk then."

"Well, let me see. Tomorrow I'm busy signing on the dole." Mary flipped through an imaginary diary with her finger. "I can fit you in between tomorrow at seven and mmmm… oh ya, the rest of my life."

"Really. I was hoping you could fit me in for a while this afternoon."

Mary giggled. "I was worried you might think I'm vulgar, but you're way ahead of me." She splashed some water in his face. "Okay so. I'll stay for the afternoon, but only because I feel sorry for you."

* * * *

When Mary was almost home she spotted her father leaning against the hedge by their gate. He waved to her and she waved back.

"How was work?" he asked. Mary scanned his eyes for something. Did he know?

"Fine. How was yours?"

"The usual."

Jack opened the gate and Mary started down the path.

"Come here to me a minute. I want to talk to ya." Jack pointed to the step inside the gate.

Reluctantly, Mary turned, strolled back up the path and took a seat on the step next to her father. Jack didn't speak straight away. He false started a few times and eventually made a coherent sentence. "You know you can tell your Mam and me anything, don't you?"

He knew something.

Mary didn't look at him. She looked at the garden. The spot where Willy had ripped off her knickers several nights before stared back at her.

Is that what he knows?

"I do, Dad."

"Well," Jack said, sighing. "Is anything bothering you these days, sweetheart?"

Mary considered her approach and decided to throw him a bone he could chew on. "I lost my job today."

Her father looked surprised. "What happened?"

My boss is a horny bastard who looks up girls' skirts!!!!

She didn't speak her mind, of course. Instead she said, "Mr. Thompson said business was going bad and he was going to have to cut back." Mary sighed for effect. "I was last in, so I was first out. Simple as that."

"Dirty bastard!"

"You're telling me."

"Screw um. You're better off outa there. If they don't want you, that's their loss." Jack put an arm around Mary and she cuddled into him. "I could ask around for you in The Cellar?"

"That's alright, Dad. I think I'll try for another shop in town or something." Mary could not picture herself packing sausages and rashers.

"Come on," Jack said, getting to his feet.

Mary jumped up and kissed him on the cheek.

"Thanks for asking anyway, Dad."

Ann came out of the pantry as Jack and Mary came in. She looked flushed from the heat in the small room.

"Good to see you in the kitchen for once, dear." Jack walked over and kissed her forehead.

"Would you like a tour? You shouldn't go in on your own. You might get lost or hurt." They exchanged sarcastic smiles. "I picked up a trousers for you today. Try them on before dinner."

"Where's Brendan and Michael?" Mary asked Ann.

"Upstairs, I think. They barely came in here."

"Avert your eyes, Mary." Jack already had his pants open.

"Ahh, Dad. For God's sake."

Mary turned her head and Jack dropped his pants. She listened as he struggled with the new trousers.

"Are you ready?"

"Okay."

Mary turned back as her mother eyed Jack from the waist down.

"They look alright," Ann offered.

Jack kicked out with each leg in turn, pulling at the waist of the trousers. The zip of the pants bulged and looked as if it would rip apart any second. "D'you know now what these pants remind me of?"

"What?"

"The Ballroom in the town of Fermoy."

Ann looked at him, a frown crossing her face. "What do you mean? There's no bloody ballroom in Fermoy."

Jack smiled. "Exactly. There's no ball room in these either."

Ann tried to stop herself, but Mary couldn't contain her laughter. Finally, Ann gave in and exploded. "I'll give you that one, Jack. You can be funny when you want to, I suppose. Now take them off. Maybe they'll fit one of the boys."

Jack dropped the trousers without warning.

"Ahh, Dad. At least a warning," Mary said, turning away a little too late.

* * * *

Brendan sat on the bed and lit another fag. Michael paced the small room, barely managing three steps in either direction. "I don't like it, Brend. We're getting knee deep into this shit, and you seem to like it all the more."

Brendan shrugged. "Hey, it's got to be done, bro. What would you suggest we do instead?"

Michael sat down on his own bed and buried his head in his hands. He was more afraid than he had ever been in his life.

He rubbed his eyes and looked at Brendan. "Where are we meeting them?"

"The Steeple Bar, by Shandon."

"At eight?"

"Yeah."

A car horn sounded and Michael recognised it instantly. "Is he going?"

Brendan jumped off the bed. "No fuckin' way."

Both of them ran down the stairs and out the front door. Longy was sitting in his car, smiling down the path at them. Brendan reached the car first.

"What the fuck are you doing here?"

Longy looked up and down the street and then leaned out the window toward them. "I'm going to the meeting with you." He winked.

Brendan shook his head. "No you're not."

"I fuckin' am," Longy said, louder.

"You're fuckin' not." Brendan reached for Longy, but Michael pulled him back.

"Okay, Longy. You can come. But we have to have dinner yet. You're an hour early."

"That's okay," Longy replied, settling back into his seat. "I'll wait right here."

Brendan started to speak again, but Michael wrestled him away from the car. When they were back by the gate Michael said, "We have to leave him go. You know him. He'll blow the whole fuckin' thing right here and now. Dad will come out and we'll be fucked completely. What harm can he do?"

Brendan grunted. "How did he know about the meeting?"

Michael shrugged. "Ahh, he must have been listening last night, in the car."

"He'll fuck everything up, I'm telling ya."

"I'll keep him in line."

"You had better." Brendan said, walking back towards the house.

****

Sergeant Higgins parked at the side of the road and climbed over the locked gate. The field was about two miles from the O'Reilly farm, closer to the city, but still considered countryside. The field was at the back of the Orthopaedic Hospital, and as Sergeant Higgins walked towards the car, he wondered how long more these fields would last. When would the demand for housing push the business of cement and bricks this far outside the city?

He could see the car abandoned in a corner of the field, well hidden from the road. Whoever had taken Mrs. O'Reilly's car from the farm had also been the person who burned down the house. The fire department had informed him earlier in the day that someone had set the fire deliberately. Mrs. O'Reilly's remains had been taken to the morgue for further examination. Higgins had spoken with the State Pathologist at four and even before he had started his examination, he agreed with the Sergeant's guess that the woman had died at least four years earlier. "She sure wasn't inhaling any of the smoke in this fire," he said.

The car was a black shell; the grass around it scorched. The domed roof of the Volkswagon had managed to withstand the heat and keep its shape. Nothing of the original colour of the car remained, but one of Higgins's team had pulled the chassis number and verified the make, model and original colour. He also confirmed that the car was registered to Mrs. O'Reilly.

Higgins moved around to the front of the car and gazed into the open boot. Of course, the boot was empty; his team would have removed anything of interest. Still, he looked anyway. He looked, as he had at the pigsty the day before, when he had noticed the dark liquid on the ground. In the end, he hadn't bothered to alert anyone on the team of his discovery. His team were at this moment searching for Mrs. O'Reilly's son, Willy. They had already learned that he had purchased a ticket for the ferry to England on today's sailing, but had not boarded the ship. Sergeant Higgins walked around the car, not really looking at it, but imagining what had happened the night before.

The sun shone into his face as it continued its slow descent. He had a briefing at eight with his team. They would have a full update on Willy O'Reilly, and he would become the primary suspect of the investigation. Higgins knew Willy was dead, probably eaten by his own animals, but he would leave the team drive on with their hunt. He, on the other hand, would conduct his own little investigation.

****

The Steeple Bar was half full when Michael, Brendan and Longy walked in. Some of the crowd stopped to give them the once over, most continued drinking. Brendan surveyed the bar and raised his hand when he saw Kelly sitting in the far corner. The pub was dull, in contrast to the brightness of the evening sun outside, but he could see two men sitting next to Kelly. One was small, a slimy looking git. The other was as big as a house. Two women could sit on one shoulder each and this giant would feel nothing, Brendan thought.

"How are you, boys?" Kelly greeted them.

The three of them remained standing, unsure whether to sit down before being invited.

"Take a seat, lads. We're all friends here."

Michael and Brendan sat opposite Kelly and his two companions. Longy was sent to the bar to call three pints.

"We just got here before you, so I haven't had a chance to update the lads here about what's going on," Kelly said. He made quick introductions, omitting Longy at the bar.

"It had better be good," Kieran Murphy said, taking a large gulp from a pint of Guinness.

"Yah," Richie Doyle, the giant, added.

Kieran shot him a look. "Do you always have to back up what I say?"

Richie didn't answer. He hid in his pint. The smaller fella impressed Brendan. Standing up to a giant was no mean feat.

"Okay, guys, relax. Here's the deal." He paused as Longy returned with the drinks. "Is he okay?" he asked Brendan, obviously not remembering Longy from the meetings. Brendan nodded.

"Okay then," he continued. "It's like this, and correct me if I get something wrong, Brend. Brendan and Michael here have a beautiful sister called Mary, who met an American last week, right here in Cork. Now, these boys and another sister called..."

"Louise," Michael offered.

"Right, Louise. They went for a drive in the countryside last Friday and low and behold they see this American in a field shooting a sniper rifle at some targets." Kelly paused, searching his guests for reactions. "With a silencer," he added.

Kieran took another drink and stared back at him, looking unimpressed.

"Well, the boys tell me of their little discovery and I get them to question him about shooting and the like on Saturday night when he came to their house for dinner. Anyway, he lies through his teeth about the whole thing. He says he hasn't shot a gun in years."

Kieran put down his pint. "Will ya get to the point, Kelly?"

"I am. Do you know who's coming here on Friday?"

"Where?"

"To Ireland."

Kieran's eyes widened and then he laughed. "Ahh. Come on. You think this fella is going to try and kill Kennedy."

Kelly scanned the bar. "Jesus, Kieran. Could you say that a bit louder, ya fucker?"

Brendan noticed that Kieran wasn't happy with being called a fucker, but he didn't admonish Kelly. Who was further up the chain of command here? Brendan wondered.

"I happen to think it's a possibility," Kelly said. "Either way. We have to do something. Our letter to Kennedy will be all over the papers tomorrow morning. In that we all but threaten Kennedy to keep his nose out of Irish politics."

Kieran shrugged. "I've read a copy of the letter and I didn't see it that way. It's harmless."

Kelly smiled. "It is on its own, but if someone, like this fucker, blows Kennedy's brains all over the streets of Cork, then that letter will be read in a different light altogether."

Kieran nodded slowly, obviously considering Kelly's words now.

Kelly continued. "The English will be thrilled. An American President slain on Irish soil, a cryptic threat sent by Sinn Fein from the IRA. They'll have America invading Ireland to kill us all. American sympathy will disappear overnight."

"You're overreacting."

"Maybe I am, but are you willing to do nothing and see if I'm right?"

"Richie, get in five pints will ya?" Kieran elbowed him gently.

Richie obeyed, jumping to his feet. He pointed at Longy. "Come on, grunt. You can help me get em in."

Longy swallowed hard and got to his feet. Brendan wasn't sure if Kieran had signalled to Richie to take Longy with him or not. He thought he had seen something.

Kieran leaned in toward the table. They all followed. "Okay, you've got a point. What do you want me to do?"

Kelly smiled. "What you and your giant do best."

Tuesday 25th June 1963

Excerpt from the Evening Echo:

SINN FEIN'S LETTER OF WELCOME TO PRESIDENT KENNEDY

Sinn Fein, in the course of a letter to U.S. Ambassador McCloskey welcomes President Kennedy on his visit to Ireland, states:-

While the Irish people have a warm personal regard for you and have exceptional ties with America, which helped build and maintain freedom, we must candidly point out that these are not the sole reasons for their enthusiasm at the prospect of your visit. The primary cause of their rejoicing is their yearning to be free and their hope that you will in some manner help to break the shackles that bind them to England.

We trust that during the course of your visit you will not do or say anything, which might help bolster British division and occupation of our country, but rather that you will add your voice to the demand of the Irish people for the right to life, liberty and the pursuit of happiness.

We wish to convey to your Excellency our very best wishes for a happy journey and an enjoyable stay amongst us.

Mary woke up without a job on Tuesday morning. She languished in bed, listening to the house come alive with the hustle of her family getting off to work. The room downstairs was a hive of activity as her father and two brothers shimmied around, grunting at each other.

When they all had departed, the house was quiet, until Mary heard her mother rise from her bed. Her mother left shortly afterwards; she was working in the sewing factory today. Mary lay still in the bed and listened to the silence of the house. Outside the odd car trundled down the street, the odd dog barked at a passer by. The only sound she could hear inside the house was her baby sister, lying across from her, breathing gently.

Slowly, Mary sat up in the bed and swung her legs over the side. Louise didn't stir. Mary slipped her feet into her slippers, grabbed her dressing gown, and quietly left the room. The house wasn't cold, the sun already heating the front rooms of the house. She reached the living room and continued into the pantry. The kettle was still warm and half full, so she placed it back on the stove and lit the gas. She cut two thick slices of bread and put them under the grill. Was this going to become the routine? she thought, as she waited for the toast to brown and the kettle to boil. Would it be two toast, always only two each morning, and then back to bed to read some mindless novel, or to simply lie there and watch the world rush past her.

The toast burned slightly and the kettle overflowed, spitting hot water onto the stove. Mary buttered her toast and made her tea. She returned to the living room and sat at the table. Her father's discarded and wrinkled day old newspaper, was strewn across the table. She took a bite of toast and reassembled the Echo. The paper was almost beyond repair. Her father didn't read newspapers; he devoured them.

The pages put back together, Mary realised that what should be the front page was actually page seven. She gave up and started reading the page she was at; knowing the order didn't matter much anyway. It was yesterday's news, but it was something to keep her train of thought away from the dark and lonely corners of her mind. She scanned the pages and read the adverts mostly. Skipping the sports section, Mary found the front page. Looking at the headline, Mary knew it was a slow news day in the world. Something about the Sweep draw on the Irish Derby reaching five million pounds dominated the front page. Mary skipped the article, wishing she had even a fraction of the money.

She read the small news piece about Kennedy wanting to build a supersonic plane. The world was rushing by, she thought. She had never been on a plane and they were already building the planes of the future. Mary couldn't imagine sitting in something going 1450 miles an hour.

She was about to close the paper and finish her toast when she saw the by-line next to the plane article. At first she was just curious, but as she read on, and each word described the scene in more detail, she felt the hairs standing on the back of her neck. The final line drove a bolt of fear into her spine and she shot upright. 'Willy O'Reilly, believed to be a resident of the burnt out farmhouse, is being sought by Gardai for questioning.'

She scanned back up through the article to the headline and her thoughts turned to Dean.

Farmhouse Burning; Arson Suspected.

* * * *

When Mary had washed, dressed and brushed her hair, she sat staring at the walls. She checked the clock and it told her that she still had a long, boring day ahead of her.

Louise made an appearance at a little after ten. They chatted for a while and then Louise left to get some food for the dinner. "You can start helping me around here, now that you're on the dole," she said before leaving.

Mary grinned up at her from the table. "I don't intend on spending my days hanging around here."

She had wanted to sit and talk with Louise, to tell her about Willy and what she was thinking, but decided against it. Instead, she waited until Louise had disappeared out the front gate, then grabbed her handbag and headed out the door as well.

The sun was hot on her face and it was quite warm for mid morning. The dew was still scattered along the grass but wouldn't last much longer; the sun was slowly creeping along the path. She closed the front door and started to walk.

She reached their front gate and she saw Angela walking up the steps to her own house. Why wasn't she at work? Something must be wrong? She decided to go over and try to patch things up. If Angela ignored her she would feel better for trying anyway.

Angela was already inside by the time Mary arrived at the front door. She rapped on it gently, subconsciously hoping that Angela wouldn't hear.

She did.

The door swung open and Mary was faced with a teary eyed little girl. Gone was the strong posture, the wilful face that Angela always had on. The girl standing before Mary was an empty shell.

"What's wrong, Ang?"

The tears came and Mary felt her own eyes well up in sympathy for a problem she didn't yet know about. Without speaking, they embraced and cried on each other's shoulders, as they had when they were kids. They stood there for five minutes, not needing to speak. The reconciliation was complete. They were friends for life, always had been and always would be. Nothing would keep them apart for long.

When the tears had subsided, they went inside. Angela was home alone; her father at work, her mother gone to town and her brother on a bus to England, to join the British army. Angela told Mary that she had walked down to Patrick's Bridge that morning with Johnny; had kissed and hugged him before he jumped on the bus to the ferry. He would be there tomorrow and sign up the following day.

"He told me that I was the only one he would really miss."

Mary made some tea and the two of them sat in the living room sipping and chatting. The house was identical in structure to Mary's. Angela's mother had bad taste in décor, but the layout was the same.

"I'm sorry about last week, Angela?" Mary offered.

"Don't be silly. I was out of line, asking you to give up the best thing ever. Christ, if I met him I'd drop you like a bag of spuds."

They exchanged smiles and Mary felt one of the burdens she had been carrying around all week, fall off her back.

"I'm really going to miss him," Angela said. "How am I going to survive in this house? I'll bet you in the next week Dad will give Mam a few slaps, and the whole thing will start up again." She took a sip of tea and announced, "I'll have to get out of here. That's all I can do. Mam will have to deal with him herself. She married the bastard in the first place. I didn't."

As she spoke, Mary could hear the old Angela making a comeback. It felt good to hear that person. It was a sign that she was going to be okay.

"Did you see last night's Echo?" Mary asked.

Angela wiped her eyes. "No, am I in it or something? Have those nude pictures I had taken been discovered?"

Mary gave a token chuckle. "Not yet and I don't think they would be in the Echo." She paused and continued, setting the tone. "Willy's farm was burned to the ground on Sunday night."

"What?"

"It was burned down. It's on the front page of the Echo. They think it was done on purpose. Willy is missing. I think they think he did it. The paper didn't mention his mother, so I'm guessing she wasn't there."

"Jesus," Angela said. "Do you think he did it, burned down his own house?"

"I don't know. Why would he do that?"

"He's a head case. Look what he did to you outside the Palm Court."

Mary sipped her tea and stared into the cup. She knew she had to tell Angela about last week and what had happened with Willy. She didn't know how to put it. She took another sip and started. "I have to tell you something now that I should have told you last week." Her hands shook visibly as she raised the cup again.

"Are you okay, Mary? It's okay, you can tell me anything, remember?"

Mary put down the cup and placed her shaking hands in her lap. The thought of talking about the event brought all the details and feelings rushing back, and she felt like it had happened the night before and not a week ago.

"Last Wednesday night, after I spent the evening with Dean in Kinsale, he dropped me off a few doors from my house." She paused and swallowed hard. Her voice was low and edgy.

Angela nodded at her, a gentle smile on her face.

"When I went in our gate Willy was waiting for me in the garden."

Angela's face turned pale. Mary knew she was thinking the worst and quickly continued, recounting the rest of the story better than she had started it.

"And he didn't…"

"No. He didn't get the chance."

"But how did you get away?"

Mary told her what steps she had taken to get him off her.

"Jesus, Mary. You're even tougher than I am. Good for you girl." Then a horrified look appeared on Angela's face. She lifted her hand to her mouth and gasped. "Oh, Jesus, Mary, I'm so sorry."

"For what?"

"You went through all this last week and then I blow up on you on Friday and storm out when you needed me most. I'm so sorry, Mary."

"You didn't know. I'm sorry for not telling you sooner."

Angela processed the information she had just received and asked, "Did you tell Dean?"

Mary nodded. She could see the hurt on Angela's face, but it was dismissed quickly. "Did you tell your Mam and Dad?"

"No. I couldn't."

Angela got up and rounded the table, squatting next to Mary. "Are you okay?"

"I am but," she hesitated again.

"But what?"

"The fire."

"Do you think Dean was involved in the fire?"

Mary shook her head. "I don't know what to think."

"When are you meeting him again?"

"Tonight."

"Ask him."

"What?"

"Ask him if he did it."

"And then what?"

Angela sighed. "Well, if he tells you he did it and he has dumped Willy in a ditch somewhere, what will you do then?"

Mary considered the question. She really didn't know. If he had done such a thing, he did it out of love for her. Willy had tried to rape her after all. She should be happy if Dean had dealt with him. "I don't know. I really don't."

"I know what I would do." Mary looked at Angela. "I'd marry him and make at least five children just like him. That's what I'd do."

Mary smiled at her. Angela had said what Mary was afraid to admit.

"I could always just say nothing and see if he tells me."

"You could, but if he doesn't, are you willing to leave it unsaid for good then?"

"Probably not."

"So ask him then. If he's the one for you, you should be able to ask him anything, right?"

Mary nodded. Angela got up, collected the cups and headed for the pantry. "Another cup?"

"Yes," Mary answered. She sat alone in the living room looking at the pictures on the wall. To her right was a picture of JFK and the previous Pope, the same as the one at her granny's. She sat and admired the two great men as Angela wet the tea in the next room.

A few minutes later, Angela popped her head out of the pantry. "How come you're not working today anyway?"

Mary grinned back. "Oh, I forgot to tell you. I was fired yesterday."

Angela looked ready to explode. "Hold on and I'll get the tea. This could take all day."

* * * *

Michael sat on the bed, gazing at the Echo in his hands. He had arrived home a little after five and had bought a copy of the Echo at O'Keeffe's shop on the corner. He scanned the pages frantically until he found the letter, printed not on the front page, as he had anticipated, but deep inside. It was tucked away in an obscure part of the paper, where only the most thorough reader would find it. He had passed it on twice before finding it.

Brendan arrived in from a late finish at the turf stores. "Is it in there?"

"Yes." Michael looked up to see the excitement filling Brendan's face. He looked like a child in a toyshop.

"Let me see it," he said, snatching the paper out of Michael's hands. The paper closed and Brendan started searching frantically for the article. After one full turn of all the pages he started in again. "Where the fuck is it?"

Michael shrugged, sitting back on the bed. "If you hadn't been so fuckin' eager to grab the thing off me, you'd be looking at it now."

Brendan stopped his search, lowering the paper from his face. "Page?" he said.

"Six." Michael didn't hesitate. He dared not.

Slowly, Brendan sat down on his bed as he read. A bed of nails could have been placed on the bed and he wouldn't have noticed. Silence filled the room. Michael lit a cigarette and lay back against the wall, letting the silence spin out.

When Brendan finally finished, he looked up at Michael and said, "There's no fuckin' threat in that. I've made more threats in letters to Santa."

"Maybe the editor cut some of it out?"

"They wouldn't dare."

"They might."

"I'm tellin' ya, they wouldn't, alright."

"Fine. Jesus, relax. It was just a thought."

Brendan lit his own fag and the two of them sat quietly dragging on their butts. Brendan finished first. "What are you doing tonight?"

"Thought I'd stay in," Michael answered.

Brendan pounded the mattress with his fist. "Christ, I'd love to be there tonight. I'd fuckin' love it."

"Yah, me too," Michael lied. He never wanted to see any of those bastards again in his life.

* * * *

Jack was sprawled across his chair, asleep, the Echo strewn across his chest; loose pages scattered around him on the floor. Louise had retreated to her room after dinner.

Mary stood at the entrance to the kitchen, chatting with Ann.

"Are you going to start looking for another job?" Ann asked.

"Not straight away. I need a break."

Ann sighed. "A break. I could do with a break." She looked at Mary and smiled.

Mary could see the tiredness in her mother's eyes, the small sacks stored under them, holding all the long hours of work. The worry of money had a compartment all of its own in there. Mary realised then that her unemployment would put a dent in the household finances, as well as adding a slight bulge to the sacks under her mother's beautiful eyes.

"I'll probably start looking next Monday. I'm just going to take the rest of this week off, go see Kennedy on Friday, and then on Monday I'll start the hunt."

Her mother paused halfway through washing a plate. "Oh yeah, I forgot he was coming this week. My mind is addled these days."

"Why don't you come to town with me on Friday? We'll go and see him together. Is Dad getting off?"

Ann shook her head. "He didn't mention it."

"Will you come so?"

Ann considered it a moment and nodded. "I will."

Mary started to leave the pantry.

"I thought you would be going with Dean?"

"No. He's going to Dublin on business on Friday, remember?"

Ann tapped her temple. "He told us on Saturday night, didn't he? See, I told you, I'm losing my mind."

* * * *

Dean arrived and was invited into the front room, where Jack entertained him. It didn't take long for Jack to dredge up an old story about when he was young. He had Dean twisted with laughter as he told him the famous horse and cart story.

After ten minutes, Jack slapped his leg, laughed and then continued. "You see, Dean. What we did that night changed Mickey Spillane's outlook on life forever." He leaned in closer to Dean. "We saved him," Jack whispered, winking.

The door opened and Mary came in, sporting a rose red dress that seemed to light up the room. Dean started to go to her, but Jack grabbed his arm. "Nearly finished now, boy."

Dean sat back down and smiled at Mary. She pointed at her watch and Dean nodded, a slight grimace on his face.

"You see," Jack continued, oblivious to the signalling. "As I said at the start, Mickey Spillane had a huge drink problem. We cured him of that problem that night. Never touched another drink in his life after that night, did Mickey. Never stepped inside another pub either for the rest of his life."

"Did you ever tell him?" Dean asked, rising off the chair and moving towards Mary.

"We couldn't. He was a changed man. If we told him the truth he would have been back on the sauce before we finished the story."

"We'd better go," Mary interrupted.

"Yes," Dean agreed too eagerly.

"I have one more beauty for you before you go."

"We have to go, Dad. Dean has made reservations at a restaurant." Mary edged Dean toward the door.

He didn't hesitate too much, just enough to give Jack the sense he wanted to stay but couldn't.

"Ahh, come on. It's the one about the priest and the eider-down."

Mary all but pushed Dean the last few steps. "I know it, Dad. I'll tell him over dinner."

Jack shook his head and started after them. "You'll tell it all wrong. These things have to be told properly."

"See you, Dad." Mary shouted and slammed the door. Dean's farewell was cut short by the closing door.

Mary got into the car and as Dean started the engine he said, "That was an interesting story your Dad told me. Have you heard it before?"

Mary huffed. "I've heard that story so many times, I'm starting to think that I'm the horse."

＊＊＊＊

The meal had everything that Mary could have ever imag-ined. Dean took her to the Arbutus Lodge; one of the most expensive and exclusive restaurants in Cork. Their waiter showed them to a table and Mary sat looking around the room, speechless. Beautiful paintings occupied every available wall space, while every corner table was adorned with breathtaking sculptures and vases.

Dean asked Mary about the priest and the eiderdown story her father had alluded to earlier. Mary started rattling off the story, too quickly at first, and then slower when Dean showed genuine interest.

When she finished, Dean laughed hard, spraying some breadcrumbs across the table. People at nearby tables looked at him with disgust. Some, who were obviously close enough to listen, were trying to stifle their sniggers.

"And Dad thought I couldn't deliver a funny story, huh." Mary sat back, happy with her achievement.

"You've got to tell me more of these stories." Dean was still flushed from laughing and coughing.

The restaurant started to empty out at a little before eleven. She looked across the table at Dean. He wasn't smiling, as he had been for most of the meal. He looked sombre as he played with the spoon in his coffee. Mary had skipped the coffee, electing to smoke one of her rare cigarettes instead. "What's up, Dean?" she asked, dipping her head to try and meet his eyes. He raised his head slightly and smiled.

Before speaking, Dean surveyed the room. All the tables around them were empty now. When he was satisfied with the level of privacy, he said, "I told you yesterday that I wanted to talk to you about something."

Panic hit Mary like a bucket of water was tossed into her face. She wanted to reach out and block Dean's mouth, prevent him from ever speaking. The night had been so perfect and now it was time to pay for that happiness. She didn't try to stop him speaking; she just nodded and sat on her hands.

"I have to return home, Mary."

The words landed like a stone on her lap and everything seemed to slow dramatically in those few seconds. He has to return to America, she thought. She said the words over and over in her head, but it was like a different language to her; the words would not sink in. What seemed like minutes passed and when Mary felt Dean take hold of her hand she looked at it strangely.

"It's okay, Mary. I want you to come with me. I'm in love with you, Mary Horgan."

The whole scene turned surreal for Mary and she felt like she was going to throw up. That would be a nice story to add to all her father's little ditties. The time she threw up on the man who asked her to go to America with him, and at the Arbutus Lodge, no less.

"Are you okay, Mary?"

She looked up and locked eyes with Dean. He smiled and the room started to come back to normal speed again. A waiter dropped a spoon on the tiled floor by the entrance to the kitchen and the noise shattered the unreal world that Mary had slipped into only seconds before. "You love me?" she whispered, more to herself than to Dean.

"I do," he whispered back, squeezing her hand gently. "I really do."

"And you want me to go to America with you?"

"Yes."

"Okay," she blurted out, as if she was answering 'okay' to a cup of coffee. "When do we leave?"

****

Somewhere in between leaving the restaurant and arriving home, the reality of what Dean had said at the restaurant started to sink in. He wanted her to go to America with him. In the car, he told her that he was leaving as early as the following weekend and that she could travel with him. Mary told him she had no passport, so her accompanying him at the weekend would be impossible.

"I have to go at the weekend," Dean said. "You apply for a passport and follow me over in a few weeks."

Mary wasn't sure where to get a passport, but she nodded her approval of the plan anyway. Deep down, beyond all the silly dreams she held inside, Mary always felt like she would never leave Cork.

Dean stopped the car outside Chez Horgan and killed the engine. They sat silently for a little over a minute. Mary sat wondering what Dean was thinking. Did he really love her? She was sure he did. Why would he ask her to come to America with him otherwise? He could easily leave and he wouldn't have to deal with telling her he was dumping her. She decided that he did in fact love her, just as he leaned in close and kissed her neck. She responded and they kissed for some time.

"Come back to the hotel with me tonight," Dean said. "Let's spend the whole night together."

Mary almost said yes. "I can't, Dean. Not yet anyway. It would break my parents' hearts."

Dean gazed into her eyes. "I suppose I can wait," he said, the disappointment evident in his voice.

"How about tomorrow night?" Mary asked.

"What about tomorrow night?"

"What if I could stay with you all tomorrow night?"

"But how?"

"I'll think of something."

The smile returned to Dean's face. "Great."

Mary kissed him gently on the lips and opened the car door. "I'll see you tomorrow night then. Will you pick me up?"

"I'll be here at around seven. Okay?"

"I'll be waiting by the gate."

Dean started the car and pulled away from the step. He turned left at the corner and Mary found herself alone, looking up the empty road. Suddenly she felt like she was being watched.

Willy!

Mary dashed down the steps and fumbled hastily for the door key in her purse. It took her three tries to slot the key into the lock. Inside and safe, she found herself peaking out the letterbox to see if Willy O'Reilly was actually outside.

Nothing.

Mary sat on the stairs wondering where Willy O'Reilly had hidden himself. She imagined that he had burned the house down and fled to England. She had been about to mention it over dinner, to gauge Dean's reaction, but he had beat her to the punch, and a hard punch it had turned out to be. Dean hadn't burned down the house, she thought. He would never do something like that.

**** **

MacCurtain Street would normally be quiet on a Tuesday night, and this Tuesday night was no exception. Dean parked the rental car about twenty yards from the hotel entrance. He checked that all the windows were rolled up and when he was finished he got out and turned to lock the door. As he turned the key, a figure leapt from the shadows behind him. The man was large, easily taller than Dean. In his hand he held what resembled a police baton. As he covered the short distance to the car, he raised the baton and brought it crashing down on Dean's head.

Dean fell against the car, slid down the side of it until his head made a dull thud on the concrete step. A car that was parked across the street lit up and the engine roared. It screeched to a halt next to Dean's car. The giant stood looking down at Dean. In one swift movement, he bent over and picked him up. He did this quite easily and carried him to the waiting car, tossing him into the back seat. Then he ran around the car and dived into the passenger seat. The car sped away, barely slowing to take the sharp corner that led to the bridge, and beyond.

**** **

At the entrance to the Hotel, Andy Dineen, the elderly night porter, who had become rather friendly with Dean during his stay at the hotel, watched all the action unfold from a secluded spot. When the car sped off with Dean inside, the old man walked calmly to Dean's car, where the car keys still dangled in the lock of the driver's door. Checking both ways, he quickly snapped the keys from the lock and stuffed them into his pocket.

Whistling as he went, he walked back to the hotel and entered the reception area. He nodded at the receptionist as he strolled past her. She returned his nod with a bright smile and a slight wink. He smiled back as he pressed the button to call the lift.

He got off on Dean's floor and wasted no time making his way to Dean's room. He was familiar with the hotel keys and found the right one on Dean's key ring in seconds. He had a master key for this room as well, but he needed the American's keys.

Checking both ways again, he slid the key home and opened the door. He flicked on the light, and holding Dean's bunch of keys in his left hand, he gently closed the door behind him.

Wednesday 26th June 1963

Excerpt from the Evening Echo:

I AM PROUD TO COME TO THIS CITY—WEST BERLINERS TOLD.

We Can Trust Our Friends. They Can Rely On Us—Brandt.

Mr. KENNEDY was cheered wildly by huge crowds when he arrived in West Berlin today. The Mayor, Herr Brandt, welcomed him, saying, "We can trust our friends and they can rely on us."

The President said in a brief statement, he was not there to reassure the people of West Berlin. Words were not so important. The record of the three powers was written on rocks.

"I am proud to come to this city. We come to a city 5,000 miles from the United States but we come to a city which we feel is part of us."

Michael opened his eyes to see his brother standing over him. He was too tired to react. He lay on the bed rubbing his eyes.

"I'm not going to work today," Brendan announced.

Michael did not reply. He knew what was coming and he wanted to go to work today. Brendan had other ideas.

"Will you take the day off and come with me or not?" Brendan asked.

Michael's head pounded as he tried to sit up. "I already took time off this week, Brendan. I'll get fired."

"Fine." Brendan turned away and started to dress.

Michael lay back on the pillow. He would take the day off if only he could lie back down and fall asleep. After a few seconds, he looked at Brendan, who was now sitting on his own bed tying his shoelaces. He sat up again. "Where are you going?"

"To see Dean."

"But Kelly told us to stay out of it."

"I don't care. I want another look at this assassin fella."

Michael swung his legs out of the bed and onto the cold floor. Brendan looked at him, hope filling his face.

"Ya coming with me?" Brendan pressed.

Michael shook his head. "No, I'm not. I'm finished with all this shit. I'm sorry Brendan, but this is way over our heads. I'm going to work." The words felt liberating, and although his voice quivered as he spoke, he felt stronger for having said what had been on his mind for a week now.

Brendan shook his head and said, "Do what you want then. I'm going to ask Longy for a loan of his car." He finished tying his laces and left the room.

Michael sat on the bed, glad he had broken the chain that had been dragging him along for the past week. He still worried for his brother though. What was Brendan going to end up doing?

Michael reckoned that they were underestimating this man from America. If he was going to try to kill Kennedy, then someone had paid him because he ranked among the best in the world, and Michael feared that his brother and a few IRA men would be no match for him.

* * * *

He emerged from his forced slumber slowly, and realised that he wasn't lying down, but was actually tied to a chair. He lifted his head and felt excruciating pain at the back of his neck. His memories were scattered, but he knew someone had clobbered him from behind. His last memory was of placing the key in the door of the car.

Dean raised his head some more and looked around the room. He was seated on a kitchen chair in the middle of a room no bigger than an average living room. The chair was the only piece of furniture. To his left was a window, but the curtains were drawn. He could see that the sun was up, but he couldn't see anything beyond the window. Slivers of light pierced the curtains and afforded the room some light. Still, it was gloomy and he had difficulty seeing into all the corners. Wallpaper peeled away from the walls and hung halfway down towards the floor. Wherever he was, it was a house that wasn't lived in at the moment. The floors were stripped down to the floorboards and a musty smell filled Dean's nostrils. It was then he realised his mouth was gagged.

He tried to move an arm, but they were tied tightly behind him. He kicked a leg forward, but nothing happened. Dropping his head again, Dean could see that his legs were taped to the legs of the chair.

The door in front of him opened slowly and a man of medium build walked in.

"Good morning, Mr. Reynolds. I hope your stay with us was enjoyable." The man stood in front of Dean and grinned widely. "Breakfast will be served shortly, but of course you won't be having any." The man laughed heartily at his own little joke.

Dean tried to talk, but the tape on his mouth did its job. The words came out muffled and incoherent.

"Just relax now, Dean. You have a long day ahead of you today and you're going to need all your strength."

Dean inhaled and caught the aroma of cooking food coming through the open door. He glared at the man standing in front of him; the man winked back.

"Maybe later we'll give you something to eat." The man paused and leaned in closer to Dean's face. "After you've told us everything of course."

Dean remained still, his eyes saying everything.

"Oh, I can see you want to kill me," said the man. "You'd love to get your hands on me now, wouldn't you?"

Dean just stared.

The stranger raised his hand and brought it down furiously on the bridge of Dean's nose, breaking it with a muffled pop. Dean's head spun to the left and the room danced in front of him. His eyes watered and he could feel the blood running past his gagged mouth. He tried to focus on the man standing in front of him. The last thing he saw was a blurry figure bent over laughing, before he drifted back into a dreamless sleep again.

* * * *

Mary was woken up by the sound of someone rapping on the front door. She heard Louise open it. The unmistakable voice of Angela filled the house. After a brief chat with Louise, Angela came bounding up the stairs and burst into the room.

"It's Wednesday," Mary said. "Why aren't you at work?"

Angela threw herself onto Louise's bed. "I took a day off. Someone has to look after you this week. And God knows I could do with some cheering up. How did last night go anyway? I've been dying to know. Did he do it or what?"

Mary knew Angela was referring to the burning of Willy's house. "No, he didn't do it," she said, a bit defensively.

Angela raised her arms. "Okay. I was just asking. No need to bite my head off."

"Sorry."

"Ahh, forget it. Where did he take you?"

Mary tried her best posh accent. "The Arbutus Lodge, darling."

Angela put her hands to her cheeks and played along. "Oh my, you went to the Lodge. I hear it's lovely at this time of year."

"Oh it is, superb really."

Angela fell back into her norry accent. "And did you shift him afterwards?"

Mary held her posh tone. "Oh no, deary. We were too busy hobnobbing with the clientele for any of that malarkey."

Louise appeared at the door. "What's all the news, girls?"

Angela spun around. "We're going to town. Wanna come?"

"We are?" asked Mary.

"I'd love to," Louise replied, ignoring Mary.

"That's settled then. The three holy sisters are going to Pana." Angela pointed at Mary. "Get dressed you and wear clean knickers. We will be trying on lots of clothes today." Angela jumped off the bed and threw her arm around Louise. "I'll take Louise here downstairs and update her on my sorry life, just so that she's not lost later, when we have lunch."

Mary got out of the bed. " There's something else I want to talk to you two about, but we'll do it over lunch. Okay?"

"Right," said Angela. "Let's make some toast, Lou. There's nothing to eat at my house these days."

****

The three girls hit Patrick Street and, although they hadn't much money to spend between them, they shopped like they were millionaires. They visited all the usual haunts and even paid a brief visit to Cash's department store, where Angela tried on three dresses before deciding they were all unsuitable, to the obvious annoyance of the lady assistant.

When they walked out of Cash's, Mary stopped and glared across the street at the sweet shop. From their vantage point, they could all see Mr. Thompson going about the daily business. Beth was behind the counter, smiling at a male customer as she weighed out a quarter pound of apple drops for him. It all looked so routine to Mary. She had left on Monday morning and now, Wednesday, business was already back to normal. The shop hadn't missed a beat after her departure. The thought that she had left no ripples of her presence there made Mary feel small and insignificant.

"Would you like me to go in and spit in his cough sweets?"

Mary turned to see Angela smiling back at her. This was Angela's way of snapping Mary out of it. " Nah," she replied. "I already licked his liquorice on Monday."

Angela giggled. "Maybe that's why he fired you?"

"Are you joking? He would have given me a raise then."

Louise caught the double entendre and smothered a laugh.

They went for lunch at the Pavilion café, the same place where Mary and Angela had split a week before. As they entered, Mary pointed across the street at Cavendish's furniture shop and explained that Dean's office was on the third floor. She showed them, although she knew Dean had no intention now of ever setting up an office there. Either way the girls seemed unimpressed and more interested in food.

Mary wondered if fate was taking a hand when they sat at the same table as last week. Would Angela storm off again when she told her of Dean's offer, and her immediate acceptance? Either way, Mary was determined to be forthright with her friend, and her sister.

They ordered tea and sandwiches and Angela flirted with the waiter every time he passed their table. She wasn't the least bit shy, and at the expense of Mary and Louise's dignity, she continued escalating her serenading of the young man until Mary told her to stop or she would leave.

"Okay," she conceded. "But, Jesus, he has a cute ass."

"Angela Browne," Mary said slowly.

Angela stopped and Mary took a large breath before starting again.

"Okay. I was telling you about meeting with Dean last night." Mary turned to Louise. "Oh, Lou. I didn't get a chance to tell you this morning." She explained about the meal at the Lodge and how wonderful it all was. Louise had a distasteful look on her face as Mary spoke, and Mary couldn't help but notice.

"Anyway," she pressed on. "Dean told me last night that he has to return to America." Mary watched them both for their reaction.

Louise reacted first. "When?" she shouted. "When?" Louder this time.

Mary was surprised by the outburst from her little sister. If an outburst was coming, she had envisioned Angela losing it.

"When is he going?" Louise leapt to her feet.

Mary remained seated, looking up at her sister. "This Saturday," Mary answered, still quite puzzled.

Louise turned pale before their eyes and Mary was suddenly worried for her sister. "Are you okay, Lou?"

Louise seemed to be gasping for air. Her mouth moved, but the words only came after a few attempts. "I'm....ahh...I'm fine...I...ahh....I have to go. I forgot something. See you later." Louise bumped her chair backward with the back of her knees.

It almost toppled, only staying upright with the help of a passing waiter. She ran from the café, almost falling when she jarred her thigh on the last table before the exit.

"What's wrong with her?" Angela asked, not seeming too put out by the whole thing. She nibbled on a sandwich as she waited for an answer.

Mary stared at the door that Louise had disappeared through and wondered what the hell was going on. "I don't know," she answered finally. "I really don't."

Angela shrugged. "Well, if you don't know, I'm definitely lost. Anyway, tell me about Deano. He's going back home for how long?"

Mary turned her attention back to Angela. She looked at her old friend and said, "Forever."

Angela's mouth dropped open. Mary knew she was getting ready to console her for being dumped. Before Angela could utter a word Mary finished the news. "And I'm going with him."

Mary waited for the grenade to explode. She had delivered it, pulled the pin and rolled that sucker across the table. Now, all she could do was wait and try to get out of the way of the blast.

It never came.

Angela's drooping jaw closed, her lips curling into a wide grin. Some tears flowed freely from her eyes and they opened Mary's reservoir.

"Oh, Mary," she sobbed. "I'm so happy for you. You're going to be so happy." She got up and rounded the table. They hugged and cried and after a few seconds Angela added, "Ya lucky bitch."

* * * *

When Dean opened his eyes again, there were two men standing in front of him. He felt the pain from his broken nose, and when he tried to open his mouth, he realised that the gag was gone. Fresh blood trickled into his mouth as he stretched and licked his lips.

He recognised the man to his left as the bastard who had broken his nose. To his right stood what appeared from a seating position to be a giant. The man was built like a small house and Dean knew he would have problems coping with him.

The nose breaker spoke first. "Dean Reynolds. That is your name, isn't it?"

Dean said nothing. He wanted to see what they knew, and what they planned to do to him, before he gave them any information.

The man shrugged. "I'd talk if I was you, buddy. It might be your last chance." He turned and smiled at the giant. The giant let out a loud chuckle, tilting his head back for effect.

Dean thought he was in a play. He felt the strange urge to laugh, but it passed quickly when the smaller man spoke again.

"Do you know why we grabbed you last night?"

They had brought two more chairs into the empty room with them. The smaller man raised his hands and sat down. The giant examined the chair before lowering his large ass onto it. It creaked loudly and swayed slightly before settling under his bulk. It looked like it would hold, but not for long.

When Dean didn't answer the nose breaker continued. "We grabbed you because someone thinks you're planning to kill Kennedy. Personally, I think the whole thing is ridiculous, but I'm employed to carry out certain tasks, not question why they are being done." He pointed to the giant. "My associate here is employed for a different reason altogether." The giant cracked a few knuckles for effect, and Dean knew instantly what the man's talents were.

"He has a boot full of little trinkets outside that he would just love to use on you. But I told him to wait, because I felt you would be reasonable and talk to us. Was I wrong?"

Dean decided to talk for two reasons. He knew they were about to start torturing him and he wanted to see if he could talk these thugs down. "I'll talk," he said, nodding slightly.

"Good lad. Now, I won't beat around the bush, friend. Is it true? Are you involved in some plot to kill the President of America."

Dean shook his head. "I'm not," he said, trying to sound convincing.

The giant smiled, obviously convinced by the answer. The other man didn't look convinced. He wanted more and wasn't going to ask.

"I'm just an architect," Dean offered. "I just came to Ireland to try and set up a business."

The small man leaned forward; his nose only a few inches from Dean's broken one. "Tell me. Does bein' a architect require the use of a rifle with a fuckin' silencer?"

Dean knew he was in serious trouble then. He had been seen practising with the rifle. Whatever hope he thought he had of getting out of the situation peacefully disappeared. He lowered his head slowly. He didn't know what to say to these men. He knew now that his fate was decided long before the nose breaker had started asking him questions. Slowly, Dean flexed his tired arms and felt the ropes around them cut into his skin. He did this discreetly and followed the same principle when moving his legs. The tape they had used on his legs was wound tighter than the ropes. He wondered which one of the geniuses in front of him had decided to use ropes on his upper body instead of tape. Tape didn't flex or loosen over time. In fact, the more you tried to get free of well wound tape, the stronger it got. Dean had always used tape in the past to detain someone. He flexed his arms again, checking for any movement in the ropes.

"You ain't going to talk, are you, Mr. Architect?" They both stood at the same time. The giant turned and headed for the door. "Maybe you can draw your way out of here?" the other man said as he joined the giant. They both laughed as they closed the door, leaving Dean to stew a little longer.

Slowly at first, then quicker with each passing minute, Dean started rocking the wooden chair back and forth. He was careful not to make much noise. He rocked the chair, hearing the wood creak and groan beneath him. As he did, he watched the door, hoping they had decided to let him think about their first conversation for a while. He needed time now, more than anything else in the world.

* * * *

The truck full of pigs backed into the yard, and the men sitting on the dock of Denny's Cellar put away their half eaten lunches and got to their feet. The young boys, who hung around the yard during the summer months, smiled happily as the truck halted a few feet from the dock. They would each get a couple of pence from the driver for cleaning out the soiled truck, when the pigs were unloaded.

Inside the truck at least fifty pigs squealed and grunted. It was said that you could sense the fear from the animals when the trucks arrived. It was as if they knew where they were, could smell the stench of death in the air.

The back door of the truck was pulled down, landing perfectly on the dock. Three men stood on each side of the walkway, making sure that the pigs took the required route. Jack Horgan's job today was to make sure the trucks were unloaded promptly, and that all pigs were guided successfully into the pen. Whacker waited inside the factory, next to the empty pen. He had worked his way through seven trucks before lunch, but to Jack he looked as eager as ever to slit some throats. The running joke in the factory was about Whacker and his wife. The consensus was that some night Whacker would end up cutting his wife's throat while she slept.

The pigs bolted from the truck, one breaking through the human barrier at the sides of the walkway. He landed hard on the concrete ground of the yard, kicking his legs furiously, trying to get off his back. One of the men dived to grab him, but he was up and away, heading for the gate that led out onto Watercourse Road. Jack looked up and saw a woman standing at the gate. She was waving frantically in his direction, and for a moment Jack thought she was trying to help stop the pig from escaping.

Jack frowned and tried to focus on the woman. He was surprised when he saw that it was Louise standing at the gate. She wasn't trying to stop the pig. She was trying to get his attention. The pig reacted to her anyway and did a full circle of the yard instead of bolting out through the gate. Some of the men followed the path of the pig awkwardly, until the animal shot in one of the open doors of the factory. One man closed the door after him and turned to the rest. "Stupid Bastard. You think he'd know that that door leads down to the pen, and Whacker."

They all laughed and returned to their lunches as the young boys climbed into the empty truck and started cleaning out the urine and shit that the pigs had left for them.

Jack walked to Louise, who didn't venture into the yard. She stood by the gate, a hanky held to her face. The smell would knock a person over if they weren't used to it. When Jack had started in the cellar first it took him weeks to get over the stench of death and blood. Those first few weeks he didn't eat much at his breaks, afraid he would throw up when Whacker went back to work.

"What's up, love? Are you alright?"

Louise was pale and beads of sweat were sprinkled across her forehead. "He's planning to go back to America on Saturday. He's planned his escape."

Jack knew who Louise was talking about. They had talked about no one else in the past few days, ever since Louise had told him about the rifle on Friday night. Mary had gone to bed early, followed closely by Ann. Then Louise had told her father all about what they had seen in the field outside Blarney. Louise could never hide anything from her father for very long.

"Calm down, Louise. It's okay. It was obvious he would have to get away from here as quickly as possible afterwards."

"What are we going to do though? We have to go to the guards."

"No. I told you already. No guards. I'll look after everything."

"But the guards could arrest him."

"For what?" Jack asked. "He hasn't done anything yet."

Louise dropped her head, clearly overcome by the magnitude of the events surrounding her. She sobbed quietly. "I can't even look at Mary. I want to tell her everything."

Jack pulled her to him and she snuggled her head into his chest. "I know it's hard, baby, but we can't tell Mary yet. I think she really loves him and I don't know what she would do if she knew. For now, I want Dean to think that his plans are his own. Okay?"

Louise raised her head and wiped some tears from her eyes. "Okay," she whispered.

"Now, I have to get back to my important work," Jack joked. "You go home now and have a cup of tea. This will be over in a few days."

Louise kissed his cheek, something she rarely did anymore, and walked away.

Jack stood by the gate, watching her walk up Watercourse Road, past the Garda station. He hated asking his youngest daughter to lie to his oldest, but he had no choice. He had sat across from Dean Reynolds at dinner on Saturday night and had drunk with him afterwards. His performance had been perfect, his true feelings well hidden. That fucker, he thought. That fucker deserves one of those Oscar things for his part.

He thought about Mary and feared the worst for his oldest daughter. She was the innocent one in all of this. She knew nothing about the real truth, and loved Dean so much already. Jack had seen it in her eyes on Saturday night. The truth was going to be a hard blow for her.

The squealing of the pigs jolted him back to the present. A truck blew its horn behind him, waiting to get in through the gate. Jack looked around and realised that he was blocking the entrance.

Some of the men stood watching him. "Have a nice dream, did ya?" one of them said.

Jack stepped out of the way and followed the full truck to the dock.

Another fifty for the knife.

* * * *

Kieran Murphy sat out in front of the abandoned farmhouse that was occasionally used by the southern branch of the IRA. Richie Doyle came out through the front door with two cups of tea. The water wasn't boiled fully, but it would do for quenching thirst. He handed one of the cups to Kieran and sat down on the other milk crate. "You didn't ask him much questions, did you?"

Kieran sipped the tea and smiled at his partner. "I just wanted to let him know what we know. Let him stew awhile now and think about his situation a bit."

"If he doesn't talk?"

"We'll do a Johnny Finglas on him."

Richie nodded, a broad smile splitting his face. Johnny Finglas, whose real name was John Burke, had defaulted on a debt the year before. The debt was owed to the man who ran north side crime in Dublin. He passed the debt onto Kieran and Richie who tried in vain to get Johnny to pay up. Johnny Finglas's body was still missing to this day. Richie had tortured Johnny, more for fun than information, and after Johnny ran out of fight and died, Richie cut him up and crammed each part into a suitcase. The suitcase was still resident at the bottom of the River Liffey in Dublin, as far as Richie or Kieran knew.

"Do you think he was actually planning to kill Kennedy, like Kelly said?"

"I dunno. He looks like a mean bastard all right. I'd say he would be capable of it."

Richie shook his head. "He must be some kind of trained assassin then. He could be dangerous, you know."

Kieran laughed. "He certainly didn't look that dangerous last night when you slapped him over the head. And he certainly doesn't look very dangerous strapped to the chair in there now."

A car backfired on the road below them and both men jumped to their feet. After a few seconds, Longy's Ford Prefect emerged from behind the ditch and turned into the driveway.

"It's that Brendan young fella," Kieran said. "Kelly mentioned that he would be coming. Wants us to show him how we work."

Richie tossed the remainder of his tea onto the ground. "It'll be my pleasure. I hope he has a strong stomach."

The car came to a stop adjacent to the house and Brendan got out. "How's it going?" he asked.

"Great," Kieran replied, smiling. "You're just in time for the main event."

Brendan looked nervous, Kieran thought. He remembered his first job ten years before, when he had puked all over the poor bastard they were interrogating. His mentor at the time had nearly burst a blood vessel laughing that night.

Kieran stepped forward and shook Brendan's hand. "Don't be nervous. You're just going to watch this time. Okay?"

Brendan nodded furiously. "Okay."

"Kelly wanted you to see this. He should be here soon himself, but he told us to get on with it once you arrived." Kieran nodded to Richie, who walked to their car and opened the boot. He waved for Brendan to join him.

In the boot were two large suitcases and a large can of petrol. Richie flipped open the first one. Brendan gasped when he saw the contents. His eyes focused on the array of knives strapped to the back of the case, the smallest one's blade at least six inches long. Richie removed a pair of pliers, a hammer and a meat cleaver. "This will do for starters," he said.

"Ahh…What's in the other suitcase?" Brendan asked.

"Nothing," Kieran answered. "That's for pretty boy, later."

Richie slammed down the boot and the three men walked towards the house.

* * * *

For the first time in two weeks, Brendan felt fear creeping back into his body. It slowly enveloped him until, as they reached the front door of the house, his body was shivering in the midday sun.

"You okay?" Richie asked.

Brendan couldn't speak. He nodded and Richie chuckled slightly. He pushed the door open and in they went.

The house was bare and Brendan looked around the living room for Dean. He felt something close to relief when he didn't see him, but his heart kept pounding in his chest and he could feel the cold sweat seeping through his hairline now.

"He's in there." Kieran motioned to a brown, paint chipped door. "Now, Brend. Don't say anything. Don't do anything. If you feel sick, get out straight away. Okay?"

Brendan didn't even want to go in now. He wanted to turn and run, get in Longy's car and go home. He wanted to, but he couldn't. He was rooted to the spot and wondered if he would be able to move when the time came to go in.

Richie stood by the door examining the meat cleaver, picking at the blade with his nails. Kieran held the pliers in one hand and the hammer in the other. "Should I get the pistol from the car?" Richie asked.

"Nah," Kieran said, dismissing him. "We won't need it."

Richie turned and placed his hand on the doorknob. Before opening the door, he turned back to Kieran and Brendan. "Let's go to work," he announced and turned the knob.

The door swung in and Brendan saw the chair first, or what used to be a chair. It lay in a crumpled heap in the middle of the room. Next to it was a length of rope and a pile of mangled tape. Kieran didn't see the chair. He had turned to Brendan to encourage him to follow them.

The door swung back venomously and crashed into Richie's face, sending him flailing backwards against Brendan and Kieran. All three of them crashed onto the wooden floor, the door rebounding back against the doorframe. The door swung open again and Brendan saw Dean Reynolds coming out. He looked into Dean's eyes and saw nothing there; no pain, anger, nothing. If he had to describe them, he would have used the word 'focussed'.

Richie had dropped the meat cleaver when the door had crashed into him. He lay on the ground holding his hands to his face. Dean bent slightly as he came out of the room, and when he straightened up again he was swinging the meat cleaver wildly.

Except that he wasn't wild.

The cleaver looked like an extension of his arm. Kieran recovered first and lunged at Dean's legs with the hammer. He missed, but Dean didn't, bringing the shiny metal cleaver down hard on his shoulder.

Kieran yelped like an injured dog, as his shoulder separated from the rest of his body.

Jesus, Brendan thought, he cut him in half. Blood sprayed from the gaping wound and Brendan scrambled backwards in an effort to get out of the way.

Kieran immobilised, Dean turned on his heels and swung the cleaver at Richie. The shirt Richie was wearing was no match for the severe edge of the weapon; neither was his huge stomach. His hands dropped immediately to his midsection, and he grappled to keep his insides from falling onto the floor.

Dean stood upright, glaring at Brendan. Brendan could see the look of recognition on his face. It was there and gone in seconds. Dean turned away from Brendan and admired the carnage he had created before him. The two hired hard men groaned loudly as they squirmed and kicked around the floor, as if they could somehow manage to escape from the injuries sustained to them. In what seemed like less than a minute to Brendan, both men lay still in pools of their own blood, dead.

Dean slowly turned and eyed Brendan. Brendan felt his bladder give and urine ran freely down his leg. He was close to the door, at least ten feet from Dean, and if he moved now he might get outside and have a chance to run. But his legs refused the task and Brendan Horgan stood motionless, gazing into those lifeless, frightening eyes.

"Now, you're going to give me some answers, boy." Dean's voice filled the silence, his expression unchanged, as he started to walk towards Brendan.

* * * *

Mary opened the front door and was glad to be home. The living room was empty, which surprised her. She had expected Louise to be there, preparing dinner with her mother. Neither one of them was in the pantry, and nothing was simmering on the stove. Mary set down her handbag and decided to start the dinner. Then she heard the key in the front door and Jack Horgan came in, followed by Michael. Both men looked tired.

They exchanged greetings and Jack asked where Ann was, sniffing the air that held no aroma of cooking food. He looked at Mary. "Have you seen Louise?"

"No, I haven't. Not since earlier today." Mary chose not to tell her father about Louise's little outburst, at least not until Louise told her what it was all about. "Look, I'll start dinner. Mam must have taken extra hours at Mrs. Duggan's."

Michael retreated to the door. "I'll be upstairs. Call me whenever it's ready."

"You could help if you want," Mary fired at him, but he was already gone.

"I'll help ya," Jack said, rolling up his sleeves. "I'll peel the spuds. You check what meat is there."

They entered the pantry and Jack started peeling spuds. Mary found some bodice her mother must have dropped home at lunchtime and dumped it into a pot on the stove.

"Are you meeting Dean tonight?" Jack asked.

"He's calling for me at seven."

Jack tossed the first peeled spud into the second pot on the stove. "How are things going with you two?"

Mary spun towards him. His head was down. She wanted to tell him now, but it felt wrong. She wanted to tell them both together, later. "Great. He really enjoyed Saturday night, Dad. Did he tell you so last night?"

"He mentioned it all right."

Silence.

"I told him the eiderdown story," Mary said, jumping into the silence. "We were in the Arbutus Lodge at the time and some of the other people heard it too. It was a real hit."

Jack smiled. "The Arbutus, huh. Can't say I've ever been in there. Where are you off to tonight then?"

"We didn't make any plans. Maybe the pictures."

Louise appeared at the entrance to the pantry. Her eyes looked puffy from crying, but she managed a smile. "Sorry for not getting on the dinner, Dad."

Jack turned to her. "That's okay. Are you not feeling well or something?"

"I feel terrible. I'm going to go back up to bed, okay?"

"Do you want me to bring up a cup of tea?" Mary asked.

Louise moved her eyes to look at Mary. A tear appeared in the corner of her right eye and dribbled down her cheek. "I'm okay," she said, turning away and heading for the door.

Mary stood by the stove, wiping a bit of spilled water from the front of it. What the hell was wrong with her? she thought. Louise hadn't hung around at the café to hear Mary's big announcement. Maybe she saw it coming and couldn't bear to hear it. Maybe that was it. Mary decided she would have a chat with her before Dean picked her up.

****

Michael came back downstairs and was surprised to see that Brendan wasn't home.

"No sign of Brendan, nah?" he asked.

"Nope," Jack answered. "Means more for us though."

The five of them sat down and tucked into the spuds and bodice. Michael picked at his food. He wondered where the hell Brendan was. He knew he hadn't gone to work. Maybe Longy didn't give him the car and he decided to go to work after all. And maybe he had to work late to make up for lost time this morning. This logic calmed Michael slightly and he suddenly felt hungry. He picked up a length of bodice.

The rest of the dinner was accompanied by trivial conversation about the day. Ann had indeed worked extra hours at the factory and wasn't happy that the dinner wasn't put on by Louise. Jack explained that Louise wasn't well.

Mary told them about the barriers being erected in Patrick Street for Kennedy's visit on Friday. "It looks like a war zone in there," she said.

Michael wondered if it would be on Friday.

"He's arriving in Dublin tonight, on the telly," Jack announced. "I think it starts at half seven."

Mary finished her last bit of food and took her plate to the kitchen. "I have to go get ready," she said passing them on her way to the door. "Dean's calling at seven."

Everyone exchanged looks around the table as Mary disappeared out the door. Michael almost choked on a piece of meat, coughing furiously to catch his breath. He knew Mary was going to be stood up tonight. He was sure of it, but that didn't stop the growing fear of seeing Dean arrive at the front door, unharmed and smiling.

And where the hell was Brendan?

* * * *

Dean didn't come to the door at seven.

He sat in his car and blew the horn twice. Mary had intended to speak to Louise when she went upstairs to get ready, but Louise had been turned into the wall, her breathing slow and heavy. She dressed and was finishing her makeup when she heard the horn.

She vaulted down the stairs two at a time and met her father at the end.

He looked serious.

"I want you home by eleven," he ordered.

"What?"

"You heard me. Eleven."

"What's up?"

"Nothing. Just do as I say, okay?" His words were harsh and his usual smile was missing. Mary was caught off guard.

"Okay, Dad," she answered.

"Good." Jack turned and walked back into the living room, closing the door behind him.

Mary could see the damage to Dean's face before she was half way to the car. He smiled, but it didn't help. His nose was turned at an awkward angle and his two eyes were already as black as coal.

He reached across the passenger seat and pushed the door open. "You should see the other guys."

Mary sat in and grimaced as she examined his face. "Who did this to you?"

Dean started the car. "I did," he said, a slight glint of embarrassment crossing his face.

"You did?"

"Yes. I was coming down to breakfast this morning and decided to take the stairs instead of the lift. Bad choice really. I tripped on a lumpy carpet and bashed my nose off the bottom step."

Mary leaned over and kissed his cheek gently. "My poor baby," she said, putting on a motherly voice. "Let's go back to your room and I'll make it all better."

Dean smiled, but shook his head slowly. "I have a better idea," he said as he drove away.

* * * *

Mary and Dean didn't see Jack Horgan standing in the doorway watching them drive away. He had told Ann what was going on the night before and she wasn't happy. She wanted to stop Mary going anywhere near Dean. Jack explained his plan, and although she agreed, she wasn't happy that her daughter was in the line of fire. To Jack though, it was simple. If Mary knew what was going on, she would surely confront Dean. Then she would be in real danger. Leaving things go on as normal until Friday was the safest way to ensure that Mary was safe. Tomorrow was Thursday and Jack wanted everything to stay the same until Dean shot Kennedy on Friday. That he went ahead with the assassination attempt was crucial now.

Jack turned and was met in the hallway by Michael. He was fidgeting with his hands, clearly upset and totally incoherent. Jack calmed him down, and after a few deep breaths, Michael started again.

"Dad, I have something important to tell you." Tears welled up in his eyes.

"Am I a granddad?" Jack patted Michael's arm.

Michael didn't smile. He shook his head and took a few more deep breaths. Jack could see he was shaking under his clothes.

"What's wrong, son?" Jack said, compassion in his voice this time.

"It's about Dean…and…it's about Brendan too."

Jack felt his comfort zone crash down around him. Michael hadn't told him yet, but Jack knew his almost perfect plan was about to take a severe beating. Jack looked to the road, but Dean's car was already out of sight.

* * * *

Sergeant Higgins waited three days before returning to the O'Reilly farm to complete his own investigation. When he pulled into the yard, the sun was still warm on his face.

He opened the boot of the car and removed a large plastic bag and an unusually long pair of steel tongs. He ignored the burnt out house and walked directly to the pigsty. The pen was empty; all the O'Reilly pigs had been moved to the neighbouring farm, until they would be sent for slaughter at the weekend.

The ground of the sty was dry and dusty from the summer sun, but at one end of the pen, where the ground sloped severely, a pool of muddy water reflected the sun into his face. The Gardai had surmised that this muddy water had saved most of the pigs' lives.

Higgins entered the pen and, starting at the opposite end to the water with bag and tongs in tow, he walked the length of it, watching the ground intently for anything out of the ordinary. The investigating Gardai had channelled all their energy and time into examining the remains of the house. Higgins had spotted the dark stain in the pen and knew that the truth lay with the swine.

The stains were gone and he found nothing else helpful to his cause on the dry ground. He arrived at the dark pool and, trying not to get wet, he started prodding the water with the extra long tongs. His first major find was an old shoe that he guessed had been there for many years. He tossed it onto the ground behind him and continued the search, slashing the tongs through the water at various angles.

To get to the far edges of the pool, he had no choice but to get wet. He dipped one shoe into the uninviting water and leaned forward to jab the tongs into the corners. He lost his balance and almost went headfirst into the abyss. The tongs struck what he thought was ground at first, and it steadied him. Then the ground he had secured with the tongs moved slightly. His balance restored, he opened the tongs wide and slowly dipped them under the water again. It took a few turns to get an acceptable grip, and when he was satisfied his quarry was hooked, he lifted the tongs out of the water.

The mangled face of Willy O'Reilly stared back at him.

Willy's right eye was gone and one of the tongs had found a home in the empty socket. The other eye was in place, but the colouring was all wrong. A grey haze clouded the eye, making it look like something inhuman. The face was gone from the nose down, but it didn't look like the pigs had chewed it off. The water drained from the head, splashing droplets onto the Sergeant's pant legs. He tilted the tongs and could see the bite and tear marks at the neck, where the pigs had decapitated him. He rotated the head and saw the bullet entry wound at the base of the skull.

After another round with the tongs, he found three fingers and a partial ankle joint to add to the head in the plastic bag. His work complete, Higgins tossed the bag and the tongs into the boot of his car and drove away. It had taken him less than twenty minutes to find the remains of Willy O'Reilly.

* * * *

Dean parked on Patrick Street, outside Cavendish's furniture shop. Mary wasn't sure what Dean had planned. She got out of the car and let her eyes rise up the length of the tall building until they reached the third floor. "What are we doing here, Dean?" she asked.

Dean came around the car and took her hand. "I have a bit of a surprise for you, Mary. It's up inside the office."

"You're still renting that place. But why, if you're going back to America on Saturday?"

Dean shrugged and started toward the door, pulling Mary with him. "I leased it by the month, so I have it until next month anyway. Come on."

They climbed the three flights of stairs, Dean leading the way. Mary pondered what little delight Dean had planned for them tonight. She imagined a bed of rose petals set up in the middle of the office, a bottle of expensive champagne and two glasses in waiting next to it. They would make love until after midnight tonight and if Dean wanted she would stay with him. Then she remembered that she had promised that to Dean already, the night before. She had not organised her cover story of staying in Angela's.

She would stay the night with him anyway, she decided. Her father would be livid, but he would get over it. He would have to, and she would be going to America soon anyway and that would be a bigger shock to her parents than spending one night away from home.

They reached the office door and Mary was bursting with anticipation. Dean held the handle, turned the key and before letting the door swing in he turned and smiled at Mary. She looked at his face, looked beyond the mashed nose and the black eyes, and she felt her heart leap in her chest. Two weeks ago she hadn't ever laid eyes on the man in front of her. Now, she couldn't imagine not being with him.

The door swung open with a slight creak. Dean held the door and motioned for Mary to enter. She slipped by him and entered the office. There was no bed with rose petals spread across it, no champagne and glasses waiting for them. Mary surveyed the room and realised that it was exactly the same as it had been last week. If anything, the place looked dustier now. She looked at the boxes and saw the one she had sat on the week before, when she had told Dean about Willy and what he had tried to do to her. The print of her bum was still on the box.

The evening sunlight protruded through the two windows and Mary's eyes were naturally drawn to them. She took another step further into the office and saw the head sticking up above one of the piles of boxes close to the window. She could see the hairline and thought at first it was a mannequin. Then it moved and Mary jumped back slightly. Dean closed the door and stood quietly behind Mary.

After a prolonged moment, Mary stepped forward again and saw the battered face of Brendan staring up at her. His mouth was taped shut and streams of blood flowed from his nose down over the tape and across his chin. She took another few steps and felt Dean moving with her. She could see the rest of her brother now, could see the lines of tape that secured his arms to his side and his legs together. He was sitting up against the wall between the two windows. Some of the tape that traversed his chest was also wrapped around a water pipe that was bolted to the wall.

Mary couldn't register what she was seeing. Her mind wasn't prepared for the images being sent by her eyes, and her brain searched for an explanation that wasn't there. She turned to Dean. His loving smile was gone. "What's?…Why?…." Mary didn't know what to say.

"Your brother there," Dean started. "He tried to kill me today."

"What! He tried to kill you?" Mary turned to Brendan. His eyes looked full of fear, but he couldn't speak, couldn't tell her that this was all a joke; what she wanted to hear.

"Yes, he did. Him and a few of his buddies. The only reason he's alive right now is because he's your brother."

"But why would he try to kill you, Dean? This isn't making sense."

Dean bit his lip and eyed Mary. "Well, Mary. Your brother thinks I'm going to assassinate President Kennedy on Friday."

"He what?"

"You heard me."

Mary's head was spinning. She felt like she was outside herself, like she was dreaming and would wake up in her bed at any moment, covered in a film of cold sweat. She stood still for a few seconds, looking at Dean, hoping for a smile or a laugh that would confirm that this was all a joke; a really bad joke.

It never came.

"Are you?" she asked finally.

"Am I what?"

"Are you going to kill Kennedy?"

Dean held his hands out like a priest at mass. "I can't lie to you, Mary. You mean too much to me."

Slowly, Dean nodded and Mary saw something new in his eyes. Bolts of fear jolted through her meagre frame and her body jerked with each one. Dean moved towards her, but she recoiled from him.

"I'm not going to kill your brother, Mary, or you. I have a job to do. That's all it is, a job. On Friday you and your brother will be free to leave this room, but until then I'm afraid you must stay here." Dean took a step towards her again.

Mary held her position, unable to move, afraid.

"This changes nothing between you and me, Mary. I love you. I've loved you since I first laid eyes on you." Dean reached out and grasped Mary's hand. "Come back to America with me, Mary. We'll leave together on Friday. This doesn't have to change anything between us."

Dean stared into her eyes and Mary knew he was searching for a reaction.

Was she with him or against him?

"Dean," she said, as calmly as she could. "I do love you, but all this is too much for me to handle."

He seemed pleased by her answer. Mary shivered in his arms as he drew her close to him. The warmth she had felt in those arms was gone now and she knew her truthful answer to his question, but she wasn't about to tell him.

As Dean hugged her tightly, Mary turned her head to Brendan. His eyes screamed at her and all she could do was wink back at him and try to tell him, with her own eyes, that she was still on his side. Her mind wandered, and she saw her dream house in America; the one she had pictured in her head so many times in the last two weeks. Except the image in her head now was different from before. No children played in the garden and the house was crumbling down around her as she sat on the porch, an old woman, alone and afraid.

* * * *

The television at the Horgan house was not turned on at seven-thirty to see President Kennedy arriving in Dublin. Louise was summoned to the living room. For the first time, Jack Horgan was afraid. Since Louise had confided in him about Dean Reynolds, he had set some wheels in motion and had felt his hand was on the steering wheel all along. Now, everything was spiralling out of control and he feared for his children's safety.

Louise came in and plonked herself down on one of the chairs. Jack saw that she was haggard looking, not coping at all. He covered her hand with his and said, "Come on now. Everything is going to be just fine."

Ann came out of the pantry and sat opposite Louise. Her eyes were red from crying. She stared at the tablecloth. After Michael had been dispatched to the phone box, Jack had joined Ann in the kitchen and updated her. It hadn't been received well. She scolded him again for not involving her from the start. "I stood by you in the past," she said to him. "Why did you think it would be different now?"

He admitted his stupidity and her eyes forgave him almost immediately.

They sat now in silence and waited for Michael.

Some deep minutes passed before he arrived back. He took the last seat at the table and said, "He's coming. He said about twenty minutes."

"Okay," Jack announced. "When he gets here, he won't talk in front of us all. I'm going to talk to him outside, okay?"

No one had objections, or if they had, they didn't dare voice them.

More unending minutes passed until a car pulled up outside their gate. Andrew Kelly stepped out from the back seat, shot a glance up and down the road before walking down the path to the house. His driver remained in the car, the engine running.

Jack scanned the table, trying to make eye contact with everyone, and failing. "Give me a few minutes, okay?" He got up and went out to talk to the I.R.A. man.

Kelly took a few steps backwards when Jack opened the door and offered him a greeting smile. He looked genuinely surprised.

"Jesus Christ. What are you doing here?" Kelly said.

Jack watched Kelly as he put the pieces together in his head.

"Oh Fuck," Kelly said, finishing the jigsaw in his head. "Brendan and Michael Horgan. They're your sons?"

Jack nodded slowly, stepping out the front door and closing it gently behind him. "Keep your voice down, Andrew." Jack moved to the windowsill and sat.

Kelly followed him, looking more relaxed now, but still surprised. He sat on the wall that bordered the garden. "Jack, I'm sorry. I didn't know they were your boys. If I did I would have sent them away. They came to me, you see." Kelly shook his head, a light chuckle escaping his mouth. "I saw something in Brendan, an inner strength. I know now where that came from."

"Look," said Jack. "Forget about it, for now. We have a bigger problem to deal with. Do you know where Brendan is?"

Kelly shrugged. "I told him to go out to the safe house today to learn the ropes from two lads I use from Dublin. They snatched the American last night, outside his hotel."

"I know," Jack cut in, urging him to get to the point.

"They were going to do some persuasive questioning today. I wanted Brendan to see it." Kelly spread his hands wide. " Jack, I didn't know he was your son."

Jack shook his head and waved him on.

"I went out there myself around lunchtime."

He paused and Jack feared he was trying to tell him his son was dead.

"The American got away."

"Brendan?"

"He wasn't there. The Dubs were cut to pieces. There was blood everywhere. I still have two guys out there now cleaning up the fucker's mess."

"But no Brendan?"

"No sign of him. The only car there was the Dub's one. I couldn't understand why the American didn't take it."

Jack bit his lip. "Because he took the one Brendan arrived in, that's why."

Kelly thought about this and nodded his agreement. "Sounds possible. There's no way he would have headed off on foot. Maybe he took Brendan with him?"

Jack nodded. "What are your plans?"

Kelly scratched his inner ear and examined his finger. "I'm not sure what to do, Jack. This bastard must be the real article."

"I read the Sein Fein letter. It wasn't that bad."

"The papers edited it. There was more. More aggressive warnings to Kennedy, but they took them out. Either way, I know now that this fella is going to try something."

"I've known since Friday night," Jack told him.

"How?"

"I still have friends."

"They must be old friends, Jack. You've been on the outside going on twelve years now."

"It'll never be long enough."

"So what do you want to do, old friend?" Kelly asked.

"I already have things in place, but I need you to keep away from the American. If we go in now, he'll use Mary to stop us, and probably Brendan, if he isn't already dead."

"Do you know where he is?"

"He picked up Mary an hour ago."

"Any idea where he would take her?"

Jack nodded. "I do. Louise told me about an office he was renting on Patrick Street, over Cavendish's. I think he's there. It's the perfect position for a shot."

Kelly stood up. "Why wait? Let's go in tonight and take the bastard out. I can have ten guys there in an hour."

Jack stood up to him. "Not while my children are there! There will be a moment on Friday when he is exposed and confused. Then we will go in together and take him out."

"Jack, Kennedy's here on Friday. We should do it before then."

"I know what I'm doing, okay. I have a plan."

Kelly sat back on the wall. "Okay, tell me about it."

Jack positioned himself on the windowsill, took a deep breath and told Kelly everything.

Thursday 27th June 1963

Excerpt from the Evening Echo:

"Took 115 Years And 3 Generations To Make Trip"
President's Delight At New Ross Welcome.

"It took 115 years, 6000 miles and three generations to make this trip," said President Kennedy in reply to Mr. A. Minihane's speech of welcome at New Ross today.

In his address Mr. Minihane said, "Mr. President, this is a great day for New Ross, for Wexford and for Ireland. At this moment every Irishman and every Irish woman not on this quay, the spot from which your great grandfather set sail over a hundred years ago, are glued to a television or radio set, our exiles all over the world, the people in Ireland, from Mizen Head to Fair Head in Antrim, from the Aran Islands to Ireland's Eye, from the Coal quay in Cork to the Falls Road and Shankill in Belfast, in spite of our differences, we are all as one today.

Mary opened her eyes and looked around the room. The sun was up, but she had no idea what time it was. Outside the window she could hear some activity, but nothing close to what Patrick Street was capable of. She decided it was sometime after dawn, but definitely before nine. Her feet were cold and her bum was numb from the hard floor. She turned to her left to see Brendan lying next to her, his head resting against the pipe he was taped to. To her right, Dean sat on one box and rested his head against another. He was asleep. The chance she had hoped for had arrived already.

Slowly, she raised her hands and started to get up. But she couldn't move. She tried again, but felt something digging into her wrists. Dean had taped her to the pipe while she slept. She struggled some more, trying to assess if he had done a good job. The tape made a crackling sound against the metal pipe and Dean's eyes opened immediately. He rubbed his eyes briefly and sprang to his feet. In seconds, he looked like he hadn't been asleep at all.

"Good morning, Mary," he said. He pointed to her restrained hands. "Sorry about that, sweetheart, but I couldn't have you running off on me."

Mary didn't attempt to answer him. Their eyes met in an unremitting stare and Mary felt real anger toward him then. She still had feelings deep down inside for him, but for now she was standing on them to reach other emotions she needed to survive.

Brendan woke with a start and almost drove his head into Mary's. She was forced to break eye contact with Dean to avoid Brendan. His mouth was still taped shut and he struggled to catch his breath through his nose. Snot exploded from his nostrils as he fought his restraints in frustration. This went on for half a minute until he was fully awake and again aware of the situation.

Dean stood by the window, surveying the street below. He looked down at Mary. "I have to go out for a while, Mary. I'll be back in under an hour." He walked to the box where he had slept and picked up a roll of adhesive tape. "I don't want to do this, but I can't take you with me, and I certainly can't leave you here to scream your pretty little head off, can I?"

"Dean, I won't scream. Please don't put that on me," she pleaded.

Dean knelt before her. "I'll be back soon and I'll bring food." He pulled off a length of tape and covered her mouth with it. He kissed her on the forehead.

He placed a fresh piece of tape over Brendan's mouth and stood up once more. He moved quickly to the door and opened it. Mary noticed that the door had been unlocked all night.

"Under an hour," he reassured her and disappeared, his footfalls echoing back up the stairway from the creaky wooden stairs.

* * * *

Jack had lain awake most of the night, speaking to Ann intermittently when she was awake. At six, he decided enough was too much and dragged his ass out of bed.

He sat in the living room reading yesterday's paper, but digesting none of its contents. The front page was dominated by news of Kennedy's arrival in the Irish Capital. Jack wondered what the headline would be on Friday afternoon. At seven, he was joined by Ann, who put on the kettle and made two cups of tea. They chatted, trying to avoid the obvious topic, trying to dance around it like two seasoned ballroom dancers. By seven-thirty, Ann was sobbing on Jack's shoulder.

Michael made an appearance after eight and Louise completed the quartet just before nine. The toast was buttered and the tea was poured. No one was going to work today, the subject was never floated; everyone knew that there would be no question of anyone doing anything normal today, or tomorrow.

They ate in relative silence, no one quite sure what to say. Jack finally filled the silence with an order. "No one outside this house is told what's happening, right?"

Everyone nodded, in total agreement.

As if on cue, Longy's Ford Prefect pulled up outside the gate. Louise was the one who spotted it. She had been gazing out the window, avoiding eye contact with anyone. "It's Brendan," she shouted, bolting for the door. Everyone jumped, causing a thunder roll of chairs on the linoleum floor. The four of them jostled through the living room door and then the front door.

Brendan wasn't in the car. Kevin Long stood at the gate, clearly startled by the reception. "Jesus, What the?" he said, taking a step backwards and almost falling over the step.

Jack pushed the others aside and vaulted the steps that brought him level with Longy. "Come in to the house, will ya," he said as he grabbed Longy's arm. Longy didn't put up any resistance.

****

Dean scanned the street. It was busy, but he wasn't interested in the general population. He was looking for the person who stood out, someone who looked out of place; someone who was watching this door. Barriers that he thought looked like giant skittles lined the street. They had been erected the day before in preparation for the presidential motorcade.

Happy that no such person existed, Dean closed and locked the door behind him and walked up the street. He was annoyed at himself and it showed on his face. He knew he had been reckless on this job, one of the biggest contracts he had ever undertaken. His employers would not be happy if they became aware of the precarious position that he had landed himself in.

His thoughts turned to Mary, and he burned inside. On one hand he scolded himself for getting involved with her, but he had actually fallen for her. She was a breath of fresh air in the smog-laden life that he led. He thought of her taped up with her brother in the office and he knew he had blown it. Mary wasn't going to return to America with an assassin. He had seen in her eyes this morning the air of contempt that was festering inside her. Given the chance, he guessed that Mary would probably shoot him dead to save her brother. He didn't think this was wrong. On the contrary, he thought it was the reason he loved her so much.

He entered the Metropole Hotel through the laundry entrance and made his way to the reception area through the kitchen. The pretty receptionist was the same girl that had returned his car keys to him yesterday. She had told him that the porter had found them on the street outside the hotel. He asked her if any messages had been left for him. She handed him a telegram from America. Dean read it, smiled and tossed it in the bin, after tearing it into little pieces.

The room had been cleaned, probably twice since he last frequented it, but all his belongings were untouched. Dean packed quickly, making sure he left nothing behind. His suitcases ready, he went to the bathroom and scanned the room for any left over toiletries. He caught his reflection in the mirror and was surprised by what he saw.

"Don't freak out on me now," he said to his reflection, and managed a slight smile.

The rifle case was where he had left it, tucked neatly out of sight under the bath. Dean pulled it out gently and verified that the hair he had placed sticking out between one clasp was still there.

No one had opened it.

He unlocked the case and lifted the lid. One of the bullets had fallen from its position, but other than that everything was in order.

After one last examination of the room, Dean left what had been his home for the last two weeks, never to return again. He paid the receptionist in cash and asked her to call a cab to take him to the airport. When she finished the call and looked up, Dean Reynolds was gone.

* * * *

"Where did you find the car?" Jack stood over Longy, who slouched in the chair at the table.

"I didn't find it. The guards did. They called me this morning and told me they had found my car on Merchant's Quay. They had it towed away to Angelsea Street. I collected it there this morning, and missed work I might add."

"What did you tell them? Did you tell them that Brendan had it?"

"Do you think I'm stupid, Mr. Horgan?"

"Convince me you're not," Jack spat back at him.

Longy looked around at the glaring faces, but didn't smile. He was afraid now.

"I told them I left the keys in it last night and it was gone this morning. I told them I was just about to call the guards myself."

Jack patted his back. "Good lad, Kevin. Now, was there anything in the car?"

"Not really." A pause. "Where's Brendan?" Longy asked, looking down at his shoes, as if he knew they had no answer.

Jack half pulled, half guided him out of the chair and led him to the door. "Brendan is fine, Kevin. You go on back to work now and I'll get Brendan to call to you tomorrow."

88889999

"But…but…what about Kennedy and that….American fella with the gun?"

"It's all been taken care of. Your job now is to keep your mouth shut about it." Jack's eyes locked on Longy's. "Okay?"

The intent behind the words, the unspoken threat, seemed to get through to Longy. He nodded, quickening his pace towards the front door.

Jack returned to the living room and the stares from his family. He glanced at the little clock on the mantle; ten-thirty.

They had a long twenty-four hours ahead of them before all this would be over. Jack knew he had the patience to wait. He wasn't so sure about the others.

****

Dean stopped at a corner café and convinced the waiter to wrap three sandwiches to take with him. He also bought some drinks and a stash of chocolate bars. This would be his last trip outside for food, so the chocolate would have to do later.

After passing the door twice and making sure no one was paying undue attention to him, Dean slid the key in the lock and slipped inside. He climbed the stairs and opened the office door.

Mary and Brendan were as he had left them and Mary's glare fixed on him from the moment he entered. Brendan barely acknowledged his return, clearly weakened from lack of food and drink. Dean put the rifle case on some boxes and the food on the floor. He squatted next to Mary and pulled the tape from her mouth. "Can I trust you not to try anything if I untie you?"

Mary's voice was raspy, her throat dry. "Yes," she managed.

They ate in silence, Mary feeding her brother, Dean sitting on a box watching her work.

When Dean finished his sandwich, he arranged some more boxes in front of him, constructing a makeshift desk. He lifted the metal case onto his new worktop and unlocked it.

Mary sat on a box opposite him, watching intently. The rifle gleamed in the sunlight as Dean assembled the pieces. He finished and held it in front of him, as he had the week before in the field.

He admired its unrelenting beauty and wished he could keep it after tomorrow. It was only a fleeting thought and he dismissed it quickly. The rifle would be destroyed shortly after Kennedy was dealt with and he would never see it again. Dean decided then that he would use the Boston gunsmith again in the future, maybe not for the next job, but definitely at some point down the road.

He felt her eyes on him and looked up to see Mary with tears streaming down her cheeks. He felt a slight pang in his heart. She was gone from him forever now. There was no way of turning things back to the way they had been. Even if he broke the rifle now, set them free and let Kennedy live, she would never be his again. His original plan was to set them both free after his contract was complete. Now, as he watched her cry and saw the hatred in her eyes, he wondered what fearful steps he would have to take tomorrow to ensure he got away clean.

* * * *

Thursday was Sergeant Higgins's official day off. He stayed in bed late and listened for the moment when his wife left for town. She had won a few bob at bingo and would waste her day shopping, until the money too was wasted. He knew she would not return home until teatime, loaded down with bags of clothes and accessories.

He had a nice relaxing breakfast alone in his kitchen; the paper sprawled across the table covered in breadcrumbs from the toast he nibbled on as he read. It was yesterday's paper, but it was all news to him. He hadn't bothered reading it last night, deciding to keep it good for today. Kennedy dominated the front page and Higgins read every article. He was on duty in the city tomorrow, like every other available Garda. He was looking forward to catching a glimpse of the President as he passed through Patrick Street.

He finished the paper and, knowing he had work to do, returned to the bedroom to put on some working clothes. He dressed in an old pair of pants, a ragged shirt and a pair of worn out shoes. The perfect outfit for a spot of gardening.

The sun was high in the sky when he strolled out to the shed and retrieved a pitchfork, a spade and a wheelbarrow. He placed the tools in the barrow and pushed it down to the end of their plush garden. Trees lined the outer boundaries, rising high enough into the blue sky to block out any curious eyes.

The end of the garden was undeveloped and Higgins was still devising a plan of attack for it. The sun had dried the dirt so much that digging would be impossible. Higgins walk back to the top of the garden and filled a bucket with some water. He returned to the spot he had chosen and emptied the water onto the cracked earth, repeating this step several times until the dirt started to loosen up.

After a long relaxing cigarette, Sergeant Higgins picked up the pitchfork and started to move the earth. The water served its purpose and the dirt came loose easily enough. It took about ten minutes to dig a hole large enough for what he needed to bury. He stopped and puffed on a fresh butt for another five minutes, letting his heart rate slow down sufficiently. The sun was hot and beads of sweat dimpled his forehead. He wiped them away with the sleeve of his shirt, tossed the cigarette into one of the flowerbeds and headed for the carport.

He had purposefully backed the car into the drive the night before. The trees blocked most of the view, but the street was visible, which meant he was visible to anyone on the street. A bread van cruised past his view and disappeared again.

Without hesitation, Sergeant Higgins popped the boot of the car and pulled out the large plastic bag. He turned as he slammed down the boot and was back in the seclusion of his private garden in seconds. He tried not to look down at the clear bag, but as he tossed the contents into the fresh hole, the remaining eye of Willy O'Reilly stared blankly up at him. It didn't resemble an eye at all really, but it stared at him all the same. He spat twice as he reached for the spade, quickly heaping the dirt he had collected onto the remains, covering them completely with the fourth helping.

When the entire hole was filled, Higgins patted the ground and moved some topsoil around the area. Instead of rushing back to the shed to put away the tools, Higgins puffed yet another butt, and when he was finished, he stamped it out on the makeshift grave of Willy O'Reilly.

Some hours later, across the city, in a remote part of a dreary graveyard, the rotten remains of an old woman were finally laid to rest in an unmarked grave, five years too late. No one attended the funeral and the priest had to help carry the coffin to the graveside. He said his few words and left the scene to let the gravediggers do their work. They covered her over and took a break by her grave to puff on a butt. When they finished, they cast their fag ends down and stamped them out on the loose soil beneath their feet; on the grave of Mrs. O'Reilly.

* * * *

The day slipped away slowly, fighting every step of the way. The sun rounded the sky and started its familiar descent down below the horizon. With the sun still visible in the sky for another hour or so, the depleted Horgan family sat down to watch JFK's continuing tour of Ireland. It was on for an hour and they watched as Kennedy visited Wexford and Dunganstown to see some of his distant relations. He made a nice impromptu speech as the old ladies fed him and his entourage tea with biscuits and cake.

The Horgans watched in silence. Jack sat in his chair and watched the President smile and shake hands with nearly everyone around him. He liked Kennedy, thought the man was making a difference to the world.

The show finished and Louise went to bed. She hugged her mother tightly and kissed her father's cheek before leaving the room. Michael followed shortly afterwards, no hugs and kisses from him though, and the two parents sat in the living room alone.

Jack switched off the television and started into the Echo. Ann took out some knitting and for ten minutes they read and knitted in relative silence. After reading the same article twice and still not absorbing it, Jack dropped the paper to the floor and rubbed his eyes. They felt heavy in his head and he wondered just how heavy they would get.

"Remember when Mary wanted to cook the Sunday dinner for the first time?" he asked Ann.

"What?"

"Do you remember when Mary wanted to cook the Sunday dinner for the first time?"

Ann smiled. "Yeah, I do."

"I'll never forget the look on her face when she walked out of the kitchen with no eyebrows and a black face."

They both smiled now, gazing into dark corners of the room, trying to call up the image of their daughter. Mary had turned on the gas in the oven that day and then went to look for matches to light it. When she returned and leaned into the oven to ignite the gas, a mini explosion sent her flying across the small pantry. Her eyebrows were singed, but the only real damage was to her pride.

"It took her awhile to get over that one," Ann said. A tear escaped her eye and followed the contours of her face. Jack saw this and he felt a vice tighten around his chest. His breath caught and he felt slightly dizzy. He hated to see Ann cry.

In recent years, Ann had rarely cried. Their life had worked out well after a rocky start. When Jack was fighting for the cause, Ann had spent endless nights sobbing at home with her mother, and later sobbing in her own house, with four young children sleeping silently in their cots, oblivious to the daily antics of their father.

All that had been fading memories until the last few days. Now Jack looked across the room at his beautiful wife and he saw in her face a familiar look of fear that he had thought he would never see again in his lifetime. That face, and the love he held inside for her, was the reason he had cut his ties to the cause and settled into a normal life.

Another tear followed the first down Ann's cheek. Jack got up and went to her. He knelt before her and lay his head on her lap.

Instinctively, she started rubbing his hair.

"It's going to be okay, Ann. I promise. It'll be all over tomorrow."

"I know, Jack. I believe you, but I can't help worrying. I want to go and get my kids now."

"We can't. It would be a disaster. We have to catch him off guard."

Ann huffed, annoyed. "I know. I know. You're right, but it doesn't feel right."

Jack tried to bring her back. "I'll never forget the time when your Uncle Tom died. That was a classic."

Ann snorted involuntarily. "You love that story, don't you?"

Ann's Uncle Tom had passed away peacefully in his house on Blarney Street. Brendan was seventeen at the time, and when Uncle Tom died, Sandra, his wife handed Brendan a wad of pound notes. "He's dead, Brendan," she said, blessing herself. "Will you do me a favour?"

Brendan nodded hesitantly.

"Go into town and buy a suit for Tom for the funeral, will yah? Good boy." She turned and walked back into the house. She hadn't waited for an answer.

Brendan, thinking the suit was for young Tom, the son of the dead uncle, decided to make some money for himself. He rented a suit from Morley's dress hire and pocketed the difference.

The next day, at the removal, Brendan walked with the crowds up the aisle to view his dead uncle at rest in his open coffin. He nearly fell into the coffin when he saw Uncle Tom, lying dead as a doornail, wearing the hired suit. His son, young Tom, was sitting next to his mother wearing an old shirt and tie. Brendan was almost in tears as he shook the families' hands and offered his condolences. They all thought he took the death pretty bad that day.

They buried Tom Reagan the next day, in the suit that Brendan had hired for the week from Morley's dress hire. Brendan tried several times to tell someone his mistake, but in the end he used the money he made on the suit and all his savings to pay for the hired suit.

Ann's smile returned as Jack recounted the story to her. She had heard it many times, in many different ways, but tonight it felt more special, like a piece of her son was being handed back to her; an unforgettable memory.

* * * *

Dean left Mary untied for the rest of the afternoon and evening. She dared not try something. She knew she could easily make it to the door and down the stairs to the street, but what would Dean do to Brendan if she got away? He had made it clear that Brendan was only alive because of her. If she got away her brother would be expendable.

Instead of trying to escape, Mary tended to her brother and watched Dean prepare his sniper's nest at the window. She convinced Dean to let Brendan keep his mouth free of tape after the sandwiches. Dean stared at Brendan and warned him of the consequences if he shouted for help. Brendan nodded eagerly, just happy to be able to breathe properly.

The day dragged and Mary regressed into her thoughts for most of it. She tried to piece together the events of the past two weeks. It had all become a blur in her mind. She had first set eyes on Dean when he had saved her from Willy outside the G.P.O.. That would be two weeks ago tomorrow, only two weeks!

She looked up at Dean as he moved boxes and set up some old mannequins at the window. Up until last night, she had felt like she had known Dean for years. Now she realised she didn't know anything about him. He wasn't an architect. He wasn't setting up an office here. He had hired this room for the sole purpose of killing Kennedy.

Had he used her to pass the time before tomorrow? She had slept with him after only a few days, and the thought of it made her feel dirty now, used.

But he had saved her from Willy and she was grateful for that. God knows what that maniac would have done to her. When Willy had attacked her for real, she had defended herself and she was proud of that fact. Had she scared Willy off that night? she thought. She was sure he would come after her again after she had hurt him so badly. Then his farm had burned down and he was missing. Mary looked up at Dean and the love that had clouded her mind was no longer there.

"Did you kill Willy?" she asked calmly.

Dean was moving some boxes into position and stopped when she spoke. He turned and wiped his dusty hands on a cloth. "I would have liked to. He was a real bad seed that boy." He sat down by his makeshift desk, placing his hand on the rifle. "When you told me he tried to rape you, I considered shooting him. It would have been good practice. But I couldn't risk it. The police would have been all over it. Then he went missing and I didn't give him much more thought after that." He raised his hand and pointed a few fingers in the air. "Scout's honour," he said, trying on a smile.

Mary turned away from him and gave Brendan a drink. Dean shrugged and returned to his work.

"You did something to her boss at the sweet shop though, didn't you?" Brendan said, speaking to Dean for the first time since entering the office the day before.

Mary spun around. "Did you?"

Dean smiled briefly and said, "That day you were fired, Monday was it? I went down and frightened the old bastard a bit, that's all."

"But you never told me about it."

Dean didn't say anything.

"And if you didn't tell me that," she continued. "Then how can I believe you had nothing to do with Willy?"

Again, Dean remained silent, gently stroking the barrel of the rifle.

"I can see it in your eyes, Dean. You killed him. You shot him with that gun, didn't you?"

Dean shrugged. "You're not going to believe anything I tell you now anyway, so believe whatever you want, Mary. He was a scumbag, so who cares what happened to him?"

Night came and Dean allowed Brendan and Mary to visit the bathroom once. When they were both finished, Dean secured Brendan to the pipe again and, turning to Mary, he apologised as he unrolled fresh tape for her. She grunted back at him and assumed the position, never letting her eyes meet his.

Sleep came slowly and in spurts to Mary. Brendan, who was physically and emotionally spent, slept heavily. Dean sat looking out the window for ages before settling down on some boxes.

Mary dreamt of her childhood and her father. He was missing a lot back then and in her dream she remembered one of those special moments when he arrived home early one summer morning. She remembered how he had swept both her and Louise into his strong arms and danced around the living room with them, kissing their cheeks repeatedly.

Mary woke, her face wet from tears. The street lights outside cast a shadow on their three faces. She felt the cold air scuttling along the ground, biting at her numb legs. She had no idea what time it was and she lay awake for what felt like hours, before sleep took her away again, into a dreamless slumber that preceded the nightmare she was dreading.

Friday 28th June 1963

Excerpt from President Kennedy's address before the Irish Parliament:

Eighty-three years ago, Henry Gratton, demanding the more independent Irish Parliament that would always bear his name, denounced those who were satisfied merely by new grants of economic opportunity. "A country," he said, "enlightened as Ireland, chartered as Ireland, armed as Ireland and injured as Ireland will be satisfied with nothing less than liberty." And today, I am certain, free Ireland—a fully-fledged member of the world community, where some are still not free, and where some counsel an acceptance of tyranny- free Ireland will not be satisfied with anything less than liberty.

Jack cooked breakfast for the whole family. He did this on rare occasions, but when he did he always made a feast. This morning was no exception, and when everyone had finished eating there was still enough remaining to feed the two members of the family who were missing from the table.

When the dishes were washed, dried and stored away, Jack went outside and waited by the gate for Kelly to come and pick him up. He kissed Ann and Louise in the house before leaving, but Michael joined him outside. The two of them stood by the gate and watched the neighbours go to work for the day. For years, Jack had never punched a clock or held down a steady job. His job had been terror and mayhem against the British invaders, and for a long time he had enjoyed it more than most.

He watched the men now, with their packed lunches of cheese sandwiches and apples, walking briskly down the street, and he wished he was one of them today. He had given up a lot for his family, and as he watched Kelly's car pull up to the footpath, his hands started to shake in his pockets. He could feel the adrenaline racing through his veins. He fought for control and didn't move until he felt he could walk without falling over.

"Let me go, Dad. I want to be there." Michael stepped outside the gate, ready to go in search of his brother.

Jack shook his head. "No, Michael. I'll look after it now. You stay here with your mother. She needs someone strong with her today."

Kelly stuck his head out of the car. To Jack, Kelly looked nervous. This had a calming effect on Jack. He wasn't the only one with the jitters today.

Jack joined him in the back seat; the driver turned the wheel away from the step and guided the car down the road. Michael stood in the same spot long after they had disappeared out of sight, kicking stones into the road where the car had been minutes earlier.

* * * *

After lying awake most of the night, Mary slept through the dawn and was awakened by the rumblings of the gathering crowds below their window. Dean had opened the window to cleanse the room of the odours that had accumulated overnight. She was still taped to the pipe next to Brendan and she felt the tightness of the tape across her mouth.

Dean had placed two scantily dressed mannequins at the window where he had arranged his sniper's nest. The rifle was still on the makeshift desk, but Dean was sitting in his nest, assessing the view below. The windows were low and Dean was bent over, looking through the female dummy's open legs at the street below. He had dressed both mannequins from the waist up only. The window in front of them was opened just enough for Dean to see out through the gap.

Mary turned to her brother and was greeted by his tired, bloodshot eyes. His mouth was also taped and all they could do was stare at each other. After a few seconds, Brendan nodded, smiling as best he could with his tired eyes. She returned the gesture and then kicked one of the boxes in front of her, to get Dean's attention. He walked over to her. She glared up at him until he finally bent over and pulled the tape away from her mouth.

"I need to pee," she said.

"Now is as good a time as any." Dean checked his watch, then cut the tape that held Mary to the pipe.

As she rose, Mary twisted her head slightly to see out the window. She couldn't see the street below. The people were lined up on each side of the road at least fifteen deep. The barriers had been ignored by most, and the guards on duty were doing nothing to push people back. The swarm of people ran all the way down to the corner of Patrick Street and Grand Parade, and beyond, she guessed. When she got to her feet, she heard a pipe band start to play below the window. The squeal of the pipes filled the room and Mary knew that if they shouted for help now, no one would ever hear them. Dean smiled when the band started and Mary knew why. She almost wet her panties before she reached the toilet.

* * * *

Conversation was scarce in the car, and when they did speak the subjects chosen were bland. Jack was surprised with Kelly. This man was supposed to be a high-ranking member of the cause, but he seemed more nervous with every passing second that carried the car closer to the city centre.

Kelly removed a handgun from his pocket and tossed it onto Jack's lap. Instinctively, Jack picked it up and a cascade of buried memories unearthed themselves. He thought back to his heyday, when he went on missions frequently, and although he also felt the butterflies churning in his stomach back then, his outer shell was always calm and composed. They were different times, he thought. When he was young, desire and the fight for freedom drove him. Nowadays, he felt that the men picking up guns in the name of their country had lost sight of the true objective. Crime was becoming a big part of the IRA now, a way to generate funds. That's not what it was about during his time.

The driver stopped the car by Murphy's Brewery, still over half a mile from Patrick Street. Gardai were directing traffic away from the city; the President's motorcade route through the town was preventing anyone from entering the heart of Cork for the next hour or so.

Jack and Kelly stood outside the car. Jack's gun remained on the seat behind him; he couldn't bear to hold it any longer than he already had.

"It's shoes and socks from here, Jack," Kelly said and they started toward MacCurtain Street.

"I've been walking all my life, boy," Jack answered him. "Haven't owned a car yet."

Kelly nudged him. "Blown up a few though, huh."

Jack didn't reply. He quickened the pace, and as they walked up Coburg Street, they could hear the music of the bands first and then the bustling crowds of people.

They reached MacCurtain Street and a wall of people blocked their progress. Jack took in the view, all the air escaping his lungs in one long, slow exhalation. He had never seen so many people in his life, in one place. Patrick's Bridge was like a human bridge traversing the River Lee, except for a small gap left for the motorcade, and as Jack allowed his eyes to follow the human path down Patrick Street, he realised that he couldn't actually see the road. People hung out of windows, sat on windowsills, hiked up drainpipes, stood on post boxes and used anything they could climb to secure a decent vantage point.

He turned and looked down the length of MacCurtain Street. Even more people lined each side of the street. Down at the end of the street, Jack could just make out a vehicle coming their way. He turned to Kelly. "We had better get going. I think he's early."

The two of them walked into the throng of people and hustled their way through the crowd. Jack was more diplomatic, excusing himself as he edged past people, while Kelly pushed and shoved his way forward. Some men turned to react to Kelly's bad manners, but when they laid eyes on the instigator, they turned away again. Kelly had a piercing look that served as a warning to what lay underneath.

When they reached the Bridge, Jack glanced into the river. Floating on the calm water below he could see at least five boats, filled with men ready to dive into the cold, muddy water to save any unlucky fallers.

Kelly shoved on ahead of him and Jack was finding it hard to stay with him. Kelly paused at the barrier that blocked their passage to the other side of Patrick Street. He looked back at Jack, summoned him forward with a nod and, after glancing both ways, he vaulted over the railing and sprinted to the other side. Some close bystanders cheered his successful attempt at running the gauntlet.

Jack reached the barrier, but it took him much longer to make his move. He straddled the barrier, and just as he was about to slide over it and onto the road, he heard someone to his right shout, 'Stop'.

The Garda was moving along the road quickly and Jack thought for a moment about diving back behind the barrier. Deciding that this was his only chance to get over to the correct side of the street, he pulled his leg over the barrier and, losing his balance, he went flying onto the tarmac. The crowd erupted in laughter, but Jack had no time for embarrassment. He gathered himself quickly and saw the Garda coming for him. Jack ran for the other side, and placing one leg on the barrier, he vaulted into the waiting crowd.

Most moved out of the way of his falling body, and Jack could see the ground coming up to meet him. Then he felt two strong arms around his midsection and he was upright again.

"Nice dive," Kelly said, dusting him off. "How about we get on with the job at hand now?"

Before Jack could answer Kelly, a deafening roar emanated from the people to their left. The two men turned instinctively and saw the President's motorcade navigating its way through the crowds. Jack could see Kennedy standing up in the back seat of the car, his bodyguards running along on either side of him. He stood out high above them all. A perfect target, Jack thought. The band on the corner of Merchant's Quay started up, cymbals bashing, drums booming and everyone cheered.

Jack and Kelly looked at each other.

"He's early," Kelly said.

"Too fuckin' early," Jack replied.

Both of them turned and started down Patrick Street. Jack led the way this time and his diplomacy faded quickly as he started bumping and pushing his way through the thickening crowds. Behind him he could hear the cheers spreading through the lines of people, like a wave heading for the shore. He tried to increase his pace, but Jack knew now that Kennedy's car would be well past them before they reached Dean's office.

* * * *

Dean opened the metal case, removed four of the mercury tipped bullets from the sponge insert, and examined them carefully, making sure each one was in pristine condition. He noticed one of the bullets had not been filed properly after the mercury had been inserted and placed it back in the case; he put the three acceptable bullets on the windowsill in front of him.

Lifting the rifle from his lap, he pulled back the bolt and slid one of the three bullets into the breech. Two remained on the windowsill, but Dean doubted if he would need them. Mercury bullets explode on impact and he would be less than 150 yards away when he fired. He left the two mercury bullets on the sill, just in case something went wrong.

The rifle loaded, Dean raised it to his shoulder and slid the silencer through the legs of the female mannequin. He pushed his eye up against the scope and the street below looked closer, much closer. He zeroed in on one man squatting on a post box about one hundred yards away. The crosshairs dissected on the bridge of his nose and Dean could see the small freckles around the man's cheeks.

He knew then that he could not miss.

He smiled as he rested the rifle back onto his lap again. He saw the disgust on Mary's face. His smile faded and they sat glaring at each other for several seconds. Dean was about to speak when the volume level of the crowd below reached new heights. The pipe band below their window started playing a familiar Irish tune. Dean broke the stare with Mary and leaned forward to look back towards the motorcade. He saw Kennedy, in the third car, standing and waving at the people. Dean pulled his head back and took a long look at the rifle in his lap before returning to Mary.

"I have to do this, Mary. If I don't, I will become a target myself."

Tears streamed down Mary's face. "Please, Dean, don't. I'll go to America with you, I will. But not if you do this."

The crowd erupted below, yanking Dean from his temporary trance. He raised the rifle once again and waited. Mary lowered her head, but Brendan sat next to her, watching Dean with wide eyes.

****

Jack and Kelly reached Cavendish's Furniture shop just as the first vehicle in the motorcade edged past them. All the TV personnel covering Kennedy's Irish visit were on board. The second car was a Garda car and the third was Kennedy's open top tour car. Jack would learn later that the car Kennedy was travelling in was in fact the Secret Service car. His usual car had broken down that morning.

The two of them rounded the corner and stood at the door that led up to Dean's office on the third floor. Jack glanced around and saw that, of the thousands that surrounded him, only Kelly was looking in his direction. They could stand there naked and no one would notice them. Kelly removed a small crowbar from his coat. He stuck it into the jamb of the door and jerked the bar backwards. The door exploded inward and, as Kelly entered, Jack looked to the street in time to see Kennedy passing by, high above the crowd. He looked like he was floating effortlessly past, his car obscured by the cheering crowd. Jack would always remember that image, and he didn't share the experience with anyone later. It was his alone to remember.

He inhaled deeply and started up the stairs after Kelly.

* * * *

Dean kept his eye pressed against the scope, trained on a spot 150 yards ahead. From the sound of the crowd directly below, he knew that Kennedy's car had already passed the window. His heart thumped in his chest and he tried desperately to regulate his breathing. He had killed before, had killed many men, using a different rifle each time, but his heart raced now, because he knew that this shot would reverberate around the world for years to come.

Slowly, he aimed at the spot in the road he had chosen as the point where he would pick up Kennedy's car. His hands felt clammy and he adjusted his grip on the rifle. The sound of the crowd and the band below was deafening. Through the periphery of the scope, Dean could see the people closing the gap on the road available for the motorcade to pass by. The barriers were five rows behind the crowd now. The shot would not be heard, but the result would cause a stampede in the street below.

An American flag flashed across the scope and Dean knew he was looking at the flag posted at the front right side of the presidential car. He moved the rifle slightly to the left and there he was, the American President, waving at the thousands that had lined the streets to get a glimpse of him. Dean could hear Mary screaming at him now. He took a deep breath as he tracked the slow moving target. As he exhaled, at a snail's pace, he gently squeezed the trigger and the rifle kicked slightly as the bullet was catapulted out of the barrel. He heard the sound of the silencer, like the muffled backfire of a car. No one on the street heard it, he was sure of that.

Kennedy raised his right hand and waved at the crowd. A woman held up a portrait of him as he passed her.

Dean had missed.

He moved quickly, pulling back the bolt and expelling the spent shell. He jammed one of the two bullets on the windowsill into the breech, relocated his target and fired again.

The rifle recoiled slightly.

Kennedy dropped his hand and nodded at the other occupants of the car. The Lord Mayor of Cork, Sean Casey, who was travelling in the car with him, smiled up at Kennedy.

Dean couldn't believe what was happening. He looked at the rifle he held in his hands and shook his head. This took all of two seconds, before he once again ejected the spent shell and loaded the last bullet available to him. The metal case was too far away for a fourth shot. It was irrelevant anyway, because the third car in the motorcade, Kennedy's car, was now at the junction of Patrick Street and Grand Parade. He was well outside the 150-yard range that the rifle had been designed for, but Dean knew he had marked harder targets in the past.

He raised the rifle for the last time as the open top car swung slowly to the left. Kennedy's smiling face was in the crosshairs and Dean squeezed the trigger.

John F. Kennedy, President of the United States of America, continued waving at the crowd as his car turned onto Grand Parade and on towards the City Hall, and the freedom of the City of Cork.

Dean Reynolds looked at the rifle in his hands. He had missed a slow moving target three times. He ejected the last bullet casing and watched as it fell to the floor to join the other two shells cooling there.

"Maybe he'll come around again and give you a fourth chance, Deano, boy."

The voice came from behind him. Dean turned and looked at the two men standing in the doorway.

He recognised the man who had spoken.

* * * *

Jack had stopped Kelly at the closed door to Dean's office. He winked at him and waited, his ear clung to the door. He nodded to Kelly, who moved into position with the crowbar. Before Kelly could smash the door, Jack stopped him and reached for the handle. The door swung open and Kelly smiled.

Jack was first into the room. He stood at the door and could see Dean rapidly reloading the rifle. He didn't try to stop him. He didn't have to stop him. He let his eyes leave Dean and search the room. He saw his two children sitting on the floor by the other window and relief flooded through him.

They were taped to a pipe running down from the ceiling. Jack couldn't see Brendan's mouth, but he knew by his eyes that the boy was smiling. He also saw fear in those eyes. Slowly, Jack raised his finger to his mouth, gesturing for them to be quiet.

Dean fired the last shot and Jack knew that Kennedy was safe now. Kelly looked ready to charge Dean, but Jack held him back.

"Maybe he'll come around again and give you a fourth chance, Deano, boy," Jack shouted over the noise from below.

The band was still playing, but the crowds had started to disperse. Dean turned and his jaw dropped open. "What the?" was all he could manage to say.

Jack reached into his pocket and took out a handful of bullets; mercury tipped bullets. He let them fall from his hand and they bounced and rolled around on the floor.

"You left these in the hotel, Dean."

Dean had no words.

Jack had.

"The night porter there is a very close friend of mine, you see. Andrew Dineen. He asked me to tell you that he thought the hair on the lock of the case was very professional. Almost caught him, you did." Jack paused and a wide smile brightened his face. "Almost," he finished.

Dean moved quickly, grabbing the case and tossing it open. Mary screamed, "No, Dean. They'll kill you."

Jack and Kelly didn't move. Dean shoved a normal shell into the breech and without hesitation, he pulled the trigger. The silencer puffed, but nothing else happened.

Another blank.

Dean flipped the rifle over and held it by the silencer, like a baseball bat. He turned to Brendan, who was helpless to move. He lifted the gun and it was clear what he was about to do. Kelly raised his gun and fired.

The crack of the windowpane was louder than the sound from the silenced rifle. The real bullet had entered Dean Reynolds body below his right nipple, came out through his back and carried on through the window. Dean leaned forward and, dropping the rifle, collapsed to the floor. No one reacted on the street. The band was still playing and the bullet that had passed through Dean Reynolds went whizzing overhead totally unnoticed, eventually burying itself deep inside a telephone pole across the street.

Jack ran over to Mary and Brendan. He pulled the tape away from Brendan's face. Brendan was crying uncontrollably and all that Jack could do was hold him. Kelly freed Mary and helped her to her feet. She didn't know this man, but she hugged him fiercely.

Then, below their feet, Dean let out a blood choked cough.

* * * *

Mary reacted first. She pulled away from Kelly and fell to her feet at Dean's side. He coughed again, a deep gurgling sound escaping his lungs. Mary took hold of his shoulder and tried to turn him over. He was too heavy. She turned and looked up at Kelly.

Kelly knelt over Dean and rolled him onto his back. Dean let out a series of moans as his back arched in pain. Mary took his hand and lowered her head in front of his. She looked deep into his wavering eyes. She needed to see something in them.

Dean gazed up at her, a faint smile appearing on his face. He coughed again and blood flowed freely from his gaping mouth. He tried to speak, but it was beyond him now. With his last ounce of strength, he squeezed Mary's hand.

She lay there, long after he had died, gazing into the deep blue eyes that kept staring back at her, although all life in them had disappeared.

* * * *

The street below was returning to normal. The bands had finished and left, the crowds had thinned and the barriers were visible again. Traffic was starting to flow through the main street. The three of them reached the front of Cavendish's shop as Kelly's car arrived. The driver jumped out and helped them to get Brendan into the back seat.

Kelly appeared at Jack's side, just before he joined Mary and Brendan in the car. "You're a regular genius, Jack."

"Not really," Jack replied.

"Ah come on. I would have gone in there guns blazing and probably been killed by that fucker. You, you had a plan, a simple but effective plan. You saved Kennedy and your kids without firing a shot yourself. Genius."

"Maybe." Jack looked into Kelly's eyes. "I want you to leave Brendan and Michael out of all this, okay. If they come to meetings, throw them out. Understand?" Jack meant this as an order, and he could see that Kelly received it as such.

"Would you consider coming back in yourself, Jack?"

"Never," Jack finished, and he didn't speak to Kelly again. The car pulled away and started the climb up the hills of North Cork.

* * * *

Ann kept them all in the house. She told them that she wouldn't have the whole road knowing their business. The three of them got out of the car and walked down the path. It was after eleven and most of the neighbours were still on their way out of town after the event.

Kennedy was at the City Hall, receiving the freedom of the city, and Jack guessed that many people would be hanging on for that. He had seen enough of the man. He would always remember the moment when he had looked back, before entering the door to the office, when he had seen Kennedy float past. Even then he had feared his plan would backfire, that Dean would have realised the bullets had been replaced in the case. He had looked at Kennedy at that moment and wondered if the man would be dead in the next few seconds.

He hadn't feared Kennedy's death as much as his own kids' demise. If Kennedy died, but Brendan and Mary lived, he could live with that, would have been happy with that. Saving Kennedy was always secondary to the safety of his children. He had put them in harm's way, and Ann had objected, but now all was forgotten and everyone had survived, except the assassin.

In the house, everyone hugged and kissed. Brendan was shattered and Ann and Michael helped him off to bed. Michael was the picture of happiness at his brother's side. He praised his bravery and hugged him every chance he got. Mary walked over to her father and whispered in his ear. He nodded and the two of them went back out the front door.

* * * *

"I know, I know. You're going to kill me." Jack held up his hands as if Mary was carrying a gun.

"Why would I kill you, Dad? You saved our lives."

"Sure, didn't I lie to your face, and his as well."

"You stopped him killing the president. It was worth it." She hugged his arm and rested her head against it. "I did love him though."

"I know, honey. And for what it's worth, I think he loved you back as well."

Mary didn't cry. She had no tears left to shed. "What will I do now?"

"What do you mean?"

"It all seems so hopeless."

"Less of that now," Jack scolded her. "Your life hasn't begun yet. Jesus, you're only nineteen. Your husband is still out there waiting for you." Jack pointed in no particular direction. "He's probably working away hard, unsure of what life has in store for him. If he could only see what's waiting for him around the corner, he'd probably keel over with a heart attack or something." Jack nudged her and Mary managed a half-smile.

Her heart was still bound in pain and she knew it was going to take a long time to release it. Angela would help, and Mary made the decision then to tell Angela everything. Angela would be her rock in the coming months.

"Were you in the I.R.A. for a long time?"

Jack had expected the question and had toyed with different answers. "Look, I'll tell you all about it in good time. Today is not the day."

"I'll hold you to that." She hugged his arm and knew that whatever shocking things he would tell her, whenever he did, she would still love him.

"You'd better go inside, Mary."

She noticed the change in her father's voice. Raising her head, she saw the Garda standing by the gate. Her face betrayed her. She could feel the blood rushing across her reddened cheeks. "Oh Jesus," escaped her mouth, before she could hold it in.

"It's okay, Mary. Go inside now." Jack helped her on her way to the door. He smiled at her as he pulled the door out.

* * * *

Sergeant Higgins carried his bulky frame down the path and sat on the windowsill next to Jack. "Is that your daughter?"

"Yes."

"Mary, is it?"

"Yes."

"She's grown to be a beautiful woman."

Jack smiled. "She certainly has."

Higgins laughed. "You're a lucky man you called me last Sunday night, Jack. You left a pile of shit behind you on that boy's farm."

"I was in a hurry."

Higgins removed his hat and played with it in his hands. Jack stared at the garden.

"Why did you do him?"

Jack raised his hand and pointed at the grass. "You saw Mary there?"

"I did."

"Well," Jack continued, still pointing. "He tried to rape her on that very spot last week."

"Did you catch him at it?"

"No. My youngest, Louise, told me after it happened."

The sergeant shook his head. "Mary looks alright now."

"She's a brave girl."

"Does she know?"

"Nah, never."

"I have no problem with that, Jack boy." Higgins paused as if he had something to add but couldn't remember it. "I found his head in the sty the other night, with some fingers and a bit of his foot. I gave him a decent burial out in my back garden yesterday."

"Thanks, John."

"They're still looking for him, you know. They think he did it all; started the fire, killed his mother, burned the house. I've checked around and as far as I could find out, he never mentioned Mary to anyone."

"Did he kill his mother?"

"Looks that way. The doctor said she was killed with a shotgun, about five years back." Higgins shook his head. "He must've kept her up in her bedroom all these years."

"I saw her. I saw her in the bedroom. Scariest thing I ever saw."

Higgins put on his hat as he stood up. "I have to get back in town. Kennedy is still at the City Hall. Jesus, the whole county came in to see him. Still, it all seemed to go as planned."

"It certainly did," Jack added, deciding not to tell his old friend about the morning's events; not today anyway.

Higgins started up the steps and stopped halfway. "Don't go killing anyone else now, Jack. Not until you talk to me first anyway. Okay?"

"Okay, John. And thanks."

"Anytime. It was like the old days again for a while. Remember the old days, Jack."

"Too well," he answered, as he opened the front door.

Higgins shook his head and sighed. "Sometimes I miss that time, Jack. We were fighting for something back then."

"We're still fighting, John," Jack answered, pointing toward the hallway behind him. He smiled as he closed the door.

Epilogue

Angela reached the top of the stairs and pushed in the open door to their new flat. They had spent most of Thursday and Friday moving their stuff in, and finally Angela held the last box in her hands.

"Is that it?" Mary asked her from the small kitchen. The flat consisted of a small living room, an even smaller kitchen and two bedrooms.

"It sure is, girl. We are now officially moved in." They both hugged each other in their sparsely decorated, but homely new flat.

Neither family had given them much grief about moving out. Angela's brother had failed to get into the British army and came home cursing the whole nation of England to hell. Things had settled down at Angela's house and she wasn't worried for her mother anymore. With Johnny there to protect her mother, her father was behaving himself.

Mary's house had returned to normal soon after June had passed into memory. One night, in September Jack had sat them all down at the table and told them nearly everything about his time fighting for the cause. They all ended up in tears that night and somehow they seemed even closer.

Mary had nightmares and they all involved Dean and those few days in his office. Brendan was very distant for a while, but he was slowly improving and he had Michael at his side every step of the way. Longy's boss finally retired and he now drove the bread van around the north side with his head held high.

"Will we go out for dinner tonight, to celebrate, like?" Angela asked Mary.

"We will not, Angela Browne. We have the rent to pay at the end of the month, and I'm starting my new job at the school on Monday. We'll have some cheese on toast and it's off to bed with the both of us." Mary had landed a teacher's assistant post at her old school.

Angela froze, trying to read Mary's face. "Go away, ya bitch ya. You had me there for a minute. I thought I was after bringing me mother along by mistake."

Mary laughed harder than she had laughed in ages. "I'll have a quick wash," she said when she could speak again. "Then we'll go to some nice place in town." She did a spin in the middle of the room. "Oh, isn't it just a great day. Nothing could upset me right now."

The big hand, on the clock that Mary's mother had given them as a moving in present, moved on another minute to tell them that the time was 5:29pm.

It was November 22nd 1963. The time in Dallas was 12:29pm...

Acknowledgements

I would like to begin by thanking all the people that read the early drafts of this novel. Tom, Edel, Mark, Mairead, Catherine, Fiona, John, Joe, Carmel, Michelle, Yvonne, Vicky, Paul, Aileen, Margaret, Patricia, Isobel, Jonathan, and a host of others, your feedback was invaluable in sculpting the book into something coherent and readable. If you are reading this it means you honoured the agreement to buy a published copy. Good for you!

Next on the list are my parents and siblings: Patrick, Kathleen, Ann and Clare. Thanks for your support down through the years.

My thanks to the Examiner Office who kindly gave permission to use excerpts from the Evening Echos of June 1963. Also, thanks to the Cork City Library local history section; a valuable source of information for this novel. And thanks to Clodagh Feehan who shared her marketing knowledge with me.

Finally, I want to thank my wife, Suzanne, who believed in me when I had given up, and grounded me when I was having notions. Without you there would be no novel, or quality of life for that matter.

I hope you derived some enjoyment from the book, even if it was only from looking for mistakes. If you did find any, blame the people I mentioned at the beginning of this piece.

If you did or didn't enjoy it, please drop me a few lines. I would love to hear from you.

MMS
July 2005
martinmcsweeney2002@yahoo.co.uk